FLYING AROUND NEW ZEALAND BY THE SEAT OF MY PANTS

Published in paperback in 2015 by Sixth Element Publishing
on behalf of Keith Reynolds

Sixth Element Publishing
Arthur Robinson House
13-14 The Green
Billingham TS23 1EU
Tel: 01642 360253
www.6epublishing.net

ISBN 978-1-908299-84-0

British Library Cataloguing in Publication Data. A catalogue record for this book is available from the British Library.

Printed in Great Britain.

CHAPTER ONE
THE JOURNEY

Lush green bush, bursting with ponga and kauri trees… ancient Maori carvings derive from these trees, as do facial tattoos and wooden artefacts. The beautiful scenery and deafening sound of silence… tranquillity can be a beautiful experience in itself. A clean, green fighting machine. Where did the nightmare or journey begin…? The beginning… at home in England, the night of the fire, twelve thousand miles away from fine wines, new buildings… compared with the historic English buildings, bright shiny and new, it's all new. Blue oceans so clear you can see the depth and wonders of the sea. Crisp, clean, golden beaches, all new and stimulating to the mind.

Free falling in a dream state, my nostrils began twitching.

"Umf!" I began tossing and turning violently, waking up coughing. "Urh, what's that stench?"

I sat up abruptly and realised something was burning. I leaned over to open the window further. The sound of sirens in the street became deafening. "What the hell! Oh shit, the neighbour's house is on fire!"

"Unravel the hose on pump two," the fireman cried. "For Christ's sake, get a bloody move on."

The neighbour's windows exploded. Guttering melted with the intense heat, flames gushed out of every opening, and then the roof collapsed.

"What's that smell?" My heart began to pound. I jumped out of bed, grabbed a chair and brought it close to the window then stared at the chaos in the street.

"Axe, axe, axe." The fireman was driving his axe deep into the front door, smoke and flames billowing out into the street, driving the man back.

This was better than a movie.

My neighbour, Bill, appeared below the window.

"Hey, Kevin," he yelled up to me. "The old guy's a gonner. Poor guy. Still, it could be worse, it could be me in that furnace. What a waste. I saw them delivering a new couch last week and now it's just gone up in flames." Bill chuckled to himself.

I shrugged Bill's comments off and continued watching, riveted at the window.

Three police cars, two fire trucks and one ambulance were now on the scene. The street was alive with blue lights, a spaghetti junction of hosepipes and a throng of people scurrying around, yelling to one another.

"The inconsiderate old bastard, I've got work tomorrow," said Bill. "How am I going to get to sleep now?"

"There's that smell again," I said through the window to Bill, "like someone cooking steaks on a barbie. It's burning flesh, I bet you."

Bill chuckled again. "Cool, what an exciting night. The old boy did have some use after all."

The fire chief yelled to one of the other firemen. "Grab another hose and aim it on the house next door, we don't want the whole street going up."

A group of firemen crowded around the second fire truck and began pulling the long hose out of its reel.

"Come on! We don't have all day! This ain't a picnic, guys!" the fire chief yelled at the top of his voice. The firemen unravelled the hose and began hosing down the house next door.

Bill disappeared for a few moments and then re-appeared with his camcorder and began filming. "This'll make a cool movie, the night the old dude died. No… the night the old dude's house burned down. No… grizzly tales, yes, that's better. I know, I'm good. I amaze myself sometimes," he remarked as he unleashed his sick sense of humour on me.

Two hours later, the drama was over, smoke still billowing out of the windows but it was under control. I got dressed and went outside.

"Good morning, mate, how's it going?" I said in a chirpy voice to the fireman.

"Please stand back!" the fireman snapped.

I stepped back just in time to get out of the way of two firemen carrying the body out on a stretcher, covered up in a body bag.

Bill was still standing there watching. "I feel good, da, da, da, I feel good, da, da, da," he sang, totally ignoring the dead body. "Looks like a nice day today. Pity I'm on my way to work, really."

"Bill! Have some feeling for the dead man, please."

"Morning," the lady next door yelled over the fence.

I ignored her. I detested my next door neighbour. Snobby was an understatement. She was forever boasting how well her husband was doing at work. She never shut up. I nearly died from laughter when I found out that the man was just a car washer. The way she talked, I'd thought he was the general manager of the garage he worked for.

I got into my car and sped off down the road, leaving the drama behind, music blaring as I went. Techno, techno, techno.

"Morning, Derek," I yelled across the workshop of Derby Motors, the car dealership where we both worked as motor mechanics. "Have I got a story to tell you! A guy died in a fire in our street last night. I was up half the night watching them try and put it out."

"You're joking?" Derek replied, shock and horror written across his face.

"I feel awful," I said. "The poor guy, he must have died in his sleep."

The morning flew by, but the drama of the night stayed in my mind as I worked. It really made me think about life and what I was doing with my own. Before long, it was lunchtime and we were sitting on the grass outside.

"Thank God it's lunch time, I'm starving, mate," I moaned, then, out of nowhere, added, "Aren't you sick of the UK, Derek?"

Derek stopped eating his ham and egg pie and looked me straight in the eye with a puzzled expression on his face.

I continued, "The crappy weather, the cramped conditions and the same old mundane routine of everything. Enough is enough! I'm ready to explode… I need a change in my life."

"Where will you go?" Derek replied.

"My sister told me that I can go back to New Zealand with her for a holiday, maybe to live," I said with a large cheesy grin on my face. "I'm fed up with the UK. There's nothing here for me anymore."

"Your Laura?" said Derek inquisitively. "It's been a while since I've seen her. What's she doing back here?"

"She's here for her mate's wedding. Anyway, enough about her and back to my plan. I fancy owning my own business. What do you think?"

Derek nearly choked on his pie. "Aye? You're as rough as guts, mate. If you had your own business, people would be suing you for gross negligence."

I ignored Derek and continued with my plan. "I'd like to specialise in something new, but I'm not too sure what. I feel I could take one aspect of what I'm doing now, fixing cars, of course, and then focus on the new. If I could bullshit my way through until I became an expert at whatever I choose, it'd be perfect. Maybe cars, maybe something new. Who knows?"

I was tapping on my cigarette packet, staring into space as I spoke. Derek's face screwed up. He frowned and stared at me.

"You're a dreamer, mate," he said. "I mean what about taxes, business plans, marketing, equipment, housing, transportation… just to name a few obstacles. Besides, if you go now, you'll miss Dusk till Dawn. It's due for release at the end of this month."

"That's a good point, it's a serious business missing a good movie. However, you're a bore, my friend. A typical Dudley," I said. "Look, all I'm saying is, I'm twenty five now and I don't want to work as a mechanic for the rest of my life. That's all. My sister's promised me she'll help me with setting up a business, she's got her own midwifery partnership."

Derek was quite intelligent but, at the same time, very unsure of himself and incredibly sensible. In fact, he can be downright boring at times. Despite these imperfections, we were best friends and had been for what seemed like an eternity.

"Think of it… the country of fine wines, lush green bush and best of all, a very low population. Oh, and kiwi fruit, of course." I chuckled, feeling very excited.

Derek stopped drinking his tropical fruit juice for a moment and turned towards me. "Go on."

I cleared my throat. "Well… with a low population, that means potential for growth. Business growth." I had a smug grin on my face. "Well, what do you think? The dog's bollocks or what?"

Derek didn't say a word.

"Do you know what I fancy doing?" I said, grinning mischievously.

"I haven't got a clue, but I'm sure you're going to tell me," sighed Derek.

"You're dead right, mate! I am going to tell you. I wouldn't mind being a mobile mechanic or fitting alarm systems. Just think of the money I could earn? I would rake the cash in." The frustration in my voice grew. "If you weren't such a big girl's blouse, you could quit this damn place and join me. Don't you ever take risks?"

Derek let out a sigh and tried to shrug off my remarks.

"Imagine it! Our own business together, mate," I said. "I mean, the UK is falling apart, isn't it? There is no Great Britain any more. It's the bloody Americans buying up everything. Well, isn't it?"

You could have cut the atmosphere with a knife.

Derek was silent for a few moments, trying his best to absorb what I'd just said.

"British standards have seriously dropped. I've had it with this country!"

Derek laughed. "That's quite an extreme opinion, isn't it? Life isn't that bad in the UK. Besides, I have my family here, and I tend to think of them before myself."

I rose to my feet and fronted Derek up. "Oh, for Christ's sake, man! You see what I mean about you being a bloody girl's blouse?

You're always worrying, aren't you? It's one bleeding excuse after another. Fine! I'll go it alone then."

Angry, I kicked an old oilcan that was lying on the grass. The silence was almost deafening between us.

Finally, Derek spoke. "Why don't you go on ahead, and if you think New Zealand is any good, I'll come out… okay?"

I hesitated for a moment. "Yeah, great idea. I'll test the water for a year, let's say, and then give you a full report on my findings. If you like what I find, you can join me."

We smiled, then sat back against the wall opposite our service bay and got on with eating our lunch.

I couldn't help continuing. "My sister paints a very rosy picture of New Zealand, she never shuts up. If I wasn't going there myself, I'd be quite jealous. I can't wait to get there."

"Aren't there more sheep than people over there?" said Derek, grinning.

"No!" I snapped. I was tapping on the cigarette packet again.

"I think there is, mate," Derek retorted. "I don't know what she's told you, but I hope you've got your facts straight."

"I have. I've asked my brother-in-law if I'd get a work permit and a job to start off with and he agrees I'll get work easily with my English qualifications. They actually mean something over there. It's supposed to be like the UK in the 60s. You know, where you go for a job and get an interview straight away then they ask when you can start. Unlike here nowadays, where it's all about two interviews and 'we'll call you', then you never hear from them again, with sixteen people turning up for the same job."

"Without the two and a half million on the dole, you mean," Derek said laughing.

"Probably because there's only three and a half million people in the whole of New Zealand and there's like sixty four million in the UK. My sister's certainly sold me the opportunities of going to New Zealand, so I'm going for it. She said that they'd support and guide me through it all, so I'm quite confident now." I was stubborn by nature and once I'd made up my mind, that was that. It was time for a change in my life and the arrival of my sister presented the perfect opportunity.

On my last day at work, I walked into the main workshop to see the entire staff of Derby Motors in there, including the general manager, Mr Pringle. Several days had passed since I'd told Derek my plans. We hadn't mentioned it again, so I assumed that he would have forgotten all about it.

"What's going on here?" I said. "Did you arrange this, Derek?"

"Okay, so what if I did?" Derek said, smiling.

Mr Pringle handed over a package, wrapped in Star Trek paper. It was blatantly obvious to me that Derek had wrapped my present. Star Trek is my favourite TV show. Sad, I know, but I love anything futuristic and imaginative.

"Go ahead and open it, then," Derek said, anxiously.

I ripped off the wrapping paper. "Wow, a beer voucher, for a non-drinker… perfect."

"I thought it was about time you got out there and had some fun," Derek said. "You know? Like socialising and meeting people? Before you leave, I will get you drunk, my friend." Derek laughed out loud.

"Hey, Kevin," Dave Berkeley chirped up, out of the throng of workers. "What are you going to do with all of those sheep in New Zealand, mate? Woohoo! You know what I mean? Nudge, nudge, wink, wink."

"Why is it that everyone in England thinks of New Zealand as being nothing more than sheep-shearing and beer-drinking?" I said.

"Because it is… that's why," Derek chipped in.

"But how do you know? Have you been there?" I was quite vexed by my co-worker's ribbing. If I'd been a cartoon character, steam would have been coming from my ears.

He nudged me and laughed. "You'll love it," he said.

I nodded. I was sure I would.

The following morning, I lay in bed, wrapped in my warm duvet, thinking of my new life in New Zealand. Then it hit me.

Doubt.

'Look! You're just nervous,' I thought. 'You'll be fine, just relax.'

Nothing like giving myself a good talking to.

I dragged myself out of bed and made a cup of piping hot tea, dunking the tea bag several times. I moved to the living room and sat smoking a cigarette, trying to bring myself back to the land of the living.

'Oh God, I'm leaving everything behind that I've worked so hard for since leaving school,' I thought in a last minute attempt to self-sabotage my trip.

In four hours time, I wouldn't have a choice.

I'd be on a plane travelling to the other side of the planet.

'Pull yourself together, man,' I thought to myself. 'What's wrong with you?'

To avoid the next four hours dragging painfully, I decided on a pleasant walk in my local park. I felt at ease with myself there and had always solved many of my troubles by walking through the park, lost in deep thought.

That time though, it didn't work. Back from my walk and only two hours had gone.

My parents pulled up in their car just as I was unlocking the front door. They followed me in, trooping into the living room after me. There was still no sign of Laura.

"God, I hate waiting around!" I said as I flopped down on the sofa. "Come on, Laura!"

I was trying my hardest to relax. The doubts about going to New Zealand popped into my head again. I just wanted to get on with it.

"Dad, so it's all set with the estate agents, then?" I said. "You know… the tenants are moving in next week and they pay three quarters of the mortgage and then, when I get a job in New Zealand, I pay the rest. In the meantime, I use savings to pay it, just till I decide whether to sell or keep letting it, renting or have my own business, yeah?"

"Yes, man, don't worry," said my dad. "I've sorted it, just relax, will you?"

"Okay, thanks, dad. You're the best."

Laura walked into the living with a grin. "Hi, Kevin, mum, dad. How are you all? Ready, Kevin?"

I sat up. "I've been ready for hours, sis. Where've you been?"

"Oh chill out, will you? You're going to New Zealand, where everyone relaxes and doesn't have a care in the world. Rushing just isn't in the vocabulary," Laura said loudly. "Come on, the taxi's waiting."

I often thought that her voice resembled a foghorn. The decibel level was certainly the same. I shrugged off her comments, grabbed my luggage and went outside to the waiting taxi and Laura's husband, John, who helped me with the bags.

Laura's mouth had certainly got louder since I last saw her. I suddenly wasn't sure about going with her because she'd changed. When we were kids, we were best of mates… peas in a pod, so to speak. Now…?

I shrugged off the doubts and hugged my mum. "I'll call you both, once I arrive in Auckland. Don't worry, I'll be fine. Now take care and I'll speak to you soon. Bye."

"Take care, son. I love you. Bye," my mum yelled after me. She tried to hide her tears, but it was no good, she began to cry.

And off we went.

Some twenty-five minutes later, the taxi pulled up outside the airport and John paid the driver and walked over to join us outside the airport. John lived in his head most of the time. He was a nice enough sort of guy, but a real daydreamer. You could scream at him beyond angry, but he wouldn't lose his cool, he was super chilled-out all the time. John grabbed the trolley with the luggage on and began pushing it towards the entrance of the airport.

Newcastle Airport was gleaming, looking very bright and shiny.

The newly overhauled building made me proud to be from the North East, all these passengers' first impression was the airport. I was totally overwhelmed with excitement and anticipation, and just couldn't wait to take off on my first overseas adventure. I'd forgotten what it was like to see and do something new and exciting. All I'd done since leaving school was work.

I had so much on my mind... business, jobs, work permits, new people. It was all just too much, so I decided to take my mind off it all and explore the airport. I pondered, looking for something interesting, trying to forget my doubts and worries. Then I found it… a large window where I could stand and watch the planes taking off and landing. I stood there, awe-inspired by the 747s roaring into life, racing down the runway. I couldn't get enough of it. I stood there for a while, watching one 747 after another until Laura appeared at the other side of the departure lounge.

"Come on, Kevin," she yelled. "Let's get going or we'll miss the flight."

Like I said, a foghorn.

I mumbled under my breath.

"Okay, I'm coming," I added, in my normal voice.

I managed to drag myself away from the window and ran to join John and Laura, puffing and panting. "Phew! Wait up you two. I'm so out of shape, I'm knackered."

As I entered the plane, I noticed that the stewardess was wearing a strange-looking dress. "What the hell is she wearing?"

John explained that the dress was called an Abya.

I was beginning to realise that there was a whole new world out there besides England. What else would I see on my journey? The stop over point in Dubai would be interesting. I felt as excited as a child at Christmas time and just couldn't wait to see the rest of the world. My sheltered life was over from this point on.

We made our way to the back of the plane, in economy class, where we found our seats. I'd requested a window seat at the travel agent a few weeks earlier. I didn't want to miss a thing. My inquisitive mind sometimes gets the better of me.

"Cabin crew be seated for take-off," the first officer said over the tannoy and the plane started to move.

My stomach flipped with the speed as we took off and I gazed out of the window, slowly watching the earth disappear.

Then there were just clouds.

A few Bacardis and coke later, I was sound asleep.

Until Laura woke me by thrashing me with her pillow.

"Laura, stop it!" I yelled at the top of my voice.

The whole economy class section turned around and stared at me.

"Who's Mr Grumpy then?" she laughed. "Just because you haven't had a smoke in six hours?"

"Annoying cow," I mumbled under my breath, then I ignored her and went back to sleep.

The rest of the trip was disappointingly uneventful really. I just got bored with the vast array of clouds floating around outside… so much for my window seat. The short stopovers in Dubai and Singapore were a welcome break, and I knew that at some point in my life I'd go back to both for a closer look. There were just so many things to see and do.

Some thirty hours of flying and two countries later, we touched down in Auckland, New Zealand.

We grabbed a trolley, loaded up our luggage and then wheeled it through customs.

I noticed a sniffer dog, a sandy coloured Labrador, checking everyone's luggage, trying to stay focused on its work and not wag its tail and get excited over the new people in the line. I walked over to the animal and began stroking it. "Here, boy. How are you, fella?"

"Let him be, mate," the customs officer said in a strong Kiwi accent. "The animal's got a job to do, mate, so let him get on with it!"

"Err, okay. No problem," I mumbled.

The customs officer moved onto the next group of people in

the line and the dog began sniffing the contents of their luggage too.

We three weary travellers walked through to the arrival section, where Laura's friend Karen was waiting anxiously. Laura waved her hands in the air and shouted at the top of her voice. "Hi, Karen. How are you, dear?"

Me and John just looked at each other in amazement.

"Oh God. How do you put up with her, John?"

"Oh, you know, I've just got used to it, I suppose. It's not that bad once you've heard it a few million times. That's just how she is."

We loaded our luggage in the back of Karen's Mitsubishi and jumped in the car. Karen was wearing a scarf, hat and a winter jacket. I found this highly amusing since the temperature was 18 degrees C and we'd just come from a northern hemisphere summer, which was about the same temperature.

"Wow!" I said as we drove along. "This place is like the Garden of Eden."

It was fresh, clean and untouched by mankind. Everything was so bright and colourful. England seemed so dark and miserable compared to New Zealand. The buildings looked no more than ten years old. Even the cars looked bright and shiny. Bright, blue skies and not a cloud to be seen. Funny really, since the Maori name for New Zealand was Aotearoa, the land of the white cloud. I'd read that on the plane over.

Adrenaline coursed through my veins. I was pumped, giddy and excited all at the same time. "I love it here! I'm going to stay forever," I said to Laura.

I was so engrossed, nose pressed against the car window, at new things and places that I barely noticed the twenty minute drive from the airport to Laura's house. Most of all, I was mesmerised by the greenery.

"Oh shit, would you look at that?"

I stared in amazement as we pulled up the driveway of Laura's house. Half of the house was set deep in the ground while the other half was a mass of intertwining beams and stilts that supported a large sun deck. The driveway led down to a three-car garage. Above the driveway was a large barbecue area, with palm trees set in large clay pots.

We got out of the car and Laura stood on the deck, admiring the view with me.

"We're not in Kansas anymore, Dorothy," I chuckled. "Would you look at that? You can see the whole valley."

"So you like it, then?" asked Laura, smiling.

"It's absolutely unreal," I said. "The house is everything that you could wish for. What's that growing in your garden, Laura? Kiwi fruit, maybe?"

"Pink grapefruit, actually," she said. "I'm glad you like it though. Now, go and get your luggage from the car then get yourself unpacked. John is going to Big Mike's fish and chip shop in a moment, so don't take too long."

Mike, I learned, was famous in West Auckland for his fish and chips. No matter what you ordered from this man, he would always reply with the same answer, "Five minutes." You could order everything on the menu for fifty people and he would still say, "Five minutes."

I nipped out to get my luggage from the car then dumped the bags on my bed. I didn't want to unpack, so I went to explore the rest of the house instead. At the foot of the hallway, I found some stairs that led down to a utility room and garage.

"Yeah, yeah, seen down here… let's have a look elsewhere." I didn't care who was listening. I was happy just roaming around the house, enjoying myself.

In the living room, I spotted a large drinks trolley filled with just about every type of New Zealand wine imaginable. "Oh, wow," I thought, "there are some serious drinkers in this house."

"You like the wine?" John said from behind me.

I jumped at the sound of his voice, I hadn't even realised he was there. "I always thought Italy or France were where good wines came from?" I said, grinning.

"Nah, not so, there's some fantastic Australian and New

Zealand wine out here, they make some damn fine wines. In fact, half of these bottles are from vineyards down the road in Oratia, Henderson and Kumeu. The climate's perfect. We usually go on the trail and taste-test once a year. The South Island has some of the greatest wines in the world… Nelson, Canterbury and Marlborough are the best places. You should try some if you get the chance."

It sounded good.

Everything sounded good.

Over the next few days, I spent most of my time sitting on the sundeck, enjoying the views and contemplating life in general.

Laura joined me on the deck and flopped into a chair. "Kevin," she said, "I've been thinking."

"That's dangerous… you thinking."

"Ha, very funny. I've think you need to get out there and see a bit more of Auckland. More than just the views of Henderson Valley, in any case. What do you think about dropping me at work tomorrow then taking the car and going exploring."

I was quite happy with Laura's suggestion. I'd missed driving over the past week. Laura's Jeep was a bit of a hairdresser's car, but free nevertheless.

CHAPTER TWO
AUCKLAND AT A GLANCE

The next morning, I dropped Laura off at the hospital where she worked and asked where I could find a corner shop.

"Dairy!" she said, getting out of the car.

"What?"

"It's called a dairy. You're in New Zealand now, so call it a dairy." She turned away to walk into work.

"Okay. Dairy? What a strange name for a shop. Are there cows there or something?" I muttered to myself.

It was probably a good thing she didn't hear.

I left the car at the house and went for a wander, eventually finding the shop and asking naively, "Forty Regal King Size, please, mate."

"G'day, mate. What's Regal King Size?" the guy behind the counter replied.

"Oh, sorry!" I eyed the cigarettes behind the counter. "Sooo… what you got? Erm, forty Pall Mall, please."

I paid for my smokes then wandered back outside.

A scruffy looking boy of twelve or so was leaning against the shop window, staring at me. "G'day, bro. Wanna buy some dak?"

"What the hell's dak?" I replied.

"Weed, bro, weed." The boy was sniggering at my ignorance.

"Err, nah. I don't think so."

"Suit yourself."

"It makes you happy, yeah?" I asked, curiosity piqued.

"It's sweet, bro. Skunk will make you happy."

"How much?"

"Fifty bucks, bro."

I pulled out my wallet and fumbled around until I found fifty dollars of this monopoly money.

"So you inject it, right?" I said.

"Ha, ha, ha. Nah, bro, you roll up and smoke it."

"Oh, so I put it in ciggies and smoke it, then?"

"Bro! You have no idea, have you, aye? You take a bud, you know the flower head, and then you break it into little pieces. Roll it up and then smoke it." The boy handed me a bag, then turned to walk away.

"Cheers, mate." I gave the boy a thumbs-up.

"Catcha, bro," he called over his shoulder.

'I must be out of my mind,' I thought. 'I don't even drink beer that much. Still, there are hardly any cops over here.' I felt free from English laws made hundreds of years ago by some landowner, some lord of the manor-come-politician repressing the people. 'Yeah, man, here we go,' I thought, 'time to get wasted.'

I opened the weed bag and inhaled the scent of the sticky buds. 'Woah, that's strong. Smells like, like… well… marijuana, I guess. Ha, ha, ha,'

Then I had an idea.

Why not just sit on the wall and roll a joint?

I emptied the tobacco from a cigarette, placed a sticky bud inside and took a huge drag. I expected an instant reaction, but no. Nothing.

"G'day, mate. Trying a bit of dac cous?" asked a man, walking by.

"Holy shit!" I said. "Does everyone do weed here? Back home, it's the end of the world and they'd lock me up and throw away the key."

"Yeah, nah, mate, you're sweet, bro, knock yourself out," said the man, laughing.

Suddenly, my eyes started flickering and my eyelids became heavy, closing and opening in super-slow motion.

'Oh shit, oh shit. There's something happening, something very strange happening.'

Then, all of a sudden, my mind was racing. Alive with thought. I was dreaming but wide-awake and, boy, was I focused, super-duper focused! Every muscle in my body was aching and then retracting from a downward position. My legs and arms began involuntarily retracting and then springing back… it was like a doctor was checking my reflexes with a medical hammer. My body collapsed in a heap on the floor, heavy while my mind floated, lighter-than-air.

'We have lift-off!' I thought. 'I guess this is what's known as being stoned.'

I giggled uncontrollably, fits of laughter, for no apparent reason. "Fuck, this is good!" I yelled at the top of my voice. "I lurve marijuana."

I had no idea how I was gonna walk back up the hill to sis's house, let alone cruise around Auckland sightseeing, but right then, I just didn't care. Ha, ha, happy days.

I picked up my stoned carcass and put one foot in front of the other, struggling with every footstep. After a few steps, I was so short of breath, I had to stop for a moment. "God," I muttered to myself, "I feel like an old man. Weed certainly takes my breath away, may not have as much next time."

As I approached Laura's house, I glanced at my watch.

Half an hour to stagger up a hill? Cool.

I fumbled around in my pocket for my sister's Suzuki keys. 'Yup, I'm actually going to drive. My sis wants me to get out there and explore… well, so be it,' I thought, as I staggered towards the Jeep and fell inside.

I reversed the Suzuki out of the drive at lightning speed and then sped off down the hill, radio blaring and arm hanging out of the window.

"I feel good, da, da, da, I feel good," I sang, as I drove.

Soon, a calming effect washed over me and I slowed right down to a crawl. I was wasted and my brain slowed to a dead stop too.

Cars were now overtaking me, drivers giving me the finger.

"Yeah, fuck you, mate!" I yelled. "I'm driving here."

I threw a cigarette into my mouth and lit it, all in one motion.

A smoke just finished the high feeling off. Like a dessert at the end of a good meal.

I could barely keep my eyes open, let alone drive. What if I was stopped while I was under the influence? I decided I didn't really give a shit. Not my country, ha, ha, ha. What they gonna do? Deport me?

Back home in England there were cars, traffic jams and industry. Not here, people were playing cricket… in the city streets. People were walking around barefoot, hilarious really. If only people from my beloved Newcastle, in their business suits, could see these people, what would they think?

The Suzuki idled at the traffic lights, somewhere in the heart of Auckland city, just before exit one, southern motorway. As my mind raced from the joint, I absorbed the new sights and sounds, cricket matches and all.

The lights changed to green.

I snapped out of my daydream and drove off slowly, making my way to the harbour bridge some fifteen minutes later.

"Finally, I get to the damn bridge. What a drama!" I said to myself.

The bridge was New Zealand's answer to the Sydney harbour bridge. 'Average, I suppose,' I thought, as I began the drive over it.

I revelled at the beautiful, bright, blue ocean below and expensive super yachts on either side of the bridge, as I drove. There were three lane highways on the bridge, the lanes separated with red and white concrete blocks that actually moved automatically, according to traffic times. Driving into the city, early morning, the blocks were moved so that there were three lanes available. On the drive home, out of the city, the blocks were moved again to make the opposite side of the bridge have three lanes.

Another snippet of information I'd read on the plane.

'Quite ingenious really,' I thought. 'Must be a British idea.'

Across the bridge, crisp, golden east coast beaches were waiting for me to explore, bright blue ocean and last but not least… naked women. The whole place was truly amazing. I hadn't been swimming since I was a kid. It was too tempting.

I turned into the car park, near an early settler group of houses, and parked the car. I stripped off down to my underwear, hoping no one was watching and then ran down to the edge of the water to test the temperature. The water was lovely and warm.

I ran into the sea, with anticipation, loving every minute of my new found freedom. I felt like a child again, wild and free without a care in the world. I swam around for ten minutes or so, one stroke, two strokes.

Suddenly, I gulped some water, then more. My breathing became more difficult and I began floating and kicking my feet, desperately trying to swim to shore. Then a strange sense of calmness came over me and I was, once more, swimming with confidence now. It flowed with ease, like a knife through butter.

I made it back to shore, sat on the warm sand and took it all in.

It was a beautiful day, sun shining and not a cloud in the sky. I contemplated my morning's excursion. 'Wait till I tell Derek about this,' I thought, 'he won't believe that I was actually swimming in the ocean.'

The traffic was light and breezy on the drive home, the drive just flowed, until I hit the dreaded, western motorway. Everything had come to a dead stop. It was a nightmare, I hardly had any fuel left and I had to pick Laura up in half an hour. I thought I'd never make it in that traffic.'

As I drove up, Laura was waiting for me in the hospital car park, and I could see the anger on her face from miles away.

"Where the hell have you been?" she yelled. "I've been waiting for half an hour!"

"The traffic was a complete and utter nightmare," I replied. "You never told me it was this bad."

"Oh!" she yelled again. "So it's my fault?"

"How the hell am I supposed to know what the traffic's like?"

Laura growled. "Come on, let's just go… I just want to unwind and get something to eat."

We got into the Jeep and as I drove it out of the hospital car park and onto the main street in Henderson, you could have cut the atmosphere with a knife, it was so thick. I just tried my best to ignore my sister and focus on driving.

When we arrived home, I went straight to my room to change.

"Don't think that you're going to get off that easily!" Laura yelled after me. "The bloody Jeep is nearly empty, you're late and you still haven't said you're sorry."

"Just drop it, will you? You're winding me up over nothing," I yelled back.

"That's not the point, Kevin. And you bloody well know it."

"Whatever, Laura. You think what you want. I'm going to watch telly with John."

Sometime later, Laura finally cooled down.

"Listen, I'm sorry I yelled at you," she said. "We lost a baby on today's shift. It doesn't happen very often, but when it does, it really gets to you." She smiled at me. "So, we're good, yeah?"

I sighed. "Let's put it behind us. Anyways, can you tell me a bit of what I need to do for my business? Like what the taxes are here, tax claims and stuff."

"Sorry but do you mind if we leave it for now?," said Laura. "I've got so much paperwork to do, it'll have to be another time."

"As long as you don't forget."

"Hey, while I remember… do you want to go with Ann and Josie to the Sky Tower this weekend? It could be fun."

Ann and Josie were the daughters of Karen and Dave, who lived just down the road from John and Laura. They had been friends since Laura and John had first arrived in New Zealand a few years ago. Karen was half Maori and half Pakiha, or European. Dave was English and had emigrated some twenty years ago with his family and, one divorce later, he'd met Karen.

"The where Tower?" I said. "Oh, is that the Tower with a casino at the top?"

"Yep, that's the one," replied Laura. "How do you know about it?"

"I saw it on my tour of the city the other day," I replied. "But in answer to your question, yes. I suppose it'll be something different to do."

"Their boyfriends are taking them, Todd and Damon. You don't mind going with them, do you?" she said.

"Not at all. Actually, I'm quite looking forward to it. I've never been to a casino before. It's a date."

The rest of the week I lazed around the house and got over my jet lag. I loved getting up when I wanted. It was much more of a natural feeling getting up at 9am instead of being ripped out of deep sleep at 7am. I was in heaven.

When the girls turned up at the weekend, they drove up in a tiny black Honda.

"It'll be a bit of a tight squeeze in the back, Kevin," said Ann. "But it's better than walking. Aye?"

"Yeah, I'm sure I'll manage," I replied.

I climbed in the back of the Honda and put my legs across the back seat. There wasn't enough room to sit normally, so there I was with my knees in my face.

Josie put the Honda in reverse and backed onto Glendale Road. She whizzed in and out of the traffic, beeping the horn at anyone in her way.

Amazingly, we managed to get to the Tower in one piece.

We made a move for the elevator from the underground car park.

Ping. 17th floor.

The main room reminded me of Las Vegas. Glitz and glamour, lights and spinning disco balls, one-armed bandits as far as the eye could see. As we walked through the lobby area, I noticed a Maori display of wooden carvings. Many artefacts, styled like a Kauri tree trunk, one chap even had facial tattoos, just like a tree bark, his tongue out and mouth wide. There was also a history of the haka – translated means die enemy – a chant to warn off their enemies. I found it all very interesting. In the far corner of the room, a Mercedes Benz was rotating on a turntable.

And then the mission of getting young Ann past the guy on the door and into the casino began. She was only seventeen, a problem because the entry age was twenty-one, so the plan was for me to take Josie's ID over to Ann, once Josie was inside.

It worked a treat too.

"That was easy," said Ann. She spotted Damon, her boyfriend, and his friend Todd at the bar and ran over to them.

I followed, a bit slower. "Hey, Damon… Todd… how's it going?" I said. "Can I get you a beer?"

"Hi, Kevin. How's your first week in New Zealand going?" Damon said. "Not working too hard, are you?"

"Nah, I haven't even started looking for a job yet. I'm just cruising, you know. Trying to suss the place out and see what's going on," I replied.

We all followed Ann, who led the way to the one-armed bandits and watched her throw huge amounts of coins into the machine and get nothing in return.

"Let me have a go," said Damon.

Damon put fifty cents in the same machine that Ann had been playing on and pulled the lever. The bars rolled around and around until it finally stopped at a losing sequence.

"Shit. Not our lucky day, is it?" he muttered.

Damon and Ann left the machine and went back to the bar, while I studied the machine.

I reckoned that the amount of money that had gone into that machine, it would pay out in the next one or two goes.

I put my fifty cents in and pulled as hard as I could. The bars rolled around and around and then it stopped.

Damn, no luck!

I tried again. But still nothing… ah, well.

So much for my calculations.

"Hard luck, bro," said Todd as we walked over to the bar to join the others.

The time was right for me to sneak off to the toilets and have a smoke. I emptied the tobacco out of one of my cigarettes and pushed a bud inside, then lit it.

"Where you been, bro?" asked Damon, upon my return.

"Urh, erm," I replied, tapping nervously on the bar. Paranoia had set in. "What do you mean? I haven't done anything wrong."

"I didn't say you'd done anything wrong, cous. Woah! What's wrong with your eyes? They're bloodshot to hell."

Somewhere under my paranoia, I knew I had to get away from them for a while so I left them at the bar and walked over to see what was happening at the lucky dip.

I stared at the Merc rotating on its plinth. "I'll have a go of that, pet," I said to the beautiful blonde behind the counter. "You've got beautiful eyes, my lovely."

"Here's your ticket, sir," the girl said with a smile.

"Oh my God, you're gorgeous." Before I knew what I was doing, I was reaching for her boobs.

She slapped my face and cried, "Piss off, you pervert!"

I grinned and went to see what the other four were doing.

"What's up, guys?" I said between fits of laughter. "Oh, playing some pontoon, are we? Twenty three, unlucky, mate."

"Come on, guys," Damon said. "Let's go and play roulette. It should be cool, aye?"

I followed the others to the roulette table, on the other side of the casino.

'Fuck, am I wasted…' I thought to myself. 'Everyone's fading in and out of reality.'

"Red thirty four," Damon told the young lady at the roulette table.

"Oi, you, bro!" a man mountain yelled at me. "Get the fuck out now! Assault one of my Sheilas, will you! I'll hurt you, bro."

I stared at the man mountain and thought momentarily of retaliating.

Ann stepped between us. "We're going," she said to him quickly. "He's terribly sorry. We're done here anyway, let's go."

"What the hell did you do?" Damon said as we walked away.

I shrugged, still not sure what had come over me.

"You owe Ann big time, bro," he said. "She really saved your bacon."

"Yeah, thanks," I replied, sarcastically.

At that, we decided to call it a night while we still had some money left and were still in one piece. We made our way out of the casino and downstairs to the car park.

"Well, that's the Sky Tower done," I chuckled to myself.

Ann, Josie and me piled into the little Honda, while the guys made their own way home. Josie drove out of the car park and onto Fanshaw Street for the twenty minute drive home.

CHAPTER THREE
THE INTERVIEW

"Hello. M1 Technical Recruitment. Ron speaking."

"Hi, err, I'd like to speak to someone regarding an interview," I said, sheepishly. "Are you the right person to speak to?"

"Yeah, nah," Ron replied in his strong Kiwi accent. "What's ya name and I'll get you in today for an interview."

I nervously told my CV to Ron, unsure how he would interpret my English work history. As the conversation moved on, his mood relaxed and the conversation began to flow. We agreed to meet at 1.30pm that day. I laughed to myself. Everything was 'dude' or 'buddy' or combinations, like 'excellent, dude'. All straight out of a Bill and Ted movie.

To fill in the time before the interview, I borrowed John's Mitsubishi Colt and it drove really well along the winding, country roads to Bethels beach.

The beaches were black on the west coast. Volcanic. Warm sand between my toes, the socks and shoes were off, warm rays of sunshine shining down on my face, with a gentle breeze flowing through my hair. Not too hot, not too cold. It was beautiful.

Down the beach, I could make out a little white caravan selling tea and snacks. The whole look was very English seaside. I almost expected to see someone wearing a knotted handkerchief on their head. I continued past the caravan and out onto the beach where there was a huge rock face. I could see some houses on top of it, nothing more than shacks.

It was very strange indeed. Who would put houses on top of a cliff? Talk about seclusion. No road, no track. In fact, I couldn't even see how anyone would get up the cliff… unless they were a mountaineer, that is?

I continued walking along the beach, seashells crunching under my feet as I walked, until I reached a cul-de-sac, surrounded by rocks and penguins jumping off the rocks into the sea.

"Wow, amazing!" I yelled at the top of my voice.

Then…

"Oh God, it's twelve o'clock already, I'll be late for my interview if I don't get a wiggle on."

I turned around and began the long walk back to the car park. In a way, I no longer felt enthusiastic about the interview, the better option would be to pitch a tent on the beach and get back to nature. Perhaps live off the land and be free as a bird, but I also remembered reality and how I had debts to pay and a business to set up when I eventually got around to it.

I left paradise behind and made my way to the concrete jungle, the western motorway, city bound. The turn-off arrived for Newton Road and then onto K Road. K Road had a funny sounding name. It went something like Karangershape Road. It was so long that most people just called it K Road.

K Road was kind of like London's Soho. Anything and everything was possible. It was quite a strange place to have a job agency really, but, hey, what did I know? Strip joints and gay video shops on one side of the road and coffee shops and a job agency on the other side… bizarre.

Several drive-bys later, I slowed to a cruising speed long enough to see a tiny sign… M1 Technical Recruitment.

Could they have made it any more difficult to find?

Beautiful blue skies, sun shining. A walk from the car to the agency would give me a chance to burn off a bit of nervous energy.

'Okay, time to relax, Kevin mate. Time for a joint,' I thought while anxiously tapping on my cigarette box. I lit up a pre-rolled joint and breathed in the smoke.

Within minutes, I could barely stand up.

I opened the large, glass door at the entrance to the building and went inside. There I found a short corridor, which led to a flight of stairs. Halfway up the stairs I saw another sign… M1 Technical Recruitment Agency. First Floor.

"Here goes nothing," I mumbled as I started up the stairs.

At the top, my eyes nearly popped out of my head. There was a reception area with a blonde-haired receptionist, sitting behind a rather tatty looking desk. It was perfectly obvious that she'd been hired for her looks and not her brains. It was even more apparent when she began to talk.

"Hi, can I help?" she squealed.

A shiver ran down my spine at the thought of listening to her whiny voice long-term.

"Is he here?" I inquired.

"Who? Ron? Are you Mr Thomas?" she replied.

"I certainly am," I said, smiling.

"Okay, Mr Thomas. If you wait just one moment, I'll see if he's free," she said. "In the meantime, why don't you take a seat over there, darling?"

Once I'd sat down, I noticed a coffee machine that looked as though it hadn't been cleaned in a year. On the table in front of me lay an assortment of grubby magazines. I picked up Mechanics Monthly and flicked through it.

I started staring at the receptionist's cleavage. She began fiddling with her necklace and, agitated, fluttered her eyes.

She leaned forward and ruffled her paperwork at the end of the desk to reveal even more cleavage as she leaned forward.

"Cheeky," the receptionist said, with a grin on her face.

"Urh, erm, what?" I finally managed to get the words out.

"You're staring at my boobs, aren't you? I don't know if you're man enough to take on someone like me, mate."

"Oh, really?" I stood up and walked across to her desk then sat on it.

She put her hand on my knee and began rubbing my leg up and down affectionately. "Do you like that?"

"What else can you do?" I replied, smiling.

"I could show you if you like? We only have five minutes before Ron's ready for you, though."

She stood up and joined me on the other side of the desk and then she bent over the desk, pulling up her mini skirt and pulling down her panties. "Go for it, big boy," she sighed.

"Here, now? Okay, if you insist," I replied, dropping my pants and banging her wildly over the desk.

"Oh yes, yes," she screamed. "You're a talented boy."

I joined in the moans and continued banging away. It was awesome…

But then I heard a firm, "Mr Thomas?"

And again, louder, "Mr Thomas?"

I blinked.

Back to reality!

The receptionist was smiling at me. "Mr Thomas, Ron will see you now."

I walked down the corridor to Ron's office, grinning back at the receptionist as I walked past.

As I walked into the office, I was greeted by a forty something year old, sitting with his feet on the desk, swigging a beer.

"Yeah, g'day, mate. How are ya, buddy? I'm Ron and you must be Kevin?"

"Err, yes, that's right, I'm Kevin. How do you do?"

"Yeah, good, mate… fancy a beer?" Ron said. "Fuck, yeah. Every fucking bloke fancies a beer. Oy, Margaret. Fetch our guest a beer will ya, darling. He looks as though he could use one."

"You offer beer in an interview?' I said. "You've gotta be kidding me, cool!"

"Yeah, mate. Glug one of these tinnies down your neck. Don't just stand there, pull up a chair, dude. Shit, yeah, it's all good, mate. You gotta have a beer and a breather half way through the day. It's in the fucking rule book, mate, aye!"

A translator was required. I had no idea what Ron had just said. I tried to keep up with the conversation. Maybe I should just humour him.

Later, I found out that a 'tinny' was a can of beer and 'glug' was drinking.

Strange people.

"Anyways, down to business," drawled Ron. "Newmarket Nissan needs a technician as soon as, mate. So, I need ya CV, asap."

I opened a large folder and pulled out my CV, then handed it to Ron.

He opened it. "Hmm, Guinetta sports cars, production line tech, that's a British sports car company… impressive, mate, impressive. I think we'll try you out with the company's general knowledge test."

He handed me the test paper and then told me that he was going for another beer.

I opened the first page and began reviewing the questions. It didn't look too bad, I suppose. I knew about the system. ECCS, good old Nissan engine management.

I picked up my pen and started the test.

It was an hour later when Ron reappeared, carrying a beer. He sat behind his desk and swigged away. "So, how ya going there, mate?"

"Oh, err, yes, nearly finished, Ron. Another two questions to answer and I'm done. Okay?" I replied.

"Yeah, mate. No worries. I'll just finish my beer then, aye?"

I completed the last two questions as quickly as I could and then passed the paper to Ron, who was barely coherent by this time. "Yeah, mate, I'm sure you've done a good job. Oh yeah, before I forget, how long did you work for Nissan UK?"

"Well, since I left school really, around sixteen years old, so nine years now, I guess."

"Shit, mate!" Ron yelled. "That's a serious amount of time, dude. You must know the product inside out by now. Shit hot? Anyway, what I'll do now is to mark your paper and then get back to you, okay? I'll get onto the service manager of Newmarket Nissan next and then set up a meeting, aye."

I nodded in agreement, then left Ron's office and walked through the reception area.

"See ya, luvvey," the blonde-haired secretary whined. She winked at me as I walked past.

"Err, yes, goodbye," I replied sheepishly.

Several days passed and Ken, the service manager of Newmarket Nissan, was supposed to have called me by now about the meeting Ron had said he would set up but so far it hadn't happened. So I took matters into my own hands.

"Hello, Newmarket Nissan. How may I help you?"

"May I speak with Ken Stillwater, please?" I replied.

There was a short moment of silence while the receptionist transferred me to Ken's office.

"Hi, Ken. How ya doing, mate? It's Kevin Thomas. I understand Ron from M1 Technical Recruitment has been in touch about a position with your good selves?"

"Oh yes, Kevin, I'm good, thanks for asking. Yes, I do know Ron and he did mention you. How about two o'clock today? Just so I can get to know you and discuss a few things, work history and so on. How does that sound, my friend?"

I gathered from Ken's accent that he was English, which I was going to use to my full advantage, of course. Fellow countrymen and all that.

"Sounds fantastic, Ken. I'll see you at two this afternoon."

Two hours passed… hours that seemed to take an eternity. Still it was lunchtime and I was having my favourite dish. Sushi.

After lunch, I made my way to Newmarket and found Nissan without any dramas. I parked around the side of the main building and went to find the service department. Newmarket Nissan was the largest Nissan dealership in New Zealand.

Or so I'd been told by Ron.

As I walked across the road, I noticed a separate used car yard opposite the main buildings. I walked up the ramp into the workshop, where I found the service reception. The reception was surrounded by glass and I walked through the sliding doors at the entrance, which opened automatically the second I walked up to them.

Oh oh, dirt bag alert!

A scruffy looking character was sitting behind an oil-covered counter. This guy was as dirty as a truck mechanic.

He was wearing a white shirt and red tie. Everyone else was in overalls. A thought went through my mind, 'I hope he's not the bloody service manager, please no. I don't want to work in a back street garage. I may be a low-life, but I do have some standards.'

The man's blond mop hadn't been combed in a year or so and it was obviously against his religion to brush his yellow teeth.

"Yeah, g'day, mate. How ya going?" the scruffy guy said in a strong Kiwi accent.

"I'm looking for Ken Stillwater, is he around?" I replied.

"Who wants ta know?" the scruffy guy growled.

I shuddered. 'This is going to be the same type of interview as M1,' I thought, 'I can feel it. This dirty guy is probably the general manager.'

"I do! My name is Kevin Thomas and I'm here for an interview for a technician's job. So, do you know where Ken is?"

"I'm Bert Perrins, the assistant service manager."

'Oh crap! I knew it! I fucking knew it,' I thought. 'This guy's a manager and he's meeting the public looking like that. My God, what is that smell? It smells like he hasn't had a shower in a month.'

I tried to brush off my negative thoughts and followed Bert to an office at the back of the reception area. As I walked into the office, I was greeted by a fifty something year old man with greying hair, dressed in a pin-striped suit.

"Hi mate, how are you? I'm Ken Stillwater, service manager of this little outfit. Grab a seat… so you've worked for Nissan before, then?"

"I have indeed, Ken," I said, sitting down opposite him. "I worked for Nissan UK for around nine years now, so I'm quite familiar with the inner workings, so to speak."

"I'll show you around the place if you want and then pass you over to Bert, so he can ask some of the technical mumbo jumbo," Ken said as he pointed to the workshop.

We made small talk while we walked around the workshop. Ken spent over twenty minutes showing me around the shop, before taking me back to his office. Then he called Bert to take over.

"Yeah, g'day, mate. How'd ya like the shop?" asked Bert.

"It's quite a size, isn't it? Looks well equipped too."

"Err, hmm, yeah. Ken has asked me to interview you," said Bert. "Tell me something about yourself, like where've you worked before?"

I was overcome by the smell of body odour. I really didn't want to be around Bert.

Why the hell hadn't someone said something to the man?

"As I told Ken, I worked for Nissan UK since leaving school at sixteen, so about nine years," I replied.

"Oh yeah, so quite experienced then?"

I could tell by his sloppy interview technique that this guy didn't have a clue what he was talking about and was just fishing and feeling his way around the interview. Time to baffle him with science and to stop being Mr Nice Guy.

"Yes, that's right," I said. "I was the hi-tech technician for a UK based company, which means that I have finished four levels of training at the Rickmansworth HQ. I am trained on the new Q32 LAN and NAT's system, along with ECCS on board computer training. I have completed twenty five of twenty five courses and have in-depth knowledge of all Nissan UK models. I also ran the workshop, acting as workshop foreman and in-house trainer, with four technicians and two apprentices under me."

Bert looked quite uncomfortable, and he cunningly changed the subject rather than continue to drown.

I was thinking it could have been a mistake coming to New Zealand if all the people were going to be like Bert and that nutcase Ron at M1 recruitment. But I decided to give it another go and not judge everyone by a few bad eggs with personal hygiene or drink issues. Besides, I needed the money to get my business off the ground.

Several days passed and I thought of calling Ken but I was enjoying my time off work, something that I hadn't done since leaving school, so I was determined to make the most of it while it lasted.

Finally, Ken faxed me the information I needed to obtain a work permit… the next challenge was to go to New Zealand immigration in town.

I found the phone number for the New Zealand Immigration Service in the phone book.

"Press one for Maori, press two for English, and press three for Samoan… then… press one for residency visas, press two for work permits," the immigration's answer service said.

'Great!' I thought. 'That didn't take long, did it? Not!'

The next few days were spent moping around the house, with an occasional walk down the road to the local dairy for some essential supplies, smokes, of course, and a spot of weed from my new, best, twelve-year-old friend.

A letter arrived while I was on my now daily walk around the block. The frustration of waiting for the immigration service had come and gone and I'd almost forgotten about it but I had the application form now, so all that was needed was to get into town and process it.

"Can I borrow your car tomorrow, John?" I said.

"No problem, mate," John replied in his usual calm manner.

"The sooner this nonsense is over with, the better. All I want to do is work and earn some bloody money!"

"Governments. That's just what you should expect from them. They take your money and give you zero in return. We had the same trouble. New Zealand and Australia have become very strict with immigrants over the years. There was a time when they paid you to settle here, now you have to be qualified and have a good job before they even entertain you. It's so that only good quality people come here. Not a bad idea, really."

It was bright and early for me the following morning, and I had one thing on my mind. Get a work permit! Today!

I arrived at the immigration building in town on Customs

Street bang on opening time… 7.30am. The reception area had five kiosks with digital displays above the kiosks. They were all set to zero. It was like a bingo hall, I was expecting someone to shout "house!" at any moment. There was a main reception area directly in front of me. I walked up to the large wooden counter with a large grin on my face.

"Good morning, I'm here for a work permit. Can you tell me what I have to do, please?" I said.

"I sure can," said the Maori lady behind the counter. "First you need to take one of these forms and then I give you a number and as soon as your number is shown on one of the above screens, then you go up to the counter and hand in your paperwork."

I took the ticket and then sat down in the large waiting area, with rows and rows of seats. I felt lost, sitting there on my own.

Within seconds, the man behind the first counter displayed my number.

Number three.

"G'day, mate. Your form, please," said the man.

"Here is my passport."

"I never asked for that, now, did I? Please may I have the application form only," snapped the man.

"Err, yes, here you go." I didn't know what to make of this guy.

"Okay, sir. Now your passport and $144, please."

"Oh, right, sorry. Here you go."

The man then stood up, turned and walked off through a doorway, while I was left guessing the outcome of my fate. Would I get a visa? I turned away from the kiosk and, to my amazement, there were now at least forty people behind me in a queue.

'My God! I've only been in here for ten minutes and it's already jam-packed.'

"Sir, your passport. Have a nice day and good luck with the new job."

I swung around to the glass counter to see the man handing over my passport. "Really, that's it? All finished? I can start work now?"

"You certainly can, as soon as you get an IRD number from the tax building in town."

"At this rate," I growled, "I'll end up paying the government to work here."

As I left the immigration building, I had two things on my mind.

First, I had no idea where the tax building was and, second, I needed some weed.

Luckily, John kept a map in the glove box of his car, and even luckier I spotted a guy who had the look of a total pothead.

'He'll do.'

The guy, a large Maori fellow, was standing on the street corner, looking very shady. "Oy mate," I said, "got any dak?"

"Do I look like a dealer, bro?"

"Err, yes actually. Do you have any, then?"

"I've only got a $20 tin foil on me. That do, bro?"

I took the foil of weed and paid him.

I spotted a quiet alley around the corner of Customs Street where, giddy with excitement, I carefully rolled up.

I had a slow ride to the Inland Revenue Department building on Simon Street. Nothing mattered now that I was stoned, and some form filling-in later, I was issued with my very own IRD card.

I was all set to start work at Newmarket Nissan.

CHAPTER 4
THE MOTLEY CREW

Bert stood at the top of the ramp smoking a cigarette and drinking a mug of tea as I arrived at work.

"G'day, mate. How are ya?" he called.

"Err, yeah, good thanks," I replied. "How's yourself?"

Bert led me into the kitchen, showed me the paraphernalia to make a cuppa and then disappeared into the workshop.

"G'day, mate," said one of the lads. "Are you the pommie guy that's starting today?"

"I'm not sure what pommie means, but yes, I'm the guy that's starting work today. I'm Kevin, by the way."

"Ross. Good to meet ya. If you follow me, I'll show you where the lockers are, so you can chuck your stuff in."

Ross was a cross between Pakiha or European Kiwi and Maori, from Papakura originally, a small town outside of Auckland on the east coast. He was roughly the same age as me so, hopefully, we'd have something in common. He had designer stubble and slicked-back hair, complete with cigarette in his mouth. He had his own unique style.

"I was expecting the workshop manager to show me around properly, but he cleared off," I said.

"Bert's a dick, mate. You'll find that out for yourself in good time. Don't trust him and don't tell him anything, he'll just use it against you. Stick with me, mate, and I'll keep you right."

I just nodded and decided to keep quiet until I found out for myself what Bert was really like.

We walked through the workshop and into a small room that was filled with lockers.

"So, you're from England, then?" said Ross with a cheeky grin on his face.

"That's right. I've been in New Zealand for about four weeks now."

"I was in the UK in 1991. It's a fucking mission getting visas, all right. In fact, it sucks shit."

I nodded in agreement.

"Shit, yeah, the UK was sweet, bro. I landed myself a cruisey job in a bar. Free piss every night, different pussy every week. Fuck, yeah, it kicked ass, all right," said Ross in his strong Kiwi accent. "The best thing was the pussy. Well-spoken English honeys, not like the bush pigs here, man. Okay, man, let's have a smoko and then I'll show you the ropes. Ken mentioned last week that you were starting, so he asked me if we could double up for a week or so."

During the morning, Ross introduced me to a variety of people, some real rough and ready characters, people I wouldn't usually give the time of day to, to be honest.

"G'day, Kevin. I'm Den."

Den was a full-blown Maori and his main function at work was selling tin foilies, which were basically marijuana flower heads rolled up inside of tin foil. Hence the name. Den was Ross's favourite supplier of weekend recreational drugs.

Den was also one of the mechanics at Newmarket Nissan. That was when he felt like it. He made more money selling drugs than he did from fixing cars.

Several of the mechanics smoked weed, as I found out, as I was introduced to them by Ross, over the course of the morning. A secret cult, if you like. Most didn't see a problem with being stoned on the job. Like Rob, for example… that guy just did not care one little bit.

Simon Dean was the dealer principal. He had lost a leg years ago in a construction site accident, so he walked with a limp. Apparently he was a real bastard.

"Don't cross him, man," Ross told me, "just stay out of his way. He's a fuckwit."

Two weeks passed at work. Talk about an easy ride. I spent most of my time talking to Ross and smoking cigarettes. I would top up a windscreen washer bottle here and check a tyre pressure there, and occasionally I went on a test drive with Ross and that was only to check out the honeys in Newmarket. Nothing too strenuous.

After years of practically killing myself with non-stop work in the UK, my life had taken an extreme turnaround.

The whole workforce seemed to be just plodding along at their own pace, as if time was standing still. Why should I rush myself when no one else seemed bothered? No matter how fast I worked, I would never earn the money I had hoped for. I found that out as the months went by when I opened my wage packets.

I became a connoisseur of relaxing and I had slowed down to a human being's pace, instead of the out of control machine I'd been in the UK.

Two types of people had emerged in my newly adopted country: the rich and successful in life, who drank too much, the alkies, and those who were super relaxed and down to earth, philosophers of life, the stoners.

Friday night arrived and it was time for the usual entertainment at C-Zone, John's place of work on Graham Road in town. Every Friday night, John's boss hosted a spread of fine wines, expensive beers and a variety of barbecue foods.

After several hours spouting verbal diarrhoea, Greg the sales manager, finally decided to let other people in the room talk.

"So, Kevin, how many beers you had, mate?" he bellowed.

"Just the one, Greg."

"Shit! Only one! The required amount is ten before you leave this building, my friend. Fuck, yeah."

Greg had an upside-down head. He'd shaved all of his hair off and then grown a bushy beard, which gave the impression that his head was turned upside-down.

"John, while I remember, I've had a great idea for my own business… mobile mechanic. I need to speak with Laura about how to go about it. Is she busy this weekend?"

"Oh, I think she's working this weekend. Sorry, mate."

"When do you think she'll be free?"

"She's booked up solid for the next month with deliveries, so try again after that. You haven't got the capital yet though, have you, so no rush, surely?"

"Okay, I'll leave it for now. Or at least until my house sells in the UK. Don't you ever see her? Like go out together and that type of thing?"

"We go to Waiheke Island once a year for ten days and the UK every second year and Australia once a year. We have things on the calendar here and there but, yes, she does work a lot."

"She's changed since I last saw her. She was the original good time girl, always out and about. Not like now, a real workaholic."

"Oh, shit!" said John, looking at his watch. "I forgot to tell you, Kevin, my mate Dave phoned earlier today and asked us to go around for a drink at his work. We have to go now."

We said our goodbyes and left. We staggered over to John's car, which was at the front of C-Zone's car park.

"I'll drive, John," I said, seriousness in my voice.

"No! It's my car, so I'll drive, okay?" snapped John, uncharacteristically.

"Look, mate! I've only had three beers and you've had at least eight glasses of wine. If I get breath tested, I'll get away with it. You won't! You've had too many."

"Oh, yeah," he slurred, thankfully seeing sense.

I jumped in the driver's seat and then backed out of C-Zone's car park very cautiously before driving off along Graham Road. Just as we joined the motorway, we saw a mobile police alcohol-testing unit.

"Oh, shit," I hissed. I slowed the car down to almost a stop and put my head out the window. "Hi, officer, how are you? What's happening here?" I inquired innocently.

The policeman was a heavyset man with a large, curly moustache, six feet tall at least and well built. "Hello, sir. Where have you just come from?"

"I've just picked my brother-in-law up from Graham Road," I replied, smiling. I desperately tried holding my breath, hoping the smell of alcohol wouldn't drift the officer's way.

"How much have you had to drink this evening?" asked the policeman.

"Well, I just had the one. I'm not too sure what John's had."

The policeman looked at John, who was fast asleep.

"Okay, sir, I'd like you to blow constantly into this device."

Damn!

I held the breathalyser firmly in my right hand and blew as hard as I could until the policeman said to stop. To my amazement, I passed with flying colours. There wasn't even a peep out of the thing.

"Okay, sir, thank you for your cooperation and have a nice evening," the policeman said, already looking at the next driver before he'd even finished talking.

I put the car in gear and drove off.

"Can you believe that I got away with that, John?"

John was too far gone to even comprehend what I'd just said, let alone figure out what I'd just got away with. He just sort of grunted in agreement and then went back to sleep.

Dave owned his own company, Apex International. They dealt with all types of gas detection, from harmful gasses underground when Australian telecom were laying new phone lines to air pollution. One of his biggest customers were the NZ police, he supplied them with breathalyser machines.

"Hi, Dave. How are you?" I said as I walked into Dave's boardroom.

"Aha, Lord Lucan and his side kick," said Dave. "Where've you been, boys?"

"C-Zone," John replied, "we stayed for a few drinks after work, but got seriously side-tracked by eight glasses of wine."

"Oh well, that's excusable then, wine makes you strong," laughed Dave. He enjoyed quoting a well-known advert for Oratia wine.

Some members of his staff were sitting at a large Waltons style table for a few drinks after work.

"Would you chaps like to test the latest in Apex alcohol breath-testing equipment," said Dave, laughing again.

"Why, certainly, my kind sir… why not, indeed," replied John in his semi-coherent state.

The manufacturer of police equipment was testing the device by getting drunk.

"When in Rome…" said John.

Victor, Dave's salesman, was Maori and a real cool dude. He was a very distinguished sort of a man, laid back attitude and chain-smoking cigarettes. He fancied himself something rotten with his fancy Italian designer suits and expensive shoes, his thick head of hair slicked back, very smooth indeed. He had an annoying habit of saying "yeah, yeah, yeah," continually until it irritated everyone to death.

"How do you find the Kiwi workmanship, Kevin?" Dave said.

"Err, well, it's okay, but a bit rough, I suppose," I replied.

Dave let out a roar of laughter and nodded in agreement. He was originally from London, he told me, but had come out to New Zealand some twenty-five years earlier with his family. One divorce and his own business later, he was at the head of the table and loving every minute of it.

Twenty minutes later, Dave was still laughing at the Kiwi workmanship comment, Victor was still saying "Yeah, yeah, yeah" and John was talking a lot of drunken nonsense.

Eric, Dave's salesman, decided it was time for a change of scenery and a trip into town was suggested. Eric was also from London but he'd only just arrived and seemed to regret every minute of his arrival, always talking about how broke he was in New Zealand and about the good old days in the UK. Dave had gone into partnership with Eric as his company wasn't doing that well, so he brought Eric from England with an injection of cash.

"Let's all go and get pissed in town," said Eric with a grin on his face. "Come on, guys, look a bit more enthusiastic. It's Friday night, for God's sake!"

Dave was planning to see a movie with his secretary, Rebecca, so he claimed. Another countryman (or woman, so to speak), Rebecca was dating Victor and was originally from London as well. I wondered whether I'd ever see anyone from the north east of England.

We waved goodbye to Dave and the others, then we left and made our way to Eric's black station wagon. I thought it looked like a New Orleans funeral car. Eric even had some New Orleans' jazz music in his tape deck to go with the whole funeral director look.

"Point Chevrolet… no wait, let's take the motorway," said Eric.

John and me grew vexed with Eric trying to make his mind up where he wanted to go. At the last minute, Eric swerved to the right and took the Point Chevrolet turn off.

"Woah! You crazy shit!" yelled John. "What the hell are you doing? Jesus H Christ! Are you trying to kill us?"

Eric had had his fair share to drink and was very drunk, so he was becoming more and more obnoxious and aggressive by the minute. There was absolutely no point in making him more volatile than he already was, by going on and on about his driving.

"Stop!" yelled John. "This is the place here. Right here. This is it. I'm sure of it."

John was freaking out so much that Eric had to stop the car and take a look. Eric was unstable enough without John yelling into his already drink-addled mind.

"Yes, here we go, here we go, here we go," John went on. "This is the place where the missus and I came for a feed, just a few months back. They serve some damn fine pizza here. Some of that real Italian gourmet shit, you know? Costs a bleedin' fortune and all you really get is a squirt of paste on your plate. Stop here, mate, and I'll stick it on the old credit card."

Eric was now in a world of his own but he finally snapped out of it and drove to a parking spot near the Sparrows Restaurant.

We got out and wandered across the road and into the restaurant, Eric and John singing, "Gin gan gooly gooly," as they walked in.

"Orwight, darling?" Eric bellowed at the waitress. "Got anyfing on toast?"

The waitress frowned. "Yes, sir. What can I get you?"

“I’ll have a nice pizza. One of them large gourmet thingamabobs,” said Eric with a large grin on his face.

John and me burst out laughing. Eric’s drunken cockney accent was just too much.

“What are you two laughing at?” Eric snapped.

“Oh, nothing, Eric. Nothing at all,” I replied.

The waitress showed us to a table and filled up our glasses with water.

“What’s this, darling?” Eric drawled. “I need something a little stronger than that to drink. In fact, to hell with the food, bring me some whisky, will ya!?”

Then he started insulting everyone.

He was totally plastered.

I decided to get out of the way and went to have a smoke. Nothing like a joint to chill me out.

When I came back, Eric was in the beer garden being sick and John was asleep with his head on the table.

“John! Wake up, mate. The pizzas are here,” I said.

John woke up instantly and started eating his pizza, as if he’d never been asleep, while I went outside to check on Eric.

“Err, yeah, nah. Fuck off or else I’ll kill you,” he growled.

“The pizzas here, but okay, I’ll just leave you to it then, shall I?” I left Eric to be sick, while I went back inside to eat.

“How’s Eric doing?” John said, smirking as he spoke. “Does he want some carrots on his pizza, or has he got some of his own?”

“He’s not well,” I said, cringing at the thought.

Half an hour passed before Eric finally managed to pull himself together and rejoin us. We’d finished our food ages ago.

“Orwight, geezers? Where’s my fucking dinner?” he said with a cheeky grin on his face.

“It’s right in front of you,” I said. “Just eat your pizza.”

“Aye! You telling me what to do?” he yelled. “You northern twat!”

“No. I’m not telling you, I’m asking you, so we can finish up and go.”

Eric grunted and sat down to eat his pizza.

Twenty minutes later, he'd finally finished and had shouted at the waitress for the bill.

"That'll be $112, please," she said.

"Aye! You gotta be kidding me?" shouted Eric at the top of his voice.

"Well, sir, this is a gourmet restaurant and we are the best in Auckland. What did you expect? Fish and chips?"

"Who the bloody hell does she think she is?" snapped Eric.

"Eric, relax, mate. I'll pay the bill," John said in his usual calm manner.

"No fucking way, mate. I pay my own way. I don't need no fucking charity. I'm paying," Eric said. He pulled out his wallet and gave the waitress $150. "Darling, make sure you give me a receipt, so I can claim it back off the company expenses."

"Certainly, sir." The waitress walked away.

After a couple of minutes, she returned with Eric's change and receipt.

Eric growled at her. "Your food was crap and your prices stink. I won't be coming here again."

"Good evening, sir," replied the waitress, smiling. "Drive carefully, won't you,"

Eric muttered something under his breath but she didn't respond. "Let's go into town and get a chinky," he said.

I'd had enough.

"I was thinking about going home now, " I said. "What do you reckon John?"

John was asleep on the table again.

"What's that, John?" I added. "You want to go home too?"

"You're just making that shit up," bawled Eric, "he never said anything of the sort."

Next stop… downtown Auckland. Eric's V8 Holden station wagon was performing nicely and he was convinced he was going to get a Chinese meal at just gone midnight.

He wasn't. The restaurant was closed.

"You've got to be kidding me?" he screamed in a fit of rage, before getting out of the car and banging on the door of the restaurant, ranting and raving. "Oy! What the hell are you playing at, you stupid shits. Back home it would be open at this time of night. Fucking Kiwis, Chinese people… they're all useless."

"Eric! For Christ's sake, man," John yelled. "Get back in the car, will you? You'll get us all arrested."

Eric showed his disapproval by pissing against the restaurant door. "Fuck you, Kiwi wankers. No fucking food, toss-pots. Take that!"

"For fuck's sake, Eric!" I flew out of the car and grabbed Eric's arm but, before I could force him into the car, he passed out in a heap on the floor, hitting his head on the pavement as he fell.

"John, you're gonna have to give me a hand with Eric. He's too heavy for me to lift by myself."

John tried to move his own lifeless carcass out of the car and managed to stagger over to me and the unconscious Eric. We both pushed Eric into the back seat of the car and then John collapsed in after him.

"Great!" I closed the back door and climbed in the driver's seat. "You fucking guys are nothing but hassle, do you know that? The thing that really pisses me off is you don't even care. You can get yourselves into bed, because I ain't doing it." I was bitching and moaning to a car full of drunken, unconscious slobs.

I started the car and drove off along the main drag, downtown Auckland. I had no idea how to find Eric's house from where we were.

'In the bush somewhere,' I thought. I was damn sure that I wasn't going to do anything more than just drop him off on his doorstep.

There was deathly silence in the car, just the hum of the engine, all the way back to the Waitakere's, where Eric lived. God knows how I found it.

The Holden was equipped with a state-of-the-art computer that kept warning me of low fuel.

John, semi-conscious, told me that it was a new car and the computer just needed calibrating and not to worry. "That's just how new Holdens are."

I slowed and turned into Eric's drive. His house was set deep in the Waitakere bush, tucked away from civilization. I pulled up outside the house and helped Eric out of the car.

Eric's wife suddenly appeared at the front door and began yelling. "Leave him there. He's not coming in the house in that state. Drunken sod. Where have you been? Dave's or town?"

"Both," I replied

"No wonder he's legless."

Suddenly Eric chirped up. "I'm fine."

We staggered into the house and dumped him in the big chair in their front room where he passed out again.

"You'll be okay with him from here, won't you?" I said.

"I'll have to be, won't I?"

I made my way out of the house and jumped into the car.

"Okay, John… now let's get you home, shall we?" I backed out of the drive and drove along West Bay Road.

Minutes later, the station wagon came to a grinding halt at the side of the road. "Fuck, no fuel! What are we going to do now? I can't really see you walking the next two kilometres up a hill, can you?"

John looked at me gloomily. "I guess we have no bloody choice, do we?" He could barely talk, let alone walk. I knew that this was going to be mission impossible.

An hour of hardship later, stopping and starting, puffing and panting, we'd managed to make it two kilometres up the hill to the house.

"Shit! It's twenty to four in the morning," slurred John. "I'm going to crash out. See you in the morning."

John stumbled off to his room, while I stayed in the living room and climbed onto the couch. I turned the telly on and, within five minutes, I was fast asleep.

A few hours later... "What the hell's going on?"

I jumped up and saw Laura standing there with her hands on her hips.

"Well?" she screamed. "I'm waiting…"

"Waiting for what?" I said.

"Don't you dare snap at me!" she yelled again.

"Chill out, for God's sake, will you?" I said calmly. "Had a bad shift? I've got a bad head and you're giving me shit!"

Laura just glared at me as if she were about to explode.

"We went out for a drink last night and Eric's car broke down, so we had to walk home. End of story. What's the big deal anyway?"

"The big deal," screamed Laura, "is that I'm worried about what you've done to my husband and his car?"

"What I've done? Your husband did this to himself. He's the one who took me out on the town with his fuckwit friends. Go on, ask him what happened."

Laura glared at me for a few seconds and then left the room to check on John.

I could hear her yelling from the bedroom.

I got up and crept through to their room to see John sprawled out on top of the bed, fully clothed and fast asleep while Laura yelled at him, fuming.

I decided it was probably about time for me to move out.

The following night, after work, I drove down the road with Laura to inspect Karen's granny flat.

"Hi, Laura. Hi, Kevin. How are ya?" Karen screeched in her usual foghorn voice.

She took us downstairs to look at the newly refurbished garage. The granny flat, or studio, to the Brits.

"What do you think?" she asked.

"I love it," I replied. "When can I move in?"

"As soon as you like really. You're the first to look and I know you, so I'm happy if you're happy?"

I looked around the flat. It had a bedroom in the corner, complete with double bed and massive shelves – which would do nicely for my videos – a sitting room complete with a yellow covered couch and yellow curtains.

'Very girly,' I thought.

In the far corner of the room was a table with… yes… a yellow tablecloth and, finally, the kitchen in the fourth corner of the room.

I was giddy at the thought of having my own space again. It'd been a long time coming but now, it was reality.

The second that I got back to Laura's house, I began putting my things into boxes and bags in preparation for my move on Saturday morning. Later, I lay on my bed thinking about Dave. If it wasn't for him, getting drunk with the architect when they were designing Karen's house, I wouldn't have a granny flat to move into at the weekend. The original plan was just for a spa but, after several bottles of fine Kumeu wine, Dave had agreed to build a spa and then an extension of the deck and then a boules court in the garden, and then a granny flat.

I wandered through to the living room where Laura and John were sitting watching TV.

"Hey, Laura," I asked. "Have you got time today to go over my business plan with me?"

"No, sorry. I'm having a cuppa and then I'm off to work. One of my women is due to go into labour, so I can't."

"Great. I'll never get set up at this rate. Just great."

She just ignored me.

"Monday, here we go, Ross. Another week at work," I said. "It's only been a few months and I've had enough of waiting to get my business going. One expense and one set back after another. If it's not immigration, its IRD numbers or my sister is working."

"No need to stress, mate. It'll come together when it's meant to," said Ross, trying his hardest to convince me. "Anyway, check out the new mechanic over there with Burt. She's a pommie chick, probably a butch lesbian… what woman wants to get her nails or hands dirty, aye?"

Burt spotted us and brought the girl over.

"Kevin, Ross, this is Kelly, she's from Hyundai down the road. Starting here today as our new mechanic. She's from Leeds, in England, originally."

"Hi, how's it going?" said Kelly, smiling.

"Not bad," I said. "Nice to meet you."

The pair then moved off to the other mechanics with Burt introducing Kelly as they went.

Later that morning, Kelly wondered over to me. "Hey, Kevin, do you smoke pot?"

"Err, yeah. Why?"

"Fancy a smoke after work? I've just harvested a crop so I thought I'd introduce you to Kelly de la weed. What do you reckon?"

"You bet!" I said.

I loved this woman the instant I met her. Why did she have to be gay?

'Just my luck,' I thought, as I stared at her. 'I meet a babe with everything going for her and she's bent. The lesbian from Leeds. Great, isn't it?"

Several hours later... Kelly rolled and lit up all in one motion. She'd obviously done it a few million times before. We sat talking in her Toyota Corolla estate for a while after work. "So, what are you doing for fun, Kevin?"

"Erm, nought really. A bit of weed, some sightseeing. Why'd you ask?"

"Well, what do you like? Do you like women?"

"I do but I'm really not into Kiwi chicks. My mate Ross said they're as rough as guts. They're like blokes, he said. He called them bush pigs."

"What do you mean? They're all right. My girlfriend's a Kiwi. Well, Samoan actually, but she's been in New Zealand since she was a baby."

"You're a lesbian, so every woman you go with is a butch dyke. You're used to it. I'm not! I like a girl to be a girl."

"Oh, thanks, love! Say it how it is, why don't you?" she replied. "Anyways, I think you should get out there, get out on the town and see what's on the market."

"Since you mention it, Rossy's going out on the town this Saturday night and he's asked me to go with him. Some club in the city is where he goes, he said, so I might just tag along with him."

"Oh, perfect. Get yourself there, man, and have some fun. You may even get laid." She leaned back in the driver's seat and took a huge drag on her joint and then passed it to me.

"I love weed, it's the only thing that keeps me sane," I said as I kicked back too. "If only I could feel this great all the time."

"Urh, aye? What's that? I was miles away. Oh yeah, I reckon, best feeling in the world, isn't it?"

I took another huge drag and then passed it back. Kelly took a drag and then gave it back to me.

"Come on, let's be having you," she said. "I'm cooking at home tonight, so I've got to be off now. You can finish the joint, I have plenty of my own."

I got out of the car, thanking her for the weed, and waved goodbye as she drove off. The car stopped abruptly then reversed back to me before the window opened and she leaned out and handed me something.

"Here, love, take it," she said smiling. "I have plenty."

"Oh shit, there must be at least an ounce of weed here. That'll last me a whole month. Thanks, Kelly. You're a legend."

The week flew by for me. The workshop was really busy. Ross was on form, boasting to the lads that he was going to get pissed that night and then he was going to get off with a long-legged lovely. No one believed him except me, who had every confidence in Ross's pulling power.

"What you wearing tonight, bro?" Ross asked with a cheesy grin on his face.

"Erm, well, just gonna throw a shirt and jeans on. What you wearing?"

"Oh yeah, same, bro, same. See you at seven, aye?"

"Righto, seven it is."

Five o'clock struck and Ross went into the locker room to get cleaned up. I followed him and began washing up. I hung my boots and overalls in my locker then I left work and walked to my car.

'A nice little joint before I drive home, I reckon,' I was thinking. 'Courtesy of Kelly's crop, I love that woman. What a babe.'

I had the joint rolled and lit before I'd even got to the car. 'I've got this shit nailed, I'm as good at rolling-up as Kelly now,' I thought, a smile across my face and feeling a sense of achievement.

I fell into my car, laughing and giggling. 'Oh yeah, it's laughing gas weed, every weed's different and this is definitely laughing gas weed.'

The drive home seemed to take an eternity, the buildings were just a blur out of my peripheral vision. The road was all I was focusing on… the white lines lighting up in my eyes. I counted them as I went, fixated.

My mood changed from uncontrollable giggles to setting my mind on the night ahead. Who would I meet? What would happen?

'Fuck that shit!' I thought.

I'd be getting pissed out of my mind and that was all. I didn't want to stuck with any girl who wanted to get all serious.

I parked my car behind Karen's, opened the car door and fell onto the driveway.

A long, hot shower and a coffee later, I was almost back in the land of the living.

'Right! One more joint rolled for the drive, bit of wax for the old hair… going for the messy look, I think, this evening,' I thought. Some smelly stuff for the pits, Lynx Africa was good enough.

I left the house and began the twenty minute drive into the city. I pulled my joint out of my shirt pocket and lit it.

‘Ooh baby, this is gonna be good.’ I thought.

I took a huge drag.

I parked in the underground car park in the centre of the city, put my three dollars in the machine and the barrier rose.

I was gonna get wrecked tonight and do the sensible thing and drive home. By the back roads, of course, so I wouldn’t get stopped by the law, ha, ha, ha. West Auckland cops are a joke anyway.

I left the car park and walked around the corner to the Underground nightclub. The club had a reputation for drug dealers and was a real hotspot for a wild night out, Ross had told me.

The bass in the music was making my chest vibrate. It was ridiculously loud.

‘Aha, the Chemical Brothers… good stuff.”

I spied rows and rows of girls in low-cut tops and short skirts, just lining up waiting for some lucky man to get off with one of them.

“G’day, Kevin. How’s it going, man?” Ross appeared from nowhere, wearing his usual, mischievous grin and his smart dress shirt with blue jeans and black slip-on shoes. “See any pussy you’d like to fuck, bro? They’re all honeys, aye?”

“Erm, yeah. Real stunners, aye. Fancy a beer, Ross? Anyways, I thought that you said all Kiwi women are bush pigs?”

“Yeah, bro, but for a fuck, who cares? I don’t have to talk to them. Once I’ve got them pissed, they’ll do anything for me. You watch. Now, let’s get shitfaced and I’ll show you how.”

We made our way through the crowd to the bar. “Two Heinekens, please,” I said to the sharply dressed bartender.

“Bottles or glasses, mate?” the bartender yelled over the deafening music.

“Oh, yeah, bottles please, mate. What do you reckon, Ross?”

“Fuck, yeah, bro. Bottles, aye?”

“You heard the man.”

The bartender handed us two bottles.

A woman pushed in between us and stared straight into Ross’s eyes. “G’day, darling, what ya up to?” she said.

"G'day. Oh, you know, just chilling. Want a beer, darling?"

"Oh yeah, that'd be cool, mate," she replied, smiling. She looked down at her legs and then adjusted her stockings while we checked out her cleavage.

"Hmm, nice view, mate," Ross said, grinning.

"Oh yeah, you're right, mate," I replied, laughing.

"You wanna dance?" the woman yelled to Ross.

"Fuck, yeah," Ross yelled back over the music. The pair went off to the dance floor, holding hands and staring into each other's eyes.

'Must be love,' I thought. I sipped my beer, looking around the room, legs and cleavage everywhere. The room was heaving with tarted-up women. Everywhere I looked. Very tempting.

"G'day, darling, fancy a dance, mate?" a gorgeous blonde said to me.

I looked her up and down, eyes nearly popping out of my head. "Erm, nah, I don't think so. I'm not much of a dancer, pet."

The woman smiled and grabbed my hand. "Come on, darling. I'll show you how."

"Erm, no, really. I mean you're very pretty and all but I don't want to embarrass myself, pet, so find someone else, please. There're lots of guys here."

"Yeah, but no one as good looking as you, mate. And now I've talked to you, I know you're English… a real catch."

"Thanks, but I'm just here for a beer, pet, and nothing else. Maybe next time, see you later."

She shrugged and went off to re-join her friends the other side of the room, staring at me as she left.

I was certain it was for the best. I ordered another Heineken and looked around the room for Ross. There he was, necking on with the woman he'd gone off with.

Shannon, I thought she said her name was.

I continued drinking into the night, while Ross slipped away with Shannon.

At 2am, I decided to call it a night. Ten beers and five hours of booming music were enough for me.

Now, where the hell was the door?

I staggered across the dance floor, brushing past attractive babes as I made my way to the exit, before falling through the door and down the entrance steps. I tried to move my intoxicated body off the floor and dust myself off.

Eventually, I struggled to my feet but still felt very unstable.

As I staggered around the corner and began my walk to the car, I remembered I had a joint in my pocket.

"Oh yes, you will be mine. Come to me, you little beauty."

I pulled it out from my shirt pocket, lit it and took a huge drag.

It was fast-acting weed, so much better than alcohol.

'Why did I drink so much? I should've just got stoned at home and watched telly,' I thought.

"G'day mate," a passer-by said to me. "On the old weed, are we, bro?"

"Urh, erm, yeah, mate," I replied, barely coherent, thinking that I'd never get used to the easy-going attitude to weed out here. It made me very suspicious.

A few moments later, I was at my car in the underground car park. I didn't know if I should be driving but fuck it. I reckoned I'd be fine… hopefully.

I fumbled around in my pocket for my keys. I pulled them out, dropping them on the floor. I was completely wasted. I just wanted to sit down and enjoy being stoned.

I picked up the keys, opened the car somehow and fell onto the front seat.

"Well, here we are," I mumbled. "Where do the keys go? Oh yeah, the ignition…"

The engine started, I put the car in gear then drove off.

'It's like getting a ship off to sea,' I was thinking desperately. 'Now, where's the western motorway? Ah yes, left turn, here we go.'

The drive home was an interesting one, to say the least. I drove on the motorway at 40kph. 60kph under the speed limit. I was barely moving, but I didn't care, I was happy. In my own little world and on my way home to bed.

On Monday, I sat with Kelly outside Newmarket Nissan, supping coffee and having a cigarette, first thing in the morning.

"So how was your night out with Rossy?" said Kelly with a hint of anticipation in her voice. "Get laid then by some Kiwi babe?"

"Erm, yeah, it was all right, I suppose. Ross got off with some long-legged chick, with boobs bursting out of her top. She knew exactly what she wanted the second she met him. I got pissed and seriously stoned and can barely remember the rest, to be honest. All I can remember is going in and hearing the Chemical Brothers playing. The rest is a blur."

She smiled. "Listen, I'm going out to The Rocket tonight with the girls, a little bar in Ponsonby. Fancy coming out with us? That's if you can handle going out a second time in a few days? Not still hungover, are you?"

"Nope, I'm not hungover. Yeah, I'll come out with you if you like as long as you bring plenty of weed."

"Nay worries, mate."

'My God,' I thought to myself, smiling, 'a dream come true… going out with a bunch of lesbians. I hope they're like all those pornos I've seen with drop-dead gorgeous babes snogging each other.'

"What you grinning at?" said Kelly.

"Oh, err, me? Nothing. See you at seven in The Rocket, then?" I jumped off the wall and went to get a job from Bert.

"Yeah, see you later."

'I love lesbians,' I thought as I pulled up at The Rocket. 'Especially ones from Leeds. I'm in love with that woman. What a babe.'

Ponsonby was very bright and shiny. Everywhere was new and improved with a mix of old buildings, lots of colonial houses, converted into apartments, with lots of brand new shops, bars and restaurants. If you were a yuppie, businessman or gay, you lived in Ponsonby. Those three types of person seemed to blend quite nicely. A straight male could be seen in a gay bar and be accepted and vice versa.

The Australians have the Mardi Gras gay parade and the Kiwis have the Heroes' Parade... in Ponsonby. A very colourful and flamboyant parade held once a year by the gay community that welcomed everyone. If half-naked men in leather hats, shorts and nipple chains were your thing, then the Heroes' parade was for you. Or if they weren't, the whole thing was either quite funny or quite offensive. Depending on your point of view.

"G'day sir, can I get you a drink?" the bartender asked, as I walked up to the bar.

"Yeah, hi, mate," I replied sheepishly. "I'll have a Heineken, please."

"Hiya, Kevin," said Kelly, as she dug my hip playfully.

"Hey Kelly, how's it going?"

"Great. I love Ponsonby and the atmosphere, I can relax and be myself. Here, let me introduce you to some of my friends."

"Erm, girls or blokes?" I replied, uncomfortably.

"Both!" Kelly snapped.

"Hello. Who do we have here, then?" asked a girl, excitedly.

Kelly introduced her as Louise.

"Hi, Louise. How you going?" I said.

"Good, mate. How'd you know Kelly? Are you close friends or something?"

The group of girls began giggling like giddy schoolgirls. Obviously, dirty minds were at play. As if having a straight relationship was strange.

"I'm Kelly's friend from work," I said. "You know, we work together at the same place!"

"Ha, ha, ha, I was only asking! Chill out, dude, I didn't detect you on my gaydar, that's all."

Louise had a crew cut, wore Doc Marten's boots, jeans and a lumberjack shirt and looked totally, stereotypically lesbian. I had poncey gelled-up hair, aftershave and a posh shirt and trousers on. I looked like a straight guy out on the pull. We were two very different types.

"This is Jackie and this is Phil, short for Philippa," said Kelly, trying her hardest to change the subject. She looked very uncomfortable at the thought of her and I being a couple.

"Have you met the guys, Kelly? They've just got engaged for their civil partnership ceremony," Louise butted in.

I looked at the two lesbians I'd just been introduced to, then across the room where two men in their mid-twenties were approaching, holding hands.

'Oh, shit, no, please,' I thought. Women I could cope with, but the thought of two guys just didn't do it for me.

"You can tell they're in love, can't you?" said Louise. "Just by the way they stare at each other and hold hands. Jerry's a florist coordinator, he does stuff for expensive weddings, and Luke's a photographer. They both live in Ponsonby. Just down the road, actually."

The men tore themselves away from each other's eyes and gently waved at the girls. Kelly nodded in acknowledgement to them and then turned back to me.

"Like I said, this is Phil and Jackie. I've known them since I came to New Zealand, some fifteen years now, good mates of mine."

It showed big time that they were a couple. Someone had attacked the pair of them with a buzz-cut shaver. They both had skinheads on one side of their head and long hair on the other side. They wore knee-high leather boots, denim shorts and white t-shirts that showed their boobs so well they were bursting out of their tops.

"Come on, let's get pissed," Louise yelled at the top of her voice. She rushed over to the bar and ordered a 'quick fuck'. Tequila and coke with a twist of lemon.

One after another she downed until she hit number six.

Kelly followed her friend like a sheep, while I made my Heineken last.

"All right, darling?" Kelly yelled to me. "Let's go outside and have a smoke."

You could always rely on the lesbian from Leeds to bring some weed. It was like cheese and crackers… weed and Kelly went together very nicely.

"What you laughing at, Mr Thomas?"

"Oh, nothing really. Just you and your weed," I replied.

We stood in the alleyway, leaning against the wall, dragging on our joint. "Shit, this is good weed, Kelly. Good crop, was it?"

"Ha, ha, ha, like fine wine and a good year. Yeah, weed's like that sometimes. I don't do anything different from a three-month period to the next harvest and yet some batches are stronger than others. Weird, aye?"

Within minutes, we were both stoned, minds drifting off, eyelids heavy and just wanting to sit down and relax.

"You look very smart, love," said Kelly, suddenly.

"Thank you and you, erm, well, you smell very nice. Very feminine."

We stared at each other, each trying to suss the other out. I was so close to Kelly, I could smell the tequila on her breath. "You're pissed, aren't you?"

"Uhm, yeah, I'm wrecked. I hate being pissed, I prefer being stoned. It's Louise's fault, she's a bad influence on me."

Then she leaned over, put her hand on my cheek and kissed me passionately.

I responded, grabbing a handful of arse at the same time as the kiss. A warm fuzzy feeling came over me… finally, my wildest fantasy was coming true.

Then, all of a sudden, it wasn't.

"Oh, no wait!" cried Kelly. "This is wrong."

"Why is it wrong? It feels right to me!"

"It's the drink making me horny… no, wait it's… fuck! I don't know what it is. Look, let's just be mates."

"Boy, you confuse the fuck out of me. You get me really excited and turn me on and then you drop me. Are you bi? Which I'm cool with… a bit of both."

"No, it's the drink, it messes with my emotions. I can't help it."

"You're a confusing woman, all right. I think you're a closet bi and you don't want to admit it."

"I'm not bi. I'm gay," snapped Kelly. "Please, just forget it."

"It's just because you're drunk, then?" I was pissed off. "Come on, let's go back in and pretend none of this happened, shall we?"

"Okay, but I do care about you… and don't think I switch teams so lightly. You're a good-looking guy, so don't get a complex, will you?"

We went back to the bar where the three girls and two guys were all dancing on the table.

"Woo hoo!" Louise called over. "Come on, Kelly, join us, let's play kiss or dare. Close your eyes and snog the brains out of someone. The one you kiss you have to spend the night with." Louise closed her eyes and snogged the brains out of Kelly while the two men snogged the other two women.

'Oh my god,' I thought, panicking. 'I'm getting the fuck out of here before the wild orgies start. I've lasted two hours in a gay bar. I deserve a medal.'

I left the bar, shouting goodbye over my shoulder as I went.

The next morning, Kelly told me she left shortly after me.

"I've decided I don't want to be part of that scene anymore…" she said, "where I'm sleeping around, not me now. Louise has always been wild. Most people calm down as they get older, she's got worse."

"It was getting too weird for me. No offence but I go by looks and sleeping with a girl with a skinhead and one that's butch like a man is just not me."

"I know, straight guys sleep with babes, if they can. I go with personality, so it's okay, you don't need to explain to me," she said. "Anyway, fancy coming out with me to a self-help group tonight? I've no one to go with."

"Erm, self-help group? What's that all about?"

"Oh, it'll be fun, it's all about these God books I've been reading… about being happy if you want to be happy. My favourite is Feel The Fear And Do It Anyway and this is the topic of conversation. They're also discussing the Chakras tonight. Are you coming, then?"

"Oh no, sounds too weird for me."

"Come on, it'll be a laugh. Go on, for me. I feel the need

recently. I've been feeling depressed and I don't know why. Maybe I need a change. Who knows?"

"For Christ's sake, all right, then. I'm gonna regret this, I know."

"You're a superstar, Kev. Pick you up at 6.30 tonight."

Kelly's car pulled up dead on 6.30pm, which was unusual for her. She was a stoner and generally kept to stoner o'clock, which was any time really.

"Hey Kevin, how you going, love?"

"Yeah good, Kelly." I jumped into her Toyota estate and buckled up. "Where's this place at, Kelly?"

"Oh, it's in Henderson. I've forgotten the exact address. Erm, Lincoln Road, somewhere or other. I've been there a couple of times before, so I sort of know the way. Should be a good laugh though."

"Err, yeah. Okay, we'll see."

We had a slow drive down into the valley of Henderson as Kelly was very stoned and in super-relaxed mode. "There's a butt in the ashtray," she drawled, "should be enough for you to get wasted, love."

"Oh great, cheers, pet." I opened the ashtray and found half a joint. "Awesome, that'll do for me."

I lit up and sat back in the seat while I sucked the guts out of the joint. Within minutes I was completely stoned and thinking of the night ahead.

Kelly drove onto Lincoln Road. "Wow, how quiet is this road? Anyway, here we are, love. Tau Paki Primary School, where it all happens on a Saturday night. Yee harr."

"Well, let's get this over and done with, pet."

"Aye! Don't you want to go in?" Kelly laughed. "Got a touch of paranoia, have we? The old weed got to you?"

"Ha, ha, ha, yeah a touch of the willies all right. I really don't want to be in a room full of people."

"Come on, love, let's go. Snap out of it!" Kelly got out of the car and began walking towards the school doors. She stopped and turned to look for me. "Come on, scaredy-cat, let's be having you."

I got out of the car and followed her into the school. I was not looking forward to it, not one little bit.

"Here we are, room sixteen," said Kelly. "Let's go and learn all about Chakras."

She opened the classroom door to a room of eight people, all sat in a circle.

"Ah, hello, you two. Please come on in," said the lady who was conducting the lecture. The room full of people all stared as we walked in.

"Hello, I'm Kelly and this is Kevin."

"Great. Come on in and take a seat," the lady said.

"Okay, love?" Kelly asked me.

"No, not really, but here we go."

"Welcome, everyone, and thanks for coming this evening, my name's Moon Child. I'd like to start off by explaining the seven points of Chakra. Your body contains seven power points where energy flows from and they are called Chakras."

"Christ Almighty, what have I got myself into?" I whispered, laughing under my breath.

"Shut up and let the woman speak, will you?" Kelly hissed, trying not to laugh as well.

"Okay, if everyone picks a partner, we'll get started with feeling each other's energy through the Chakras," Moon Child said to the class with a big show of bright white teeth. She had a nervous twitch with her glasses and kept adjusting them every time she gave a suggestion to the class.

"She's gay, you know?" whispered Kelly.

"How do you know?" I replied.

"I've got a built-in gaydar that allows me to detect any gay women. And she's gay, love. Maybe this is all just a ruse to pick up women."

"Okay, guys," said Moon Child. "Choose your partners and don't be picky."

I found a girl, no more than twenty years old. Quite a geeky type of girl, wearing large, dark-rimmed glasses.

"G'day, mate, erm, err, I'm Clara. What's your name?"

"Hi, Clara, I'm Kevin. That's my friend Kelly over there, she dragged me here tonight so no embarrassing stuff, please."

"No, no embarrassing stuff," Clara replied.

I sat down on a rickety, wooden chair and tried to relax while Clara stood behind me and held one hand over my heart and one hand over my forehead and then closed her eyes.

"Anything there, Clara?" I said, holding back the laughter.

"Wait… I can feel it. Oh yes, here it is. You're very kind and thoughtful with a heart of gold. That's two points of Chakra. There are five more to get a feeling for. How about I feel the energy from your groin area?"

"Urh, erm, what?" I gulped.

Clara put her hands over my groin and closed her eyes again and began trying to feel something.

"How about this time, Clara? Anything interesting?"

"Oh yes, you're a great lover. A powerful, assertive man and you're going to meet a nymphomaniac who'll make love to you over and over again."

"Oh yeah!" I jumped up, feeling very uncomfortable and ran to the door. "Err, yeah, got to go to the bathroom. Shit! It's locked. Hey everyone, the door is locked."

Moon Child came over and tried the door. "Oh, so it is. We're locked in."

"I know, I'll climb out the window," said Kelly, laughing out loud. She opened the window, struggling to climb out, her arse in the air as she fell out and down into the bushes below. "Fuck!" she yelled.

"Kelly, you okay, mate?" I yelled into the darkness.

"Err… yeah, I think so. It's just my ego that hurts. Hold on while I go and find someone to unlock that door." She stood up and disappeared into the night, picking bits of bush out of her hair as she went.

We waited patiently for Kelly to reappear at the window but it never happened. Ten minutes went by and then a key turned in the lock and a caretaker and Kelly appeared at the classroom door.

"Sorry, guys," said the caretaker. "I locked up not realising there was a class tonight."

"Come on, Kelly," I said, "let's get out of here before I die of laughter."

"Oh, please," cried Moon Child, "please, everyone take your seats again and we'll continue what we were doing before the interruption."

"Okay, let's go," Kelly said between fits of laughter.

"Well, that was a success," I said, laughing out loud. "You weren't wrong, Kelly, it was a laugh, all right… a blast."

The next day, we downed tools at lunchtime and headed out of Newmarket Nissan and onto Broadway. The street was its usual, busy place, lots of traffic, crowds of people hustling and bustling going about their business… shop-till-you-drop women, young and old, men too, window-shopping for their wives or girlfriends.

We walked into the mall together, talking. There was a German brass band playing for some charity or needy cause. Kelly threw a couple of dollars into the bucket as she walked past. "Well, could be me that's in need of charity someday, so I give a bit here and there, thinking someone might do the same for me."

She walked over to the food court and paused for a moment while she decided what to have. "Erm, oh, what the hell! I'll have a green curry, what'd you think?"

"Sounds hot to me. I'm sticking with a butter chicken."

We stood in the short queue, pointing out what we wanted to the Indian lady behind the counter.

"That'll be four dollars each, please," the lady said.

We paid then went off to find a table.

"Let's sit here, shall we, love?"

"Yeah, why not, overlooking the wishing fountain, perfect. I've got a new sideline, for some extra cash," I said as we sat, "since there seems to be nothing but the minimum wage here."

"Oh yeah, what's that, love? Oh, my God, this green curry's gorgeous. Wanna try some?"

"Nah, you're all right. As I said, I'll stick to my butter chicken, thanks, mate. Anyway, my sideline's selling WOF test certificates to Larne's mate. Gotta make some money somehow."

WOFs were what the New Zealanders called MOTs.

"What!?" she said. "Are you mad? If you get caught, you'll be fucked, love. Be careful."

"Larne approached me last week saying he could get me about forty WOF tests to sell and it'd be $50 a pop. His mates would pay me for the tests if I just wrote them out for their cars."

I put a forkful of curry into my mouth. "I think it's hilarious that I was never interested in being an MOT tester in the UK because I hated paperwork," I said, still chewing. "Becoming a WOF tester is gonna be another feather in my cap, I've got a real use for WOFs. Maybe it's the business I've been looking for, sales… a great idea."

"I don't know, love, I'd be too scared to do anything like that. Selling WOFs is definitely not me, be careful."

"I need to make some money or else the move to New Zealand is pointless. I should have stayed where I was."

Kelly suddenly roared with laughter.

"What's so funny?"

"Just thinking of Moon Child and being locked in the class room. As funny as."

"The funniest bit would have to be when you fell out of the window into the bushes. That was funny. Yeah, it was an entertaining night, all right. What about when my partner put her hands over my groin and said I'd meet a nympho who'd make love to me over and over. What a nutter! No more Kelly nights out, please, or any more nights out full stop. I'm fed up with going out. I'm having a few nights in from now on."

"You bore! Get a life, will you?"

CHAPTER 5
THE BUSH WALK

"Hi Kevin, how are you?" bellowed Karen. "When are you gonna move the rest of your stuff into the granny flat?"

"This is all of my stuff. What else do I need?" I replied.

"Oh, err, okay then. I'm glad you're here, Kevin, Dave's away on business in Sydney, Singapore, Egypt, the UK and then finally Fiji, so it's good to have someone in the house for security."

"It must be a hell of a business trip," I said.

"He's trying to sell his latest product to the world. I'm going to Sydney tomorrow on business as well, but I'll only be gone for two days. If you like, you can use the spa and the swimming pool."

The following morning, I thought I'd walk down to the Waitakere Dam and get back home for around 4.30pm, just in time for my sister's birthday party at her favourite restaurant in Henderson. I threw some things in my backpack and locked up the flat.

The walk down to the dam was an easy one as it was all downhill. The long trek back was what worried me. I had visions of crawling back up the hill on my hands and knees.

"Wow, would you look at that!" I yelled.

Standing at the foot of Cascade View, I took a deep breath and inhaled the clean air. I could see how much care had gone into preserving the natural beauty of the valley. It was as if the designers had gently moved a little ponga tree here and a little kauri tree there, then this gigantic concrete dam had been plonked in its place, leaving the bush looking untouched.

"I've been missing this all my life. The great outdoors. I love this country," I shouted at the top of my voice. The words echoed around the valley.

'Maybe, I could have my own bush walk tour and charge tourists for showing them around,' I thought. 'Learn a bit about the history of the place and do some talking and a sales pitch. What a great idea for a business, much better than fixing cars.'

It was the damned money though, this month's wage package was dismal… no bonus, no overtime, just a crappy basic wage that wouldn't even be a minimum wage back home.

'Wait till I sell my house in the UK, that'll make some money…' I was deep in thought at this stage.

I carried on walking along the winding gravel track, until I came to the top of the gigantic dam. I wanted to get a bird's eye view of the millions of gallons of water below. I paused for a moment, took a few snapshots of the lush, green scenery, wild untouched bush, ponga and kauri trees growing wild then moved on.

"I feel alive," I yelled again and again, my voice echoing around the valley.

I looked across the valley and spotted some train tracks leading into the side of the mountain. I couldn't resist going to explore.

The tracks didn't look rusty, so I reckoned there must be some sort of train still in service. What worried me was that, if I followed the tracks into the tunnel ahead, would I encounter a train half way through?

Well, it was a risk I'd have to take.

I walked along the tracks, towards the entrance of the tunnel, took a deep breath and entered.

The tunnel was unbelievably dark. Not just dark, but fucking dark, as John's friend, Greg, would say. Slowly, my eyes adjusted to the lack of light and I could make out insects crawling on the walls. They were the size of my fist, at least.

"What the hell…"

I continued deeper and deeper inside the tunnel, until I saw something glowing on the roof above me. "My God! What the hell is that?" I muttered. "It's a bloody glow-worm, I'm sure. Wow."

I was getting over the initial shock of being in a cold, damp, dark tunnel, when it hit me… I actually felt quite at ease with myself. I'd totally forgotten the fear I'd felt at the beginning of my little adventure.

I walked out of the tunnel into a little clearing with a rickety old shack that was partially hidden by bush overgrowth.

'It's a shed! What the hell is a shed doing in the middle of nowhere? Maybe it's a railway workers' hut and they keep their tools inside? Or, maybe, it's a vagrant's shelter and he's hiding in there, waiting for someone to go inside.'

I passed by the hut and then stopped dead in my tracks.

It was no good, I had to satisfy my curiosity and take a look inside. I slowly opened the door, fearing the worst. The door made a loud creaking noise as it opened, which grew louder and louder, the further I opened it. I pushed myself forward and stuck my head inside, half expecting to have my head chopped off by some deranged vagrant, high on cocaine or LSD.

Just before I went inside, I remembered Kelly's self-help book entitled Feel The Fear And Do It Anyway. At this point, the self-explanatory title of the book came to mind. I had certainly felt the fear, I just needed to push myself that little bit further and do it anyway. Which is easier said than done.

I let out a frantic cry of fear and leapt inside the shed. I did it! I was pleased there was nobody here, because I would have felt pretty stupid if someone had seen me act that way.

But I would have been wondering who or what was in there for the rest of the day, if I hadn't investigated. 'Maybe there is something in this alternative mumbo jumbo after all?' I thought.

Five minutes later, I'd completely forgotten about my little shed experience and had found something else of fascination.

A picnic area.

"This place gets stranger and stranger," I said out loud. "How bizarre."

Who would put a picnic table and a brick barbecue three hours walk from the nearest road and four hours from civilization?

I was not even going to think about the strange-looking hut I could see. It was all just too bizarre. Time to escape from reality, I decided.

I went over to the shelter and sat down then lit a pre-rolled joint. I just wanted to kick back and admire the scenery that was simply oozing out of everywhere I looked.

'I know,' I thought, 'I'll write a letter to Derek and let him know all about the great times I've been having exploring New Zealand and going out on the drink. I'll let him know I'm just looking for a payout, like the sale of my house in the UK and then he can come out and visit and we'll start up a business together. Being out here really makes me think of bush tours. It could work. Who knows?'

The wacky-baccy took effect and I was soon on another plain. I decided it was time to move on further down the tracks.

I stopped after a while and looked around in the bush, not exactly sure where I was and thinking I should head back. It had been an adventure. At least I'd have something to tell everyone at Laura's birthday dinner.

Then my brain started whirring. Why should I backtrack three hours the way I came? Why not just go straight through the bush?

I eyed a track that led into the bush and hesitated for a moment. The track was muddy with several large potholes scattered here and there and dense bush. But I didn't care anymore. My devil mind had already taken control. I would never hear the end of it from Laura if I didn't turn up on time, so I had nothing to lose really.

Or so I thought.

Feeling brave, I took a step back and made an almighty leap over the first pothole, only to fall flat on my back in a pool of mud.

"Great!" I yelled, then, "Just my bloody luck, it's starting to rain."

If I could just make it a bit further into the bush, the huge ponga trees deep in the bush should shelter me.

The bush was pitch black. It spooked me to begin with but, within minutes, my nerves and my eyes became accustomed to the dark. I fumbled around, finding my way with surprising ease.

The trees were the size of houses. Trees that had been growing for a few hundred years, their trunks as wide as double decker buses, and they had obviously been untouched by man for centuries. Just allowed to grow and grow and grow out of control.

Walking through the dense bush, I became aware of the undergrowth going uphill and that the trees were becoming closer together.

I didn't have enough energy left to climb in between trees and up a steep hill.

I was too exhausted.

"Where's my bloody camera?" I said suddenly. I had only just finished paying for the bloody thing. I wasn't going to lose it now. I turned back the way I had just come and headed back. As I walked, I kicked the bush back, looking for my camera. Just as I had given up all hope, there it was, behind an overhanging branch.

'Hallelujah. Now I can get back to finding my way out of here. It can't be much further, surely.'

I continued my trek, back up the hill in the hope of finding my car. The hill became steeper and steeper and more overgrown until I had to crouch to avoid the gorse scratching my face.

I'd been told by John that the gorse had been brought over by English colonists a century or so ago. It may look very pretty in an English garden with an English climate, but in a sub-tropical environment, like New Zealand, where there is plenty of rain and sunshine, it grew like wildfire until it became as big a pest as the New Zealand possum.

I paused for a moment and then looked up at the never-ending hill, all covered in the damned gorse. I was tired beyond belief. I had to take a little breather or else I would simply collapse from exhaustion.

I couldn't help but think of the lecture that I'd receive from my sister for being late for her birthday dinner.

If I was still alive at the end of this ordeal, that was.

Soon, I had to crawl on my hands and knees. I was cut to ribbons by the gorse, bleeding from most parts of my arms and face. I was beginning to think this crappy adventure was never going to end. Or was I going to die here?

'The bloody English should be shot for bringing this damned gorse here!' I thought in frustration. 'How ironic!'

After several hours of crawling around in the dense bush, I decided that my bloody arms and face had had enough torture for one day and I collapsed in a heap on the floor.

I lay in a muddy ditch, staring up at the dark sky and thinking how the hell I was going to get out of my predicament. I hadn't even noticed that day had turned to night because, until now, I had been so completely focused on getting to the top of the hill. I lay there in despair, wondering what time it was and what everyone at Laura's birthday party would be doing.

It was dark, raining, and I had no idea where I was, not forgetting that I was only dressed in shorts and a t-shirt. I'd found a new level of frustration.

I looked around for some dry kindling, desperately wanting to start a fire to thaw the bitter cold I was now feeling but everything I found was soaking wet from torrential rain that afternoon. The situation was hopeless. I had no choice but to grab a large bunch of branches and pull them over my weary body. I pulled my arms inside my t-shirt. At least my arms would be warm.

I lay there trying to find a comfortable spot, but it was no good, the patch of ground I was on was just too damned uncomfortable. I knew that I just had to switch off mentally and close my eyes to forget the hopeless situation. I didn't manage to get in a deep sleep but I did manage to get a few winks, in between the nightmares.

The night was a cold and restless one and, to add to my troubles, I was convinced there was someone, or something, else in the bush with me. I didn't know what it was but there was definitely something amiss. I tried my hardest to ignore my racing thoughts of panic and kept telling myself that this was what I did best… survive the impossible.

Sometime in the dark of that night, I woke, turned around, and to my horror discovered that I'd been sleeping on a fallen tree. The tree had fallen half way down the side of a mountain and had come to rest almost vertically.

"My god, that was close," I said. "And now I'm talking to

myself. Must be lack of food and water sending me doolally."

I leapt to my feet in a fit of panic and, in the process, fell some twenty feet off the tree trunk and onto some rocks. I lay there motionless, in agony.

"Fuck!" I screamed.

From the pain in my leg, I was pretty sure my ankle was broken.

How was I going to go anywhere now?

I was completely screwed.

I lay on a patch of sodden grass, staring up at the sky and thinking about how stupid I'd been to have taken the short cut, instead of going through the pouring rain, back the way I'd come.

I reached inside my pocket for a cigarette.

"Shit. I smoked my last ciggy yesterday, brilliant," I yelled in anger, as I threw the empty cigarette packet into the bush. "Not to mention smoking my last joint too. Brilliant!"

I removed my shoe and nursed my swollen ankle. The situation was looking pretty grim and I decided the only thing I could do was to stay put until help arrived. I tucked my arms inside my t-shirt and then pulled some branches over myself to keep warm.

Next came the rain. Huge drops bouncing off my face with no mercy.

"Oh God! Can things get any worse than they are now?" I moaned.

The next morning brought rays of hope, in the form of sunshine. At least the weather gave me a brighter start to the day. All I needed now was for a search and rescue team to find me. Even the temperature felt like it had risen slightly.

'Right! It's time to do something to help myself or else I'm not going to survive another day. I need to find water. Not too sure what I can do about food, though?' I thought assertively.

I managed to forget my hunger pangs by focusing on the pain in my foot.

'This would be bloody funny if it were someone else. Laura will have panicked by now, I know it. She'll have the entire world out looking for me.'

It was just a matter of surviving until someone found me.

'I'm Going Slightly Mad'… what a great Queen song. Freddie Mercury must have been lost in the bush when he wrote that song, no food or water, wandering around aimlessly, out of his mind. I chuckled, deep in my mad thoughts.

I started laughing, beginning to feel crazy. Slowly but surely losing my mind. I was so unfocused now that I couldn't even think straight. It was starting to sink in just how serious my situation actually was.

'The Waitakere Dam should be behind me,' I thought, 'so, hopefully, I can find a stream somewhere.'

I managed to stand and wandered off to look and, to my amazement, found one within only a few minutes of looking.

I couldn't believe it. The water had been right in front of me all the time. I just needed to test the purity of it and hopefully I wouldn't die or grow a third eye.

I crouched down and leaned over the stream to scoop up some water.

It was stale and mouldy.

I yelled as I spat it out.

I sat there contemplating my next move.

I decided I was going to drink it anyway. What did I have to lose?

I was damned if I did and damned if I didn't.

I scooped another handful of water up from the stream and drank it, screwing my face up before taking another handful.

Then another and another until I had quenched my thirst.

The daytime temperatures seemed to have increased and I needed to dry my t-shirt, so I hung it over a large branch. Pneumonia was the last thing I needed right now. As I removed my t-shirt, I noticed how badly damaged my body was. There were scratches all over me, not to mention the bruises and the sprained ankle. I wasn't sure how much more I could take.

I sat down on some grass and leaned against one of the huge ponga trees.

It was all too much for me, so I decided to try to have a short nap to forget my troubles.

After a few hours of sleep, I awoke feeling quite refreshed. There was a distinctive chill in the air, the temperature had dropped. Thankfully, my t-shirt was now dry, so I put it back on. I knew the police wouldn't even start looking for me until I'd been missing for twenty-four hours. It had roughly been forty-eight hours so, in theory, it was just a matter of time before I was found.

The light was rapidly fading, so I decided to hop over to the largest tree I could find and take shelter. I knew that I had the basics: water, shelter and a clearing in the trees a few metres in front of me in case of any airborne search and rescue teams. I also knew that, because of the fading light, this meant another night in the bush. No one would look in the dark. Not forgetting my new problem… my ankle, and how I couldn't even put my shoe back on because my foot was so swollen.

My mind was racing with all sorts of possible survival tactics. Like what the hell I would do if no one found me? How would I get out of this on my own? How long would I be able to last on stale water? The list just went on and on until eventually I fell asleep.

Grunt. Snort.

The sounds came from the bush.

I woke up and jumped to my feet.

Grunt, grunt.

Something moved in the bush to the left of me.

I stood perfectly still.

Frozen with fear.

A pair of beady eyes stared at me through a large clump of overgrowth. What the hell was it? Then another grunt from behind, then to the left and then to the right of me.

My God. There was more than one.

Oh shit.

Suddenly, a huge pig leapt out of the bush and ran straight past me. Then it ran back into the bush. I stood there, terrified.

What the fuck…?

The animal reappeared, this time from my left hand side. It came around to face me. I could hardly bear to look. I opened one eye and stared the beast straight in the face.

Oh shit, it was a pig with huge tusks. It must have weighed at least 300kg.

I slowly backed away from the pig, one step at a time, shaking with fear. I thought about running, but decided against it, I'd never outrun the beast, especially with a fucked ankle. And where would I run to anyway?

Suddenly, a sense of bravery came over me and I opened my eyes. "Go away, pig, go!" I said.

What was I doing? I was talking to a pig, for God's sake.

I began flapping my arms frantically in the air, and then hobbled forward towards the pig. "Come on, pig, get lost!" I yelled.

The pig ran into the bush.

I sat down with a thud and then leaned against a tree. That was intense.

"Go on, pig, run away, you girl's blouse," I shouted out, laughing in relief.

Sleep was totally out of the question now that I knew I wasn't alone. The thought of the pigs coming back was enough to keep anyone awake all night.

The night dragged on. Several hours had passed since my close encounter and I was on the brink of giving up all hope of ever being found.

Then… I heard it.

The sound of a helicopter circling above me.

I jumped to my feet and waved my hands frantically in the air then I had an inspirational thought… I could flash my camera at the helicopter and this would, in theory, either be spotted through the bush or picked up by their heat-seeking equipment. I'd seen that little trick on TV.

The helicopter flew straight past me and into the distance without showing any sign of spotting me. I sat down again. I knew there might be another opportunity to flag the chopper down, so I pulled down a wiry tree and tied my t-shirt to the top of it. It sprung upright like a flagpole.

According to 'Barry Crump', a well know Kiwi bush expert, if you follow a stream, eventually you will come out at a farm or at least some sign of civilization. It had "saved my life many a time" he wrote. The question was… should I risk getting myself in even more trouble by following Barry Crump's theory or wait till the chopper flew overhead again. I decided to stay put for now.

I stopped thinking and started listening.

Yes, another chopper.

Now, where was the damn thing?

I rose to my feet and stood staring up, trying desperately to scan the sky section by section, searching for any sign of a helicopter.

I spotted it.

'Aha. It's a red one, I bet that's the West Pac Trust rescue helicopter that I've seen on TV,' I thought.

As the helicopter came closer, I confirmed that it was the West Pac.

'I'm saved. All I need now is for these guys to see me and it's all over.'

I began flashing my camera frantically, over and over in the direction of the helicopter. I jumped up and down on the spot, my ankle screaming, desperately trying to increase my body temperature, in the hope that I'd be seen on their heat-seeking equipment.

The West Pac circled me a few times and then flew off in the direction that it had just come from.

"Come back," I yelled. "Please!"

I felt completely screwed. And I had zero energy left to go anywhere.

This was it, this was where I would die… right there in the Waitakere Ranges, Auckland, New Zealand.

I screamed as the chopper flew off and hung my head in

despair then fell down with the weight of the blow. It was all too much for me.

A few moments later, I passed out from exhaustion.

"Are you Kevin Thomas?" a voice yelled from the bush.

I couldn't believe my ears, I thought I was hearing things.

"Stay there. We're coming to get you," the voice yelled again.

A thought flashed through my mind… what if I wasn't Kevin Thomas? Would they just have left me there?

"It's going to take a while to get to you. The bush is really dense, so sit tight until we get there," the voice yelled.

"Okay," I yelled back.

The sense of relief was overwhelming. I couldn't believe anyone had actually found me.

"Kevin. Are you still with us, mate?" the voice yelled.

"I'm still here." Not that I had a choice of going anywhere.

I could hear voices directly in front of me, possibly on walkie-talkies. I figured that the search and rescue guys were talking to their home base or one of the two helicopters that was circling overhead.

I heard one of the rescuers give some coordinates to the pilot of the West Pac helicopter, then I saw it: the bright, red chunk of metal hovering overhead. The engine was louder than you could ever imagine.

Just at that moment, a hand came through the trees holding a bottle of water. It looked like a scene from Excalibur. Not a hand with a sword coming out of a lake, but a bottle of water coming through the bush.

"Hi, Kevin. How do you feel?" said a young woman. "Here, take some water, you look as though you could use it, mate."

She was the first of three search members that came through the bush and stood beside me.

"Here, take off your shirt and shorts. You're soaking wet," she said. She started undressing me, which made me feel incredibly uncomfortable in front of the other members of the team. She tried to take off my undies next.

"Hey! Trousers and shirt, yes. Undies, I don't think so," I yelled.

"Okay, relax, mate. Here, put this jump suit on," she replied, handing me an orange-coloured flight suit.

A man wrapped me in a silver space blanket. "There you go," he said, "this should warm you up. We'll get you out of here as soon as the pilot figures out where we are. I'm George, by the way." He pulled out his walkie-talkie from his backpack. "Yeah, mate. We're directly below you. Over."

I couldn't hear the full reply, but, by the puzzled expression on George's face, I gathered that the pilot still couldn't see us.

A couple of guys from the search and rescue team began chopping down a small group of trees, just in front of me. After two or three trees had been felled, one of the guys lit a flare and waved it above his head.

"West Pac chopper. Ground team here. How's that, mate?" George said.

"Yeah, nah. I still can't see you guys, but whatever, I'll just have to wing it," the pilot said over the radio.

"We're directly below you, so hover at the following coordinates and then lower your man down," George said. "We need to get the guy out. He's sprained his ankle and can't walk. He's also suffering from blood loss, starvation and mild hypothermia, so he's going nowhere on foot, mate."

"Roger that," the pilot replied.

A large Maori fellow appeared at the side door of the West Pac and then hung over the side of the helicopter. He began lowering himself down to our position and then attaching a harness to me.

"George, why didn't the guys in the chopper see me with their heat seeking equipment a couple of hours ago?" I asked.

"The bush has so much life, it gives off a huge amount of heat. On an open motorway, they would see a car, no worries, but in the bush not much chance really because it's all red and all heat from life," George replied.

"We'll be taking you to Mechanics Bay, which is our HQ," the large Maori fellow said. "We have paramedics to check you out and, if necessary, we'll take you to hospital, okay?"

"Hey, has anyone got a smoke?" I yelled. "I'm dying here without one."

"Don't you think that's the least of your worries, Kevin?" George said, trying his hardest not to laugh.

I didn't see the funny side of it. I was serious about the smoke. I'd forgotten all about my physical pain in the excitement and began thinking how cool it would be to ride in a helicopter for the first time. I looked up at the dangling rope from the helicopter hovering above me.

'I'm going to learn how to fly one of those. Mark my words, I will,' I thought.

"Okay, Kevin. Here goes, mate," the Maori fellow said.

He gave the thumbs up to the pilot and the cable began to winch us up to the helicopter. "Hold tight, Kevin, here we go, mate."

Half way up, a strong gust of wind caught us and made the cable sway out of control. "Don't panic, mate, she'll be all right," the Maori fellow said, with a smile on his face.

"To be honest, I'm not very reassured, but whatever you say," I replied.

We made it to the helicopter and climbed aboard. I sat on the helicopter seat, exhausted. The other guy followed and sat next to me on the rough and ready looking bench. He handed me a set of headphones to dampen the horrendous noise of the engine.

I looked around the helicopter and couldn't believe how unrefined it was. There was nothing they didn't need on board, just the bare essentials. The helicopter had plenty of electronic equipment in the cockpit but nothing in the way of cosmetics. No cushions on the seats, no soundproofing, no nothing. The most prominent thing was the noise, it was deafening beyond belief. All that could be heard was the loud whirring noise from the rotors above my head. I was too excited to care. I just sat back and enjoyed the bird's eye view of the Waitakere Ranges.

"Oh look. There's my car down there," I screamed at the top of my voice.

"What?" the paramedic yelled back.

"I said that's my car down there."

The paramedic seemed totally uninterested in my car, he was more concerned about my cuts and bruises and treating them.

I looked down, to where my car was in relation to where I was found and I couldn't believe how far off course I was. It must have been at least ten kilometres away from where I was supposed to be heading.

"Two seconds to fly past my car, three days on foot through dense bush," I said.

I remembered my nicotine craving and shouted to the paramedic for a smoke. Unfortunately, the guy was a health freak, the same as the search and rescue guys, and didn't have any. "Fuck! Does anyone smoke anymore?"

Some fifteen minutes later, the helicopter landed with no dramas at Mechanics Bay. Still wrapped in the space blanket, I opened the sliding door of the helicopter and hopped out. Then, with the paramedic's help, I hopped over to the entrance of their HQ.

"If you take a shower, Kevin, I'll be able to see what's superficial and what's serious, mate," the Maori fellow said.

I looked in the mirror in the bathroom of the HQ at my blood-stained face. I couldn't believe how much of my body was leaking blood.

"You're English, aren't you?" said the paramedic.

"Err, yep. Why?" I replied.

"You must be the last person on the earth to know. Princess Diana was killed in a car crash in Paris this morning."

"What! You're kidding?" I said, shocked and bewildered at the news.

"Yeah, nah, it's all over the news, mate. When you're showered, you can read our paper in the smoko room," the paramedic said.

The paramedic left the room while I undressed. I stepped into the shower and, boy, did it feel good. I stood in there for quite some time, just enjoying the feeling all over my body.

"Hey, Kevin, you finished yet, mate?" the paramedic yelled. "I need to check you out, buddy."

"Yes, I'm coming," I yelled.

I finished drying off and put on the clean jumpsuit that the paramedic had given me. I walked through to the canteen to find two men sitting at a table.

"Okay, matey, take a seat and I'll have a look at your cuts and bruises," the paramedic said. "Right, your ankle is not broken, just badly swollen. What I'll do is strap it up for you and you can stay off work for a week. Your cuts don't look too bad, except for a few on your hands and face, so this is going to hurt like hell but, in the long run, it'll prevent infection."

I sat there as he put cream onto the cuts.

"Well, Kevin, I think you're a lucky man. In fact, I can't believe that you survived," the paramedic said. "Most people who go missing for more than a couple of days are carried out of the bush in a body bag. Anyway, I have no objection for you to go home now, just get plenty of rest and drink lots of fluids to rehydrate, and stay warm."

"We have a spa at home," I said. "I'm just going to chill in that for a few days, I think."

"Lucky you. Sounds like a plan," said the paramedic. "Anyway, I've called your local police department and GP for a check-up and the cops are on their way from Henderson. In the meantime, drink your soup and relax, mate,"

I picked up the NZ Herald and began to read about the death of Princess Diana.

In the meantime, George had arrived at HQ and had walked into the canteen. He tapped me on the shoulder. "Come on, mate, your ride's arrived," he said.

"Okay, guys, got to go and thanks for everything," I said. "I really appreciate you, well, err, you know, saving my life. Cheers and I'll see you later."

I left the canteen and followed George outside into the car

park, where two cops were admiring the rescue helicopter on the landing pad.

"G'day, mate. How ya going?" said the older cop.

I knew straight away that these two cops were from West Auckland, they were so relaxed. The way they acted, it was like they had never seen the city before, let alone a helicopter up close. They were a little bit countrified, to say the least, but friendly enough people and they'd driven all the way from out west to Mechanics Bay to pick me up, so not all bad.

The two cops soon grew tired of the helicopter and noticed me standing there, looking quite sorry for myself.

"Oh yeah. Sorry, mate. How's your foot?" the younger cop said.

"Sore," I said. "Where's your car?"

One of the cops helped me to the police car and sat me in the back seat.

"Thank God. I'm finally on my way home, I'm going to sleep for a week," I said. "And for God's sake! Please stop at the next gas station so I can buy a pack of bloody smokes. I'm dying here."

"Nah, mate, no can do," the young cop said. "It's not permitted to smoke in the patrol car, so I'm afraid that you'll have to wait till you get home."

The drive didn't take long, down the western motorway and then through the winding, country roads to West Bay Road. I was dreaming of the cops putting the blue lights on and them thrashing the cop car around the streets but, no, it was not to be. Not important enough.

A few moments later, we arrived on West Bay Road and then turned into Dave and Karen's driveway. As I stepped onto Karen's porch, Laura ran up to me and gave me a big hug.

I saw someone taking pictures of me out of the corner of my eye. I turned around to see someone pointing a microphone in my face.

"Who's this?" I said. "I don't want the attention, I just want a bloody smoke."

"Hi, Kevin, I'm John Stevens from the Herald. I'd just like to ask you a few questions, if I may?"

The reporters continued pressing me about my ordeal, despite being told several times that I was disorientated and hungry and needed to rest.

Eventually, they got the message and left.

Once we were inside, Dave began making me soup and sandwiches. He went berserk with preparing the food, his way of dealing with the stress maybe.

"You stupid idiot, Kevin," Laura said.

Karen even took thirty seconds off work to make a phone call to me. I was well impressed by her thoughtful act… not.

All I wanted to do now was soak in the spa then sleep for the next twelve hours.

Then, I could write my letter to Derek.

I definitely had something to tell him now.

CHAPTER SIX
SOLO FLIGHT

"Okay, guys, you have two and a half hours starting from now," the examiner told us.

I turned my paper over and studied the questions with intense focus and concentration. Navigation was all maths, which was never my strong suit at school, so I didn't realistically expect to achieve a very high grade, but, it was one of the criteria and I really did want to fly, so I put my head down and pressed on.

Two and half hours passed quickly. In fact, it flew by. I was quite pleased with my effort and thought I'd done well. I put the chair under the desk and walked over to the examiner's desk. "There you go, all finished, mate."

I arrived home some forty minutes later and found Karen watering her plants in the garden.

'That woman never stops,' I thought. 'She just keeps going and going, like a Duracell bunny.'

"Hi, Kevin, how are ya?" Karen asked through the spray of the sprinkler. "How did your exams go?"

"Oh, you know, so, so," I replied. "The RTF exam was the one that I want to pass the most. That would be Radio Telephone Flight Test in layman terms. But no worries if I don't pass first time around, I can always take it again."

I left Karen to her gardening and walked around the side of the house and into the garden. My new dog, Sylvester Stallone, greeted me as I opened the gate. Sly couldn't help himself, he always went berserk when I arrived home, wagging his tail, jumping up and getting very excited. Ross had brought him round one day after finding him wandering the streets. Sly was great. I wish I'd got a dog earlier.

"Calm down, Sly. I've only been gone a morning."

Sly wagged his tail and did his 'golfer about to tee off'

impression, stomping on his left legs and then his right very quickly, side to side, just like a golfer.

I opened up my flat and walked inside to make myself a cuppa. A few moments later I wandered back outside to sit on my deck and reflect on my morning. I stared into space, thinking about flying. Despite being lost in the bush and nearly dying, bush walking had become my second passion in life, so I decided to take Sly on a walk in the Waitakere Ranges that afternoon.

Two weeks later, the mail arrived. I had passed three out of six exams, so I was half way there with the theory work. Soon I would be moving on to the practical, which was what I really cared about.

That night I tossed and turned in bed. I couldn't stop thinking about flying.

The following morning, I decided to drive out to Arrow Moore flying school and talk to Barry, my current instructor. The instructors were constantly leaving for airlines or rotating their students, so I rarely had the same instructor for very long.

"Barry? Err, I think he's flying right now," the girl on reception said. "Hold on while I check. Echo Victor Charlie, Arrow Moore base, request position."

"Arrow Moore base," replied Barry, "EVC overhead, 1,500ft, descending none traffic side for runway two four."

"Copy, Kevin Thomas is here to see you," the receptionist said.

"Copy base, see you in zero eight," Barry said.

"He'll be down in eight minutes, Kevin, so just hang around until he lands."

Even the radio terminology excited me. I loved the thought of being a pilot and couldn't think of anything more exciting than learning to fly.

I walked outside and sat on one of the benches to wait for Barry to land, dying to tell him that I had passed the mandatory three exams I needed to take a solo flight.

Arrow Moore had loudspeakers mounted on the walls

outside, which allowed everyone to hear every aircraft radio communication in the vicinity and I followed the radio com intensely, listening for Barry's position reports.

"Arrow Moore traffic, Echo Victor Kilo, finals, two four, full stop," came the voice of Barry over the loud speakers.

I watched with great anticipation as EVC came into land. The student who was flying the aircraft looked to be doing a pretty decent job of landing, the touchdown was perfect.

The aeroplane rolled onto the forecourt and parked up next to the fuel pumps. The student shut down the engine and then stepped out of the little Cessna 152. Barry spotted me, still waiting for him on the bench outside the school.

"G'day, Kevin. What's up, mate?" Barry said.

"I've passed my exams now, so as soon as you set me up with a B-category instructor, I'll be going solo, mate."

"Let me finish here and I'll come and fill you in on the details, okay?" Barry left me and walked inside to the reception area.

A few moments later, he came back out. "Right!" he said. "I'm reasonably happy with your take-offs and landings, your circuits are good and so are your radio calls. All we need to do now is to revisit everything next Wednesday, say around 5pm. Then I'll get Natalie, who's a B cat, to test you. How's that sound?"

"It sounds awesome, mate. I can't wait," I said, feeling like a giddy schoolgirl.

The following Wednesday evening, as 5pm approached, I was ready to clock off work and begin the wacky races out to Arrow Moore. It always felt that way to me as I fought my way through the traffic on the motorway.

"G'day, Kevin. You're on the ball, aren't you?" Barry said.

"I wasn't going to be late for my first solo, Barry. Not on your nelly," I replied, smiling.

"First, I'll run over the circuit procedure with you and then, blah, blah, blah…" Barry's voice faded into oblivion. All that was on my mind was my solo flight. I didn't really care about the theory part of it. I just wanted to get airborne.

"Excellent, let's get out there and have some fun," Barry finished.

"Aye. Oh right, yeah, I'm ready." I snapped out of my daydream and returned to the land of the living.

We left the briefing room and went outside to find EVC. I carried out the standard pre-flight checks and refuel then climbed in the left side and waited for Barry to join me.

"Okay, Kevin, let's rock," Barry said.

He climbed into the right hand side of the Cessna and put his headset on. Within minutes we were airborne.

"Excellent take off, Kevin. Well done, mate," Barry said. "Just make sure that you do the same with Natalie and you'll get your solo flight today."

"Arrow Moore traffic, Echo Victor Charlie, overhead, 1,900ft, descending none traffic side for runway two one." I began my descent back into the circuit. I always found this procedure as confusing as hell. There was so much happening all at once in the circuit, so I had to be completely focused at all times.

My touchdown was perfect, or at least I thought so. We rolled up to the forecourt some seventy minutes after take-off.

"Excellent work out there today, Kevin. Go and get a drink, have a smoke and relax, then I'll come and get you. Okay?" said Barry.

I jumped out of EVC and walked over to the reception area to have a smoke. A short time later, Barry reappeared with a rather nice looking, thirty-something year old lady.

"Hi, Kevin, how are you? I'm Natalie," she said in a soft-spoken voice.

"Oh, hi, Natalie," I replied, trying to look at her eyes and not her boobs. I felt very excited by her presence. How the hell was I ever going to stay focused on my flying with her as a distraction?

'Lady flight instructors should be banned,' I thought.

"Shall we go, then?" Natalie said. We walked over to the Cessna and then climbed in.

"Plenty of juice, Kevin?" Natalie said.

"Yep. She's got an hour and a half left from the first flight we had. I've carried out another pre-flight check, just as a precaution." I cranked the engine then taxied out of the forecourt and off towards the runway.

"How do you know that two one is in use, Kevin?" Natalie said.

The inquisition had begun.

"Because we always take off into wind and the windsock indicates the wind direction is 210 degrees, which is south west, or runway two one," I replied.

I finished my pre-take off checks and then looked to my right for any aircraft on final approach. There weren't any, so I made a radio call and moved out onto the runway.

"Arrow Moore traffic, Echo Victor Charlie, rolling, two one, remaining in the circuit," I said over the radio.

"Good job, Kevin," Natalie said. "Now be careful on take-off because there's a crosswind of eight knots, which is enough to rock a little Cessna around."

The Cessna gradually reached fifty-five knots, I pulled back on the stick, smoothly lifting the nose and leaving the runway behind.

"Well done, Kevin, everything is good so far. Now, let's see how your landings are," Natalie said.

I turned onto the crosswind leg of the circuit and then onto final approach, I made a call to the circuit traffic then began my descent.

"Carb heat off, lower twenty degrees of flap and positive power changes to control my rate of descent," I said assertively to Natalie.

"Good, now, make sure your nose is in line with the runway threshold and watch your approach speed."

I nodded my head in acknowledgement. I didn't want to be put off by someone talking, so I tried my best to shut Natalie out.

As I flew over the fence that separated the road and the runway, I eased back the power and then gently pulled up the nose. The aircraft levelled out and glided in to land. The main gear touched down first and then the nose wheel followed.

"Okay, power up, we're going around again. I just want to make sure you can do the same again."

I gradually applied full power to the Cessna and, as soon as I reached the rotate speed of fifty-five knots, I gently pulled back on the stick.

"Another perfect circuit and landing, mate. Stop on the grass while I get out and then you can go off by yourself."

"What?" I said.

"I said 'off you go'," Natalie replied.

I didn't quite understand Natalie's haste, but hey, who was I to argue? I spun EVC around and headed back to the holding point. I was crapping myself big time, but I had to push on, because no one else was going to do it for me.

I made a call to the circuit traffic and then began rolling. EVC reached the rotate speed and then I pulled back on the stick.

"Wahoo, I'm airborne," I yelled. "I'm doing this myself. Awesome!"

I climbed to 500ft and then turned onto first base. Within a few minutes I was on the downwind leg of the circuit. I made another radio call to traffic and then turned onto final approach.

It was awesome. It made me feel so free and alive… better than sex, better than driving a fast car, better than anything I could think of.

I turned onto final approach and made a final radio call, then lowered 10 degrees and then 20 degrees of flap, turned the carb heat off and then set the nose in line with the runway threshold, just as I'd been taught. As soon as I was over the fence, I eased off the power and gently pulled up the nose, so the aircraft was level, keeping the stick pulled back until the main gear touched down and then the nose gear.

I slowed down and turned off the runway onto the taxiway. I headed towards Natalie, who was waiting for me on the grass verge opposite runway two four.

"Awesome, Kevin. How did it feel?"

"Absolutely fantastic. It's the best feeling in the world. I can't believe I did it."

Natalie climbed into the aircraft and then told me to take her back to the flying school reception. "Now, where's your log book, so I can sign off your first solo flight at 16.5 hours? You're all set now, a free man. You can go flying any time you arrange things with Barry. Happy with that?"

I finished taxiing back to the flight school and then parked the aircraft next to the gas pumps as I normally did.

I climbed out of the plane and spotted Barry.

"Hey Barry, sorry to interrupt, mate. But I thought you'd like to know I passed."

"Well done, mate, I'll see you out here next week, then?"

"You bet," I replied.

I left the reception area and walked outside to my car. I sat for a few moments to reflect on the morning's achievements.

I couldn't believe what I'd just done. Hmmm… who could I tell? My sister? Nah, she'd be working.

Maybe Kelly would be impressed?

When I arrived home, I found Karen in her garden, as per usual. She never stopped and, if she wasn't moving the house to the left or something, she was telling someone else what to do. This time she was washing the outside windows. Dave must have been laughing when he married her. He never did anything except get drunk and crash out on the couch. She did it all.

"Hi, Kevin. How are ya?" Karen screamed in her usual, loud voice.

"Well, since you mention it, I just happen to have been flying a light aircraft around Papakura by myself! What do you think of that?"

"What! They let you go up by yourself?" she screeched.

"Yep, they sure did. Pretty cool, aye? I could hardly contain myself it was so cool."

"Well done," she bellowed. "Good on ya, mate."

I felt the need to phone my parents in the UK and let them know what their son had achieved. Their phone rang and rang, but all I got was an answer machine.

Shit, shit, shit.
Where was everyone when I needed to speak to them?

CHAPTER SEVEN
THE BREAK IN

"Kevin, wake up!" Karen screamed, as she turned into a raving lunatic.

'No, go away and leave me in peace. It's too damned early,' I thought.

Or was it just a dream?

Sly the dog was going wild, running around and around the flat and then jumping up at Karen. The whole situation was total panic and chaos.

"Kevin, Kevin, some baaarstoods stolen my car and smashed up our gate," Karen yelled.

"Aye! What are you on about?" I replied, frowning. "For Christ's sake, it's five in the morning. I don't care. Just go away and come back in two hours."

"Please, help me," she screamed in my ear.

I mustered enough energy to sit upright. "What's with the baseball bat?"

"So I can hit the baarstood with it, that's what's up with it."

"Oh my God. I don't have the energy or the interest for this. Please go away."

"Please, Kevin, come outside with me and bring Sly, and then he can bite the thief."

"Sly only bites if another dog threatens me. He won't bite a person, because he's a big softy… but… whatever you say."

I crawled out of bed and shouted Sly. Karen hung onto my arm as we went outside, her eyes wide, looking for any movement in the dead of night.

'What the hell am I doing here?' I was thinking. 'I mean… Karen's the one with the baseball bat and she actually weighs more than me, so she'd do more damage than I would. What a pair of clowns.'

We walked slowly around the side of the house and into the

garden. I couldn't see a damned thing. It was darker than hell. I tripped over a watering can. "Shit! Who left that bloody thing there?"

"Sorry, it'll probably have been me," Karen whispered in my ear.

We both tiptoed to the gravel driveway and then stopped abruptly. Karen was still stressing and anxiously looking around for the thieves.

"Hello. This looks suspicious," I said sarcastically. "The gates are smashed up and there are deep tyre marks in the gravel."

"That's what I've been trying to tell you! You see… my bloody car's gone. We've been robbed and my bloody husband is still fast asleep on the couch. He came home late last night, pissed out of his mind and obviously didn't hear a thing. Great man he is."

"Well, they've obviously gone, so come on, let's get in the warmth," I said.

We went back in the house to phone the police.

"Urh, aye. Orwight, Kevin. Orwight, darling," Dave said in his strong, east London accent as he awoke from his coma.

"You baarstood," yelled Karen. "You were pissed last night, weren't you, aye? You didn't even notice that we've had a fucking break in."

"You what. What's been taken?" Dave snapped.

"Only my bloody car, that's all." Karen walked through to the kitchen to get her phone book from her purse. "I may as well call the insurance company. Oh no, they've taken my purse and credit cards too." Karen started crying, which took me by surprise. She was usually as hard as nails.

Dave sniggered in his usual heartless manner.

I didn't know where to put myself.

"My laptop's gone too," said Karen, as tears rolled down her cheeks.

"How the hell did they get in?" I replied.

Dave let out a roar of laughter. "Unlucky, still it could be worse, it could've been my stuff they swiped."

"I don't know what the hell you're laughing at, they've taken your wallet and credit cards too," she said.

Dave looked at her as if he was going to slap her, but then just shrugged it off and seemed to get over it, just as he always did.

"Well, I suppose I'll have to call the cops then, won't I?" said Karen.

Meanwhile, I had decided to check around the house for any signs of entry.

"Karen, Karen," I yelled. "I've found out where they came in. Come and see."

Karen ran to the front of the house, to where I was standing. The lock on the front door had been drilled out. I opened the door and went inside the corridor to the main house. I felt like Sherlock Holmes, tracing the steps of criminals.

"Elementary, my dear Watson."

"What? Who?" Karen snapped with a frown on her face.

"Kiwis have no sense of humour," Dave butted in. "She won't get what you mean, mate."

"Shut up, you pommie baarstood!" Karen yelled at him. She turned to me. "Anyway, what's so bloody funny, Kevin?"

"You can picture the scene, can't you?" I replied. "I'm fast asleep and they are drilling door locks right next to my granny flat. Dave fast asleep from his night out with the boys and the crooks walk straight past him. And the only one who noticed anything was the one who was too scared to deal with any of it… you. Hilarious, when you think about it."

Karen went back in the house to use the phone, while I went back to my flat. Maybe I should have felt guilty for getting stoned and sleeping through it all but, on the other hand, who gave a shit? If her own bleeding husband couldn't wake up and stop them or even care, why should I?

I sat on my deck near the back patio doors and lit a cigarette. It was just about daylight. I could hear the muffled voice of Karen talking on the phone, and assumed it was her credit card companies. I just wanted to go back to bed and catch up on my sleep.

'Shit. It's Monday and I should be at work,' I thought suddenly. 'I suppose that I should give Ken a call and let him know what's happening.'

Bang, bang, bang.

"Friggin hell, now what?" I sighed. "Is there any end to the noise and chaos this morning?"

I got up and answered the door.

"All right, Pete, what's up?" I said. It turned out to be the guy from next door, so I invited him in and took him through the corridor of the granny flat and into the main house.

"I was just wondering if you guys heard the commotion last night," Pete said. "After all, it was coming from your driveway."

Everyone gave Pete their full attention.

"Yeah, man, around 4.30 this morning I heard this horrendous noise that I can't even describe, so I ran outside to check it out. There was this Honda all smashed to pieces. Boy, what a mess. Then there was a Mitsi V3000 with its arse end hanging off. It looked like the Honda had drove into the Mitsi when it was backing out of your driveway. But it was too dark to be sure of anything really. Just as I was about to go and call the cops, the Mitsi drove off into the Waitakeres. I didn't even think it was possible, the state that the thing was in."

"Aye! My frigging car is smashed up," yelled Karen.

"Your car?" Pete said. "I thought it looked familiar, but like I said, it was dark."

"Yes, my car. It was stolen from our bloody driveway last night. Someone broke into our house."

"Oh right," Pete said, frowning as he tried to piece things together. "It all makes sense now. Anyway, this Honda was obviously coming back from Piha, so I assumed the guy that was driving had been drinking hard and lost control. After the Mitsi took off, I thought the best thing to do was to follow them."

"Do you want a cup of tea, Pete?" said Karen.

"Thanks, but no thanks. Anyway, I chased them for a couple of miles before they stopped in one of those apple orchards off West Bay Road. God knows how he made it that far. Sparks were flying everywhere from the petrol tank, it was scraping along the road. Crazy, I know."

"My God, you're kidding me," Karen replied.

"Once they dumped the car, they ran off into the night," Pete said. "By the time I got home, the cops were already on the scene breath-testing the young guy in the Honda. Unfortunately for him, he'd been to an all-night beach party and had been drinking hard, so they arrested him and took him away in the paddy wagon."

I could see the smirk on Dave's face and wondered what he was thinking. Maybe he was thinking about who he could tell this great story to. I could never tell if Dave was lying or not, the man was a legend in his own lifetime at winding people up. A real bullshitter.

"Okay, let's get going, Kevin," said Dave. "We're off to find Karen's car or we'll never hear the end of it."

We drove onto West Bay Road and headed for the apple orchard, two minutes up the road. Sure enough, there was Karen's car, abandoned and looking very sorry for itself in the orchard.

"Can you believe the state of it?" said Dave. "Have you ever seen a car so smashed up?"

The rear of the car was completely gone, the boot and rear suspension were now in the back seat.

Dave looked around the wreck. He was trying his best to be interested in finding Karen's purse, but he soon became bored and got back in his car to make a phone call to a towing company. Meanwhile, I decided to search a little wider afield for the purse.

Eventually, a big, red tow truck turned up, backed up to the rear of Karen's car and hooked up a winch. The driver pulled the mangled piece of metal that was once Karen's pride and joy onto the truck and then drove off.

As soon as we arrived home, Karen began screaming at us.

'Oh joy,' I thought. 'Karen in full swing, that's what we want… not.'

"Did you find it? Is it repairable? Did you find my purse? Blah, blah, blah." Karen droned on.

"Urh, what?" I replied. "Oh, well, I'm not sure if it's repairable, and no, we never found your purse."

Dave just said "Yeah" to everything, as he always did. He wasn't even listening, he just pretended so that he could keep Karen happy.

I left Dave to handle Karen's mouth and returned to my flat. I sat outside on his deck, listening to Karen giving Dave verbal abuse for not listening and not caring about her beloved car. Dave was deadly quiet. This guy could take any amount of crap from anyone before getting riled. He had to really, being married to her.

I left them to it and went along the drive to the mailbox.

Bills for Karen. Bills for Dave.

'Hmm, what's this? Yes, Derek's written. Finally.'

I took the mail back to the house, left the others' mail outside the door to the main house then excitedly took Derek's letter to the sun deck to read it.

What?!?

Derek had met someone and was getting married.

Brilliant…

He wrote that he was staying in the UK with her, no chance of him coming out to NZ.

Great.

Then… He would be going on a honeymoon to the Dominican Republic.

Brill, that's all I needed.

It looked like I was on my own with the business lark.

If only I could decide what to do… not to mention my house sale in the UK had gone tits-up and I had to give it back to the mortgage company because I just couldn't afford to keep propping it up. The rent just wasn't enough to cover the mortgage.

How the hell was I ever going to get out of this rut of being a mechanic without Derek's input?

It was time for a joint to drown my sorrows.

I called my boss to let him know I wasn't going in, then decided to spend the rest of the day relaxing and playing on my Playstation.

All I wanted to do was kick back and not even think about work or Karen stressing over her car.

CHAPTER EIGHT
FIRE ON BOARD EVT

'Flaps down ten degrees, then twenty degrees, fifty knots approach speed, keep the nose pointed at the threshold of the runway and now a radio call,' I was thinking.

"Arrow Moore traffic, Cessna one five two, Echo Victor Tango, finals zero three, full stop," I said over the radio.

Adrenaline pumped through my veins… it was awesome. Totally out of this world!

The Cessna touched down perfectly, main gear first and then the nose wheel. I taxied to the flight school and parked.

'Ignition off, then back on, radio and transponder off, flaps up, masters off. That'll do for me, great practice flight. Hope my flight to Tauranga in a few days' time goes as well,' I thought. 'I need this flight to get one step closer to obtaining my private licence. Who knows, maybe I could make this my business and charge people to fly them around the beautiful east coast and then take them into the city air space as well. It could work.'

"Hi Sarah, it's Kevin Thomas. How you doing? Is Richard in?" Richard was my new instructor, since Barry had landed himself a job with South African Airlines.

"Sure, Kevin, hold the line, please," Sarah said.

"Hello, is that Richard?" I said on the phone.

"Yeah, mate, speaking. How's it?"

"Hi Richard, it's Kevin Thomas. Thought you'd like to know I have twenty seven hours flight time logged and several practice cross country flights under my belt, so I was wondering when I could be checked out for a solo cross country flight."

"Oh yeah, nah," said Richard, in a typical Kiwi response. "Come out this weekend and we'll do a test run. I'll be a complete bastard and test you, okay?"

"To be honest, mate, I went out yesterday and had a great flight, so I'm ready to go solo. What do you reckon?"

"Yeah, nah. Sounds like a plan, no worries, mate. Tomorrow it is."

My financial situation was sort of under control now, so why not go for it, I thought. After all, it was only the bank's money.

"If I owe money, let them worry about it, I say," I chuckled to myself.

The following morning, I was organised and ready to go, bright and early. I grabbed my pre-packed equipment bag and headed off to Arrow Moore.

Arrow Moore School was a huge place with every facility you could imagine, from a huge runway for those naughty little lapses of concentration to a 747 flight simulator. Big bucks to use.

"Christ Church Information," I said.

"Go ahead," the controller replied.

"Echo Victor Tango, Cessna one five two, AD 005 to TH eta 050, TH 030 to TG eta 010, TG 060 to TH, eta 020, TH 020 to AD 005."

I loved this pilot talk. No one else had a clue what I was saying.

"Yeah, mate, read back, Arrow Moore AD depart five minutes past the hour to Thames TH estimated time of arrival ten to the hour 50 full stop at Thames for four zero minutes, depart Thames TH half past the hour. 10 Then pretty much the same in reverse, yeah?" replied the controller.

I laughed. I was totally amazed at how easily controllers could decipher a bunch of numbers and letters into actual meanings. They were just so quick with their interpretation of what most people would think was a rocket scientist formula.

"Roger that."

"Mate, somewhere along that route the wind's zero two zero degrees west, at four knots, yeah?" the controller said. "Okay matey, you're all set with CCI Christ Church Information and remember to report before and after take-off. If no reports are received every half an hour, then we send up the West Pac search and rescue helicopter. So stay safe and enjoy your flight."

"Okay, speak to you en-route over the radio," I replied.

I put the phone down and thought how proud I was of myself. I had submitted my first flight plan with no assistance. I gathered my papers together and chucked them in my bag on the way out of the door. I grabbed the keys for EVT from behind reception and headed out to the forecourt to find my aircraft.

Echo Victor Tango was in pristine condition. The club had just refurbished her. With her bright red paintwork and brand new interior, she was a very swanky looking aircraft. I had no hesitation in being the first person to fly her.

All I needed now was my flight instructor, Richard, to sign me off on my first solo cross country. And now I'd done my pre-flight checks, I should really ask Trudy where Richard was.

Trudy made a call. "Hi Richard, it's Trudy at the school. You have a very anxious student here waiting to go to Tauranga, where are you?"

"Aye. Who, what?" a very sleepy Richard replied.

"Your student's name is Kevin Thomas," Trudy said. "It's in the booking sheet for 10am till 4pm. What's happening, mate?"

"Oh yeah, I forgot to tell him to blast off without me, I'll keep track of him from base and through CCI."

"Has he been cleared for solo cross country yet by a B-cat?" Trudy replied.

"Oh yeah, nah, he'll be right, mate. He's a shit hot student, so I'll take responsibility for him, no worries."

"Well, if you're sure, Richard. I'll pass the message on. Catcha, dude."

"Oh, Richard, come back to bed," a female voice said in the background. "I haven't finished with you yet, baby."

Then the phone went dead. Trudy laughed and then looked at the shocked expression on my face.

"Oops, sorry, mate," Trudy said. "Maybe I shouldn't have put him on the speakerphone when he's at his girlfriend's house. You heard the man… do you feel confident enough to blast off by yourself?"

"I was born ready for this. I've been waiting my entire life for this flight."

"Okay, off you go and be careful. If you get in trouble, land at an airport or call us with a status, okay?"

I left reception and climbed into EVT, which was waiting for me on the forecourt. I flicked the master switch on, primed the fuel and started the engine. It spluttered and coughed for a few minutes and then began idling nicely at 800rpm.

Off with the park brake and push the power forward. "I'm off, yee har."

I taxied the aircraft through the narrow gates and out towards runway two five.

I loved going fast down the taxiway. I was always in trouble from my instructor for speeding. And since there was no instructor now, I could do what I liked.

Oh yeah, I loved this freedom.

Once at the holding point, I spent time going through my usual engine run-ups and pre-take off checks and then taxied out to holding point two five on the main runway.

A quick look to see if there were any aircraft on final approach, nope, none, then a radio call to the traffic and I was away.

I pushed the throttle forward and began slowly moving along the threshold onto the runway. "Arrow Moore traffic, Echo Victor Tango, rolling, two five, vacating to the south east," I said over the radio.

The aircraft hurtled forward. I felt the familiar thrust of the engine that made the aircraft veer to the left. To compensate, I had to apply large amounts of right rudder to keep her straight. I reached rotate speed and then gradually pulled back on the stick. I was airborne.

"Arrow Moore traffic, Echo Victor Tango, downwind 1,300ft, vacating to the south east."

I banked hard right and then flew straight over the Hunua Ranges and onto the east coast of Auckland. The view was spectacular from 1,500ft. I could see lush, green hills to the right and a bright blue ocean on my left.

I couldn't go any higher than 1,500ft until I'd cleared Whenuapai's air space. Whenuapai was a military base and had quite a few restrictions in, over and around their airspace, their rules. However, I knew to play with their controller, so I could have some fun and work the system.

"Whenuapai tower, Echo Victor Tango," came my radio call. "Cessna one five two, Hunua ranges, 1,500ft, request clearance into the zone, on track Thames."

"Echo Victor Tango, cleared into the zone, 1,700ft, stay on track, report overhead runway," the controller said in a very military manner.

If you asked, you got, it seemed.

"Cleared into the zone, on track, 1,700ft, report overhead runway," I repeated back to him.

Excellent, I was cleared into their airspace. Cool.

I applied more power, so that I could climb up a few more hundred feet, and then I altered my course towards Whenuapai's runway. Today was a quiet day at the airbase. No Tornadoes or F16s flying around, just a little Cessna plodding on through.

"Whenuapai tower, Echo Victor Tango, 1,700ft, overhead runway."

"Echo Victor Tango, stay on track, report clear of zone," replied the controller.

"Stay on track, report clear of zone, Echo Victor Tango."

Huge military planes were on the runway below. I didn't recognise them but I didn't care, I just wanted to see the base from the air and to say that I'd been there, done that.

I made a call to the tower, now I was clear of Whenuapai's airspace and then altered my course, back to the south east. Next stop, Thames.

I descended to 500ft over the crystal clear water. I desperately wanted to get some snaps of Marlin fish swimming around in the firth of Thames. The water was so bright and clean that I could see right the way to the bottom of the ocean.

The scenery around Auckland just seemed to get better and better the further afield that I went. I could see everything from up there. There was Rangitoto to the right, yet another one of these dead volcanoes in and around Auckland. There was even a small island at the back of it, where someone lived. The owner must have been a serious recluse and love his privacy.

'My God, I'm here already.'

I'd been so absorbed in the scenery, I didn't even notice the time.

"Thames traffic, Echo Victor Tango, Cessna one five two, 1,800ft, ten miles north west, joining overhead."

I hated this runway. It was just so damned confusing. It had several grass runways either side of the sealed runways. That's tarmac runway to us Brits. Today, runway three six was in use, or that's what I thought at first glance.

'Hmm, this is confusing, maybe if I circle around the runway for a while I can figure out where the damned wind is coming from, so I can land.'

I spotted the windsock, but remembered from my last trip that the sock was seized and no longer swivelled around according to wind direction. I had no idea what way the wind was blowing. It could have been runway 360 degrees or runway 240 degrees wind direction. Who knew?

I noticed the clouds were being blown from the north. The closest runway was two eight, which in laymen's terms meant I was going to land in the direction of 280 degrees or north west.

"Thames traffic, Echo Victor Tango, overhead 1,800ft, descending none traffic side for runway two eight."

I eased off the power and lowered the nose. I had to descend to the circuit height of 1,200ft. The Cessna swayed round violently, winds picked up to twelve knots or more, so it was becoming increasingly difficult to control the aircraft. I had flown in bad weather like this before, was reasonably confident I could land safely, so I continued my descent.

"Thames traffic, Echo Victor Tango, finals two eight, full stop."

The Cessna glided onto runway two eight and touched down smoothly. I slowed to a taxi speed and headed in the direction of the Thames clubhouse.

I jumped out of the Cessna and stretched my legs. There was no one to be seen around the airfield. It was completely dead. Not even the clubhouse had anyone inside it. I walked over to a large hanger and sat on the grass verge opposite to think.

Where had the time gone?

It was 2.30pm already. I had to get going if I was to stick to my flight plan.

I jumped into the Cessna and belted up. I arranged my charts so that I could read them with ease en-route and reset my altimeter for Thames air pressure to 20ft above sea level.

'Masters on, fuel primed, gauges reading pressure and charge rate at 12 volts. Radio is off and go to start,' I thought.

I cranked the engine and she fired up straight away.

'Hello. What's this?'

I wasn't getting much of a charge from my generator. I flicked the gauge with my finger a few times but it made no difference. 'Hmm, I need to check my flight manual, I think.'

Here we go, charging… if the charge light is malfunctioning, shut down the engine, turn off the master switches and then restart the lot. The flight manual read: Do not fly with this error!

'Oh I see, so don't fly, aye? Best make sure that it's fixed then.'

I shut down the engine and turned everything on again, just like rebooting a computer.

It appeared to be working fine now. I had no idea what was wrong with the thing but I didn't care, I just wanted to get going. The only thing on my mind was informing CCI about my location. If I didn't report every half an hour, they would contact search and rescue so I had to get going. I continued with the usual take off checks and procedures, I just wanted to get airborne now and stick to my flight plan estimated times of departure and arrivals.

"Thames traffic, Echo Victor Tango, rolling two eight, departing to the south east," I said over the radio.

I applied full throttle and roared down the runway until I

reached fifty-five knots and then gradually pulled back on the stick.

"An excellent take off, if I may say so myself," I muttered.

"Thames traffic, Echo Victor Tango, airborne two eight, 500ft, vacating to the south east." I released the flaps during the climb and reset my radio to Christ Church Information's frequency.

"Christ Church Information, Echo Victor Tango, airborne Thames, this time, 1,000ft climbing 1,800ft, tracking south east Tauranga," I said.

"Echo Victor Tango, Christ Church Information, Thames, 1,000ft climbing, en-route Tauranga. How's the weather there, mate?" the controller replied.

"The weather's clear leaving Thames and Piroa ahead, so it looks fine to me. I can't see Tauranga yet because of two big hills."

"Cheers, mate, catcha later," said the controller.

"Only in New Zealand would you get a response like 'catcha, mate'," I chuckled. I continued flying towards the small town of Piroa, which was world famous in New Zealand for its lemon and Piroa fizzy drink, hence the name L&P. There was even a large L&P can on the outskirts of town to show their pride in their product.

"Tauranga tower, Echo Victor Tango," I said.

"Echo Victor Tango, Tauranga tower, go ahead," said the controller.

"Tauranga tower, Echo Victor Tango, Cessna, 1,800ft, overhead Piroa, request clearance into the zone, tracking to Tauranga International."

"Echo Victor Tango, cleared into the zone, continue 1,800ft, report ten miles out," the controller said.

"Cleared into the zone, 1,800ft, report ten miles out," I repeated.

I was really quite chuffed with the way things are going.

Not bad since I hadn't really been checked out properly and just sort of thrown into it by Richard.

The transponder light suddenly began flickering on and off.

"What the hell is that?" I yelled.

I thought things were going too well.

The charge light had come on again.

I had to do something and do it fast. I tried to shake off the fear and realised that, if I didn't get the radio back on soon, I would have to turn back. CAA rules state that no aircraft may enter controlled airspace without a two-way radio.

Tauranga was only a small airport, but still an international airport, so I'd have no choice but to get that damn radio working. The last thing a controller needs is a little Cessna flying around unannounced, especially when there are 747s flying in from Australia or Singapore.

What was the procedure again? Oh yeah, restart the avionics.

I flicked the master switch on and off, but it was no good. I had to turn around. I had no radio, no transponder to send signals to the tower's radar system, no nothing.

Now the bloody flaps didn't work.

Brilliant.

How the hell was I supposed to slow her down when I landed?

I had no choice, I had to turn around and circling around over Piroa wasn't really helping.

I made a hard bank to the left and pointed the aircraft towards Thames.

If I headed for Thames, I might be in with a chance of surviving this little crisis. It should only take me fifteen minutes.

"Now what?" I yelled.

Thick, black smoke had begun to appear from behind the dashboard.

Could things get any worse?

I could see Thames' runway in the distance, I only had a few miles to go and then I'd be safe.

Just as that thought entered my mind, flames burst out of the avionics.

I screamed in pain. It was unbearable, my hands were burning up. I switched all of the electronics off, in the hope that I could fly visually and see landmarks instead of using navigation. The cockpit was filling up with toxic smoke from the melting plastic dashboard.

Fuck, fuck, fuck.

I had to find somewhere to land.

My hands were red raw from the heat of the fire.

Emergency frequency 7777mhz, which was a locator, or black box, for want of a better word. Hopefully Tauranga would pick up my squawk code and alert the necessary emergency services.

I reached desperately behind my seat for the fire extinguisher. I grabbed the pin and pulled. Foam sprayed everywhere, now I couldn't see a damn thing but at least the fire was out.

Thames was directly below me now, so all I had to do was land, which was easier said than done.

I swung the aircraft round and nosedived towards the field below.

A field would do.

I was obviously not going to make the runway so a field was as good as anything. I levelled out and began floating in mid-air.

Gently back on the stick and there's the sink effect I was waiting for, touchdown and beautifully done.

What a drama!

Thankfully, everything electrical had stopped smoking now.

I pulled out the medical kit and sprayed my hands with anti-inflammatory spray.

Time to access the damage.

No transponder, no radio, no flaps, no gauges, no mobile phone to call for help, and one melted dashboard.

I opened the door and stepped outside, threw a ciggy in my gob and lit it. I took a large drag and then exhaled.

'Well, do I fly it back to Auckland blind or do I walk to the nearest house and phone the club?'

I sat smoking my cigarette for a few moments, contemplating my dilemma.

'If I don't get the aircraft back to Arrow Moore, they'll charge me for the use of it, so I'm gonna have to risk it… best get going.'

The airspace was uncontrolled, so no radio required. I could slow the aircraft down by using my throttle and not the flaps, so just the fire to contend with.

'Suppose I should wipe all that gunk off the screen and I might actually be able to see where I'm going,' I thought.

I dived into the Cessna and belted up.

"Masters on, ignition. Oh yes, we have contact, away the engine goes. Okay, a maximum performance take-off, I think, for a short field take off, here goes."

The Cessna roared down the field, hitting every bump and pot hole in the field as I went. My heart was in my mouth and I was dripping in sweat.

"Come on, you hunk of junk," I yelled as I pulled back on the stick. "Yes! We're airborne, and I didn't even hit the hedge at the end of the field. Oh, I'm good."

The aircraft climbed to 2,000ft and banked hard right and then levelled out. "Okay, heading one six zero degrees, Auckland here I come."

The flight back to Auckland dragged.

Finally, with the day's drama on my mind, I landed without event and parked up next to the clubhouse.

"G'day, Kevin," Trudy yelled across the forecourt. "How was your flight?"

"Ha, don't ask," I replied, jovially. I tied the aircraft down and went to fill in the logbook and then to try to explain what I'd been up to in the club's aircraft.

What a day.

CHAPTER NINE
NORTH HEAD

Oh shit. Another bloody credit card bill. God only knew how I was going to be able to pay this one.

I was coming apart at the seams, my mounting credit card bills were now out of control and I was sinking fast. I had used all of my savings to pay for my flight training and there was nothing left. The sale of my house in the UK didn't make any money at all. I'd had to just give it back to the mortgage company. So I had two choices left. Either stop flying until I had enough money, which would be never, living in this country, on this crappy wage with no overtime or bonus, or find a school that would let me fly and just drip feed my account. I was determined to get my licence and then charge people to go flying as my new business venture.

I really needed a commercial licence to do that legally but if I said the people going with me were buying me an expensive lunch, that'd be a way around that legality. A hundred and fifty dollar lunch that was.

It'd taken me three long years to adjust to life in NZ. I'd gone through lots of struggles and turmoil and I wasn't going to give up now. The only thing missing from this bloody country was the money!

It was Saturday morning and I decided to go for a drive up north on a whim. I loved to just jump in the car and take off. The sense of freedom was what it was all about. I certainly needed a good feeling at the moment, with all of the financial frustrations in my life.

'Learn to fly with North Head Aero Club,' read the sign.

I slowed to a cruising speed and tried to think where the hell I was. But it was no good, I was completely lost. I had to make a mental note of this place, so that I could try and find it again but, for now, I just wanted to have a quick look at the club. The country lane, just off the motorway, led to an old farmhouse, which had been converted into the club.

The runway wasn't as at big as Arrow Moore, but was big enough to put a Cessna down, maybe even a Beechcraft, if you were lucky. There was a balcony upstairs and what looked like a barbie and a couple of wooden tables outside the clubhouse.

It was perfect. I had already made my mind up that I was flying here, so I decided to investigate further. Inside the reception area was a fine display of accessories and flight equipment, there was even a notice board that listed cheap houses close by to help students ease the cost of flying.

"Hi there, can I help you?" the girl on reception said.

I explained to the girl that I had previous flight experience and was looking for a new school to finish the last part of my training. She explained all about the facilities of North Head and how much each flight cost, how many aircraft they had and a whole variety of other interesting and useful bits of information.

I grabbed the chief flight instructor's business card from the reception desk and put it in my shirt pocket.

This was the place. I knew it.

After the North Head experience, I continued my drive north, towards Whangarei township, where I was heading in the first place. It was good to get back to nature. It revitalised my mind and soul, just by being there.

I spent most of the day at Whangarei, checking out the Maori displays and historical information and pictures of British troops and the Maoris with facial tattoos. It was the peace and quiet I really enjoyed the most.

On the way up to Whangarei, I stopped at a little beach called Tutu Kaka.

It was paradise.

Golden, crisp, clean beaches, untouched by man, with a bright blue ocean and palm trees lining the promenade, beautiful.

After lunch, I lay back on the beach and thought about the final three exams that I had taken at Arrow Moore. If I passed those babies, I was all clear of Arrow Moore flight school and I could move onto North Head. Nothing else mattered to me, I had become totally obsessed with flying.

"G'day. You must be Kevin Thomas?" said the man.

"Yes, that's right. How are you?" I replied.

"My name's Joe Schofield," he said, "and I'm going to help you get through the last part of your flight training. Here are the keys to HVY Cessna. It's parked on the forecourt. Can I see your logbook, please? I'd like to review it while you carry out a pre-flight check."

Joe came across as a bit of a nerd, but he was friendly and, most importantly, he was professional. You could ask him anything. He certainly studied hard and stayed updated on his flying. You'd have to get up pretty early to catch Joe out.

Several weeks had passed since I'd stumbled across North Head and today marked a monumental occasion. My first flight at my new school.

The Cessna 172 looked huge, compared with the little 152 that I was used to flying at Arrow Moore. Everything was different… the instrument panel, the cargo bay, the fuselage, the wingspan and the engine. I felt like a child with a new toy, it was all new and exciting and I couldn't wait to get airborne.

"How ya going, mate?" Joe yelled across the forecourt.

"I've checked for water in the fuel, the windscreen is clean, three hours of fuel in the tanks and half an hour safe. I've also checked the oil level and engine bay condition, which are all good," I yelled back.

Joe climbed into the passenger side while I climbed into the captain's side, of course. I loved the sound of that word… captain. It made me feel very strong and powerful. In fact, it fuelled my ego, if I were honest.

"Okay, Kevin, the controls are not too different from the 152. You may think that they are, but they aren't really," Joe said. "You have the avionics here, which I am sure you are very familiar with. The flaps are electronically controlled rather than lever and cable controlled. Now, feet on the brakes and crank the engine till you get her to fire."

I nervously cranked the engine and it roared into life then the nose dipped violently forward.

"Woah! Feel the power from this baby," I yelled. "It's like stepping out of a Mini and getting into a Ferrari."

"I see you've noticed the wind sock and wind direction, so you know which runway to take off from."

Within minutes, we were airborne and flying around Papakura on the east coast of Auckland. After several manoeuvres, I brought the Cessna back to base.

All went well during the flight, considering that this was my first flight in a Cessna 172. I walked through the reception area and into the car park. My mind was racing with thoughts of how much work I still had left to do.

"Hi, Kevin. How are you?" bellowed Karen. "A letter came for you this morning. Here." Karen handed me the letter and then went back inside the main house.

I took the letter and went into my flat. I jumped on the couch and opened my mail.

"Yee ha. I've passed."

I had passed the final three exams I needed to move forward with my flying. Finally, I was free from the money pit of Arrow Moore flight school.

CHAPTER TEN
THE STRANGER

"Hi, mate, I'm Kevin Thomas." I held out my hand to the new guy at work and shook his hand.

"Orwight, geezer. I'm James Doyse." James had touselled, blond hair, scruffy clothes, and basically looked like a tramp. His eyes were bright red for some reason and, in fact, he looked ill.

"So you're English then, James?"

"I sure am."

"James, you're obviously a man of very few words, so I'll leave you to it, shall I?"

An hour later, I spotted Kelly arriving. Late, as usual.

"Morning, Kelly, how's it going?"

"Yeah, not bad," she said in her usual depressed and miserable voice.

I had noticed Kelly was always depressed. I read in the paper that New Zealand had a high rate of suicide because so many people smoked marijuana and I thought of long-term users like Kelly. Apparently it caused depression and mood swings. She told me that she had smoked it for about fifteen years, pretty much since coming to New Zealand. I didn't know what to think after reading that article. I hadn't noticed any change in myself – although other people may have disagreed – so I ignored it. Besides, I loved the feeling of being stoned.

"Can't be all that bad, surely," I said.

"What's so fucking good about it, aye?" she growled. "I'm fucking here, aren't I?"

"Okay, I'll leave you alone then."

Another loner.

She wasn't on flexi-time, but 'Kelly time'. She did as she pleased and got away with it. No one dared say anything to her because they knew that they would get a mouthful. I knew that this girl had some serious, underlying issues to deal with, so I left her alone when she was in one of her legendary moods.

Just before morning smoke break, Bert introduced James to everyone. I could clearly see that Bert wasn't really interested and just wanted to be off doing his own thing.

"Yeah, good day, Kevin," Bert said. "This is James, he's starting work here today as the new groomer."

"Yeah, I know, we've met. Hey, man, how's it going?"

"Hello again."

Bert's vocabulary was limited to grunting and clicking noises. He wasn't really capable of saying anything else. I felt it was a serious concern that Bert was the workshop manager. He was so scruffy and unpresentable to the public. How did he get away with it?

Kelly was quite happy to see a new face in the workshop. I wasn't too sure what her story was at times. She had a heart of gold one minute and loved people and then the next minute she was the moodiest person on the planet.

'Maybe it is the weed,' I thought.

All the smokers were sitting outside on the little wall, chuffing away on their cancer sticks. James walked by everyone, including me, on his way down to the car park, eyes bright red and bloodshot.

"Hey, Kelly. Feel better now?" I said.

Kelly had just arrived on the scene carrying a mug of coffee in one hand and a roll your own cigarette in the other.

"Aye," she snapped. "What the fucking hell do you mean by that?"

"Oh, err, sorry. I thought you were feeling shit this morning, you know with the hell attitude that you gave me."

"Call that an attitude? You want to see me in a real mood, mate," she replied.

"I went flying at North Head this weekend," I said, trying my hardest to change the subject. "Also, I got the results for the final three exams that I took at Arrow Moore. The plan now is to revise my past flight experience and then go in for a flight test within a month or so."

"So will you take me flying then?" Kelly said with a grin on her face.

"You'll be the first on my list," I replied. "Anyway, how's your weekend?"

"Crap! I'm having trouble with my girlfriend. We're not getting along."

"Oh, yeah? What sort of trouble?"

"Oh, don't worry about it. I don't want to talk about it to be honest."

Kelly went quiet after that and, within a couple of minutes, she left, leaving me to talk to Rhys, one of the mechanics. I tolerated Rhys most of the time, just to keep the peace.

Suddenly, James reappeared, looking like he had been dragged through a hedge backwards for the second time in one day. His eyes were even redder than in the morning and this time he had tears rolling down his cheeks.

"Hey, James, are you okay?" I asked. "You look like crap, mate. What's wrong with your eyes?"

"Oh, err, nothing, geezer." James rushed back to the wash bay and started washing a car that had just been serviced.

"He's fucking stoned, mate," Rhys chirped up from his state of silence. "Well and truly wrecked. Can't you tell?"

"How can you tell?" I said.

"His eyes are fucked, mate. Didn't you see how red they were? It's called china eyes. He's probably just been down to the car park for a toot on his peace pipe. Weed is for fags, I reckon. Drink's a real man's drug, not some pussy shit like weed. It turns you into a lovey-dovey faggot."

"Rhys, you're such a charmer, mate. Zero decorum, do you know that?" I said.

"What the fuck is decorum, you fucking stupid pommie baarstard?" Rhys spat back.

I laughed. "How do you manage on this shit salary, Rhys? There's no bloody jobs in the paper that would pay me the money

I used to get back in the UK and I'm sick of these crap wage packets."

"You wingeing pom. Are you ever happy?"

I dismissed his comments and walked through to the kitchen, where I found Kelly talking on the phone. She was always on the bloody phone just lately. Whenever I saw her, she was on the damned phone.

"Come on, you guys. It's half past," roared Bert.

Bert made me laugh. He was always winding people up with his bad attitude, especially Kelly.

"Did you hear me, Kelly? Back to fucking work, lovey," Bert yelled in her ear.

Kelly turned to Bert and snarled. "If you say one more fucking word, mate, I'll fucking kill you!"

"Move ya fucking arse, dearie," Bert said back.

"That's fucking it!" Kelly screamed. She slammed the phone down and turned nose to nose with Bert. "You fucking dick! Fuck off, will you? You fucking wanka. You dirty, smelly, fucking tosser. I fucking hate you. You fucking toss-pot."

I was cringing in the corner, trying to think of a happy, happy place.

Bert yelled back at Kelly. "Get the fuck out of here now, missy! You little tart!"

I looked at Bert and then put my coffee mug in the sink and quickly disappeared before he could say anything to me. I walked out to the workshop and went back to the job that I was doing before my break. There I found a very anxious James waiting for me.

"Orwight geezer. Got any dak?" James said.

"Any what?" I replied, frowning.

"Dak, dak, you know, weed," he said.

"Erm, in a word, no. I know who will have some though… the biggest pot smoker around. Kelly, of course. She's crying her eyes out in the toilets right now, so I wouldn't disturb her."

"Aye. She's crying? Why?"

"James, if you slow down on the pot, you might be able to stay focused on one thing for more than two seconds without your mind drifting off. Listen… I said Kelly has some but she is in the toilet crying at the moment, so go and stand by her work bay until she comes out, okay?"

"What. How do you know I'm stoned?" James said.

"Earth calling James. Are you listening? I can tell… because your eyes are bright red, mate."

"Shit. I meant to get some Clear Eyes this morning from the chemist, but I forgot," James said.

"Gee. I wonder why you forgot. It wouldn't have anything to do with the huge amounts of marijuana that you smoke every hour, would it?" I replied.

"I need that amount of shit to get through the day, man."

"I'd say you've had enough for one day, mate. Go and stand over there. Wait for Kelly, please. I have too much work to do."

"Fuck, fuck, fuck. I need some now, dude. It's my first day on the job, man, and I can't get fired, not yet, no fucking way."

James walked over to Kelly's work bay, ranting about how he couldn't cope or get through the day without a hit. I couldn't believe this guy. He was completely off his face.

Kelly came out of the bathroom, moaning about Bert. I butted in on her moaning and directed her over to James. She obliged and went up to the roof with him for a smoke.

"This place is full of crazy people," I thought as I watched James and Kelly go.

As soon as 5pm rolled around, I clocked off and ran down to the car park. I sat on the bonnet of Kelly's station wagon, waiting for her to come down.

Ten minutes later, James appeared from nowhere. This guy reminded me of the cartoon character Mr Magoo. He hadn't got a clue where he was, or where he was going. He was in a permanent daydream.

"Orwight, geezer. Come for a spot of weed, have we?"

"I sure have, mate, have you seen Kelly? She irritates me… the way she's never on bloody time," I said.

"Relax, dude, this is a no stress zone, okay?" replied James.

"Maybe when I've had some of the green stuff, I'll think differently."

"Yeah, man, that's the spirit."

Kelly eventually appeared, plodding along with her head down, looking ten years older than she actually was.

"Sorry, dudes, I was distracted by one of the salesmen who's having a problem with his girlfriend," Kelly said. She opened her car doors and let us in. "I'll break, you roll, Kevin. It'll be good practice for you." Kelly began breaking up a few buds of marijuana on a magazine and then passed it over to me.

"Come on, man. What's the fucking hold up?" said James anxiously from the back seat.

"You're like a junkie, James. Just chill out," I said.

"Kelly, I need twenty two smokes of weed just to stay sane in the fucking Matrix, man," James yelled.

"Aye," we said in chorus, before looking at each other and bursting out laughing.

"What are you talking about, James?" Kelly said, as she tried to hold back her laughter.

"The Matrix, man. Don't get me started," James yelled sharply.

"Erm, yeah. Okay, James," I said. "Had a bit too much weed, have we? Feeling a wee bit paranoid?"

"Just fucking roll the joint, geezer and don't give me any shit," James shot back. "The world is just like the movie, The Matrix, and everyone is being held captive to work in The Matrix."

I finished rolling the joint and then lit up. I took a long drag and then passed it to Kelly. She took a few drags and then passed it back to the frantic James.

"You sound like a vacuum cleaner back there, James, are you okay now?" Kelly said.

James didn't reply.

"Hey, man, pass the joint, will ya?" Kelly said. "I've had a stressful day too, you know. You only wash bloody cars, I fix the damned things. That's stress, love."

James handed Kelly the joint and then began acting weird, in and out of control.

"He's gone," I said, trying not to laugh.

"So, Mr Thomas, what are your plans for the future?" James asked from the back seat.

"Well, I'm training to be a pilot at the moment. I plan to take it further, to the commercial level, which will be quite cool, don't you think?"

"Captain Thomas… tally ho, chocks away," James said, in between fits of laughter.

I turned slowly and looked at James. "You're gone, man, completely gone."

Kelly was having a giggling session with herself at this stage.

The whole car had a happy feel to it.

"Good morning, ladies and gentlemen," said James, "thank you for flying relaxed airways. This is your First Officer Geezer speaking. Your pilot today is Captain Thomas. I would like to inform you that Captain Thomas has issued an order to the flight crew. All crew must be completely wasted before take-off. Captain Thomas is in the process of hauling on a joint, so you can all rest assured that he will be fully relaxed in case of an emergency."

Kelly nearly burst a blood vessel, she was laughing so hard.

"Could you imagine being on a flight in the future and then you hear this plonker's voice on the intercom? Captain Thomas. Wouldn't you just die?" James said.

"What did you mean," Kelly asked curiously, "when you said The Matrix, James?"

I turned and looked at Kelly. "Don't get this guy going, Kelly. He's obviously a raving loony."

"Oy, geezer, I'm right here, you know!" James yelled. "Don't talk about me as though I'm not here, dude."

"Okay guys, chill out," Kelly yelled back. "Let's have another smoke and you can tell us all about your Matrix theory, James."

James lit the joint and sat back to enjoy the effects of the weed. "You know the movie The Matrix?"

"Yeah. What about it?" asked Kelly.

"Well, that's how life and work is in the real world. Can't you guys see that?" James said.

"See what?" I said.

"The movie was about human beings being held captive and under the control of machines. We all live in boxes and think the world is normal, but it's not. It's all about control. People go about their business and just accept everything they encounter as normal," said James.

"Who are they, James?" said Kelly.

"The fucking clones and the fucking agents who keep us under control," said James.

"Who the hell are the clones and the agents?" Kelly said, trying not to laugh.

"Watch the fucking movie. I've said too much already," James said in a paranoid tone of voice.

"Come on, tell us," begged Kelly.

"All the people are the clones. Doing the same thing every day for fifty fucking years. For what? A gold watch at the end of it. They are conditioned the moment they are born, with propaganda shit from society. The agents who pose as government officials are really the fucking agents who control everyone in the Matrix. It's exactly like the fucking Matrix!"

"Do you know what, James? If I were you, I'd keep those deep thinking opinions to yourself, mate. Otherwise, the agents may come and lock you up," I said in between fits of laughter. I thought my sides would burst, I laughed so much.

"Why not just say you don't want to work and that you're a complete and utter lazy bastard?" Kelly said in her usual, logical manner.

"Aye!" yelled James.

"You're looking for someone to agree with you on justification for not working, aren't you?" she said. "You've made up this elaborate story in your head to justify your actions. Yes?"

Kelly was always a deep thinker, and the level of conversation in the car was way over my head.

"What was that? Could you start again from the beginning, Kelly? I wasn't listening," I said, trying not to laugh. I had drifted off somewhere along the way and completely lost the conversation.

"You mean you never heard a word I've just said?"

"Nope. Not a word," I replied. I began laughing uncontrollably.

"You bastard, Kevin." Then Kelly began laughing too. "I said, 'I've voted for the Marijuana Party.'"

"The what? Marijuana Party, what's that? Need I ask?"

"It's a political party, kinda like the UK Green Party, but they want to legalise weed. They have candidates in parliament that will stand for office and legalise weed. Cool, aye?"

"You're joking? Sounds awesome. Where have I been? I must have missed all the adverts and campaigning, must have been stoned for a few weeks. I usually think all politicians are the same and only out for themselves, there's only Labour that actually does something for the people, so the Marijuana Party sounds as though they could do some good. Could you imagine everyone on pot, everyone super-chilled-out and happy? Ha, ha funny… don't you think?"

"Life would certainly be a lot different with weed legalised."

James had fallen asleep in the back of the car. He looked like he was set for the night.

"Oy, geezer! Get up, you lazy bastard." Kelly wasn't going to take that from him, no chance. "Come on, let's be having you. I'm off home now to the missus."

James's corpse slowly moved into life and he opened his eyes. "Urh, what? You're going?"

"Yeah, man, let's go, chop, chop. I've got to be going," said Kelly.

I opened my door and said my goodbyes to everyone and then staggered over to my own car. I stopped, turned and then looked back at Kelly's car. James was on the floor where it had been a few moments earlier. He looked like death warmed up. He tried his hardest to get to his feet, but failed miserably.

"Sorry, James, I'm too wrecked to deal with your shit right

now, so you're on your own, I'm afraid." With that, I fell into my car and drove off.

The following morning, my mouth was so dry it felt like I'd swallowed a carpet burger, and my whole body was as stiff as a board from the huge amount of pot. I knew that I had to stop smoking because I also knew that I had a lot of revision to get through before the next day's flight.

CHAPTER ELEVEN
THE FLIGHT TEST

“Hey, George,” I said. “Taking care of the place, mate?”

The clubhouse cat was the only living thing in the building when I arrived at the aero club.

Brilliant. No distractions.

Somebody had already printed the weather report and kindly left it on the table in the briefing room. I sat in my favourite chair by the window and reviewed the report to see what my chances were of making my cross country flight today. It looked like it was going to be a sunny day with a bit of cloud, so great, I was going as planned.

I extracted the information I needed from the array of numbers and letters in the weather report and began working on my fuel and course calculations. Things like true airspeed, and various navigational coordinates, contributed towards working out a heading. I wrote my calculations on my flight planner and finished in just under an hour. I then grabbed the keys to EAY and walked outside to carry out a pre-flight check. Everything was flowing at the moment, I’d done exactly the same thing yesterday, so there was no thought, I just did it. All that was remaining was to arrange my topographical charts and visual flight guide.

“Let’s rock,” said Mike, appearing from nowhere.

“Masters armed, amp meter reading a charge, radio’s off, fuel primed, throttle full and free, prop clear and cranking,” I said in a newly found, confident manner.

The nose of the Cessna dipped violently forward as I started the engine and then I released the park brake and taxied out to the runway.

Joe was taking his B cat flight exams so Mike would take me out today. I was used to this chopping and changing of instructors by now, so I didn’t mind too much.

"Okay, Kevin," Mike said, "let's get airborne, and then take us out to the training area."

"Full power, keeping straight with rudder and rotate at fifty five knots," I said, trying my hardest to focus on the procedure. A few seconds later, we were airborne and climbing to 1,500ft.

"Hornet nzvta, Whangaparoa, 200ft, mac 2, eta zero three," came over the radio, breaking the silence in the Cessna's cockpit.

"Oh shit!" I yelled. "A hornet is coming through here in three minutes time."

"Hornet nzvta, Cessna 172, Echo Alfa Yankee, beware section v62, far south, 1,500ft." Mike stopped me from replying and gave the call himself.

"Echo Alfa Yankee, hornet nzvta, changing vector far north section v62, 200ft," the pilot of the hornet replied.

Mike clicked the radio button twice, as a quick way to acknowledge the other pilot's decision to change course.

Vrrrrroooooooom.

Bang.

The hornet pasted through area V62 at sound-breaking speed and left me and Mike with our jaws on the floor in total disbelief.

"My God, that was fucking awesome," I yelled in delight. "Have you ever heard or seen anything like that in your life?"

"God, no. That was out of this world," Mike said, excitedly. "How fast was the hornet going and how low was he?"

"I reckon it was fast," I said, nodding my head in agreement.

It took a few minutes for us to get over the awe inspiring jet, flying twice the speed of sound, but slowly we snapped out of it and returned to reality. Our focus returned to our small, slow Cessna world.

"Okay, that's good enough for me," Mike said. "Now take us back to base and I'll get you to show me a forced landing without power, okay?"

I swung the aircraft around and headed back towards base.

"Area V62 traffic, Echo Alfa Yankee, 800ft, south east, vacating north, training area," I called over the radio.

The flight back to base was by the book, which pleased Mike.

He didn't say anything, but I could tell from the smile on his face.

"North Head traffic, Echo Alfa Yankee, twelve miles north west, 2,500ft, joining overhead," I said.

I continued flying directly for the runway, trying to see which way the windsock was pointing and listening out for other aircraft making calls to give me a clue which runway was in use. I established that runway two one was in use and began setting myself up for an overhead descent.

Then Mike switched the fuel off, killing the engine and I jumped into life, beginning my emergency procedures.

"North Head traffic," I said, "Echo Alfa Yankee, late downwind, forced approach two five."

I sized up the runway for my FLWOP – forced landing without power – and continued with my check procedure to try to re-start the engine.

"Masters are on. Cycling carb heat. Checking the fuel tap and pretend that it is on even though I know that you have just switched it off. Pre-start, so checking the runway is clear. Yes it is and no one else is in the circuit. Runway two one is in use, I'm at 1,000ft, too high and too fast. Solution is to lose some altitude and speed by making a zig-zag approach."

"Good, mate," said Mike, "don't go too far with the zig-zags though, or else you'll not make the runway."

I made a few more zig-zags, decreasing my height down to 300ft and then made an imaginary crosswind leg of the circuit. Shortly after that, I turned onto final approach.

My airspeed was at fifty-five knots, which was still too fast, so I raised the nose slightly and shed five knots. I had to pretend that I had lost all electrics, which meant that I would have no flaps to slow me down. My airspeed was crucial to a controlled landing.

"Okay, 50ft and forty seven knots, levelling out and waiting for the sink effect," I said confidently. "Then we go into the flair, nose high and main gear down."

"Awesome, mate, well done," Mike said. "A perfectly controlled landing. Do that on your flight test tomorrow and you'll be sweet, bro. Okay, fill out your log book and I'll sign you off, so we can pass you onto Bill Begg tomorrow."

The only thing that I really cared about was my flight test. I just couldn't believe it. After all my hard work, tomorrow was the day that I'd been waiting for. It seemed like an eternity but here it was.

I planned on having an early night so that I'd be fresh for my flight test.

Thank God, they only drug-test commercial pilots in New Zealand and not pilots on a private licence.

I was undressed and tucked snugly in bed for 9pm that night.

After a long and sleepless night, morning finally arrived. I was beyond anxious about my test but it had to be done. I dragged myself out of bed and made myself a cuppa. All I could think about was my flight test at 11am. I was quietly confident, but nevertheless, I was still nervous. All I had to do was stay calm and I would get through it, I knew it.

Bang, bang, bang.

I went to see who was at the door so damn early.

"Orwight geezer," James yelled, laughing uncontrollably as he spoke.

"What the hell are you doing here?"

"I have some vintage weed with me and require a certain Captain Thomas to help me smoke it. Can you oblige, old chap?"

"Come in, Doysey."

James went straight through to my flat and began breaking up his weed on top of the stove. He put two knives on the ring of the stove to heat up and then began rummaging around in the bin for something.

"What are you looking for?" I said.

"I'm looking for a coke bottle, so that I can use it for a funnel, man. Who got out of the bed the wrong side this morning, aye?"

"Look, man. I've got a frigging flight test this morning and the last thing I need is to be fucking stoned," I snapped.

"Okay, dude, no stress. I just want to use your stove and then I'm gone. I didn't know that you had plans. I just thought we could chill and then go for a drive, that's all. No stress, dude."

I wasn't really too happy about this guy just landing on my doorstep without any notice. Not to mention bringing drugs into my house, especially with the wicked witch from the west on the warpath. Karen, that was.

"I was speaking to my ex-wife in Canada this morning," James said. "She reckons she hasn't found anyone but I think she has and she's just not telling me. I really miss her, she was my soul mate. It's just all the baggage that comes with a relationship that pissed me off. All I really want is a fuck. You know that's what every guy who's honest wants from a woman, not all that talking and emotional shit that comes with marriage."

"Look man, just smoke your shit and then go, okay," I said. "I don't mean you any harm, but you know you've got to go as soon as you're done. I'm off for a flight test and I don't want you to mess things up for me."

"Okay, dude. As I said, just chill out, I'm gone as soon as I've finished these spots."

James began rolling his weed into tiny balls and then placed them on top of the stove. He cut the top off of the plastic coke bottle that he had found in the bin and then placed it in his mouth, acting as a funnel. He placed the hot knives on the balls of weed and spotted them.

Cough, splutter.

"Holy shit, man, this is some good shit all right. Try some of this, dude," James said. "It'll blow your mind."

"Are you deaf?" I said. "I said that I'm going for a flight test in two hours time. No!"

But I stared at James, contemplating if I should or shouldn't. The devil voice inside me told me to stop being a wuss and just get on with it. The good side kept saying not to do it.

"I told her I've been with someone since her, she seemed to take it well, but she was a strong old girl, so I'm sure she can take it. I bet she has met someone."

"Fuck it," I said, "one hit before take-off won't hurt me."

I leaned over the stove and picked up the knives and then took a deep breath and sucked in as much smoke through the funnel as I could.

"You should get out there and meet some cute Kiwi chick," he said, "there's plenty out there and, with your accent, it'll be a novelty for her. I tell you, you'll score dead easy."

"Yeah, nah, I struggle with the whiney accent, mate, they are okay until they open their mouths. I think I'll just stick with English babes, unless I just fancy a fuck."

"I tell you, that's all I want from a woman. All that talking and bitching and moaning that women do just doesn't do it for me. A fuck's all I need."

"Where the hell did you get this shit from, dude?" I said in between fits of laughter. "It's as strong as hell. I do believe that you're trying to kill me."

"Shut up and have some more, dude," James said as he started coughing again.

I grabbed the two hot knives and placed them on the balls of weed. Then I put the funnel in my mouth and took a huge lungful of smoke.

"Oh my God, that's just taken the linings off of my bloody lungs, mate. I feel absolutely hammered now," I yelled, crying with laughter. "How the hell am I going to drive to the airport? Let alone fly an aircraft and pass a flight test now."

"As the locals say, 'she'll be right, mate.'" James tried his hardest to put on a Kiwi accent, but his strong London accent was just too much to hide.

I chucked my things in a bag and stood there for a few moments, trying to figure out what the hell I was doing.

Oh yeah, flight test. Got to do a flight test.

James looked at me and saw how absolutely smashed I was. He couldn't hold it in any longer, so he let out a roar of laughter. "Man, you are messed up. You're never gonna pass this damned flight test now, dude. Not in a million years."

"Cheers, you bastard. I'll kill you if I don't pass," I said in between fits of laughter. "I've got to go. Lock up or whatever you like on your way out and don't let Sly out, okay."

"Urh, aye, whatever," he said before he instantly fell asleep on the couch.

I grabbed my bag and left. I wasn't looking forward to my flight test, now that the Londoner had messed up my brains but it had to be done, so I went anyway.

"Hi Kevin, how are ya?" bellowed Karen.

"Hey, Karen," I replied.

"Are you okay? You don't look okay. What's wrong with your eyes?"

"I've got my flight test now and I'm shitting myself. Wish me luck," I said.

"Break a leg," Karen yelled as she left the passageway.

She stared at me as I walked past her to my car. It was quite obvious that she knew I was wasted but she never said anything. No doubt she would tell my sister the next time they saw each other. At that point in time, I really didn't care what she did.

I drove out of the driveway and onto West Bay Road and then headed out to North Head aero club. I felt absolutely wrecked. Why had I listened to James? I was going to blow my flight test now, I was sure of it.

When I arrived at the club, some forty minutes later, I had almost made it back to the land of the living. The walk from the car to the reception area seemed like an eternity, it was almost as if time were standing still. The effects of the weed, no doubt. I made it to the reception area and, thankfully, there was nobody around, so I just helped myself to EVC's keys that were hanging on a hook behind the reception.

"Ah, good morning, Mr Thomas," said Patrick. "All ready for your flight test, are you?"

I cringed. I thought that I was going to get away with not being seen by anyone for the next hour or so, unfortunately this was not the case. It couldn't be the guy who cleans the floor that said good morning to him, no, it had to be the chief flying instructor, Patrick.

"Yeah, good day, Patrick. How are ya?" I said, trying my hardest not to give my present condition away.

"Yeah, good, mate," Patrick replied.

"I'm off to do a pre-flight and then I'll come back to check the weather, so I'll see you in a bit."

"Okay, matey, take it easy today and you should be right," Patrick said.

I grabbed the keys and went outside to check EVC. All I could think about now was how much I hated James for messing me up before such an important event in my life.

'Alrighty, she's all fuelled up and ready to go,' I thought. I didn't feel too bad by this stage, most of the effects had worn off and I was somewhere near myself again.

I went back into the reception area to fill out the paperwork for the morning of flying and was met by a guy with a bushy beard.

"G'day. You must be Kevin Thomas?" the bearded guy said. "I'm here to give you a flight test."

"Oh, right," I replied. "Hold on a moment, I've seen your face somewhere before. I know, you were on that Ozzy telly program… where they dared a guy who was scared of heights to fly an aircraft. You must be Bill?"

"Yeah, that's right. That was a few years back when I actually worked here. Anyway, we'll get right into it, Kevin, okay? By the way, what's wrong with your eyes?"

"Oh, err, late night studying all night, you know."

"Well, if you say so. You look knackered to me. Are you sure you're okay to fly?"

"I feel fine in myself, so yes… I'm okay, erm, yeah, I'll be fine. No problem."

"Okay, Kevin, off you go into the flight planning room."

I sat down in the flight room feeling quite nervous about the whole thing, but I knew that I just had to get on with it.

"Okay, matey, what I want you to do is to plot a course and fill out a flight plan as if you were flying to Stuart Island," Bill said.

"Erm, yeah, sure," I replied.

Bill left me to it and went to grab a coffee in the reception area. I suddenly realised that I had been tricked… Stuart Island was not on my topographical map. I had only purchased the North

Island map as most student pilots had. We only needed the North Island, because we weren't experienced enough for a long flight down to the South Island.

"Aha, very clever, mate, very clever," I chuckled. "This Bill Begg character won't catch me out."

I looked at the wall in front of me in a daydream, trying to think where I could get the information. Then I saw the oversized topographical map on the wall.

"Well, I'd say that I've just passed my test," I thought. I jotted down the co-ordinates from the wall map and continued plotting an imaginary course for Stuart Island.

"How ya going, Kevin?" Bill said as he walked back into the flight planning room.

"All finished, would you like to check it?" I handed him the flight plan, then Bill began laughing.

"Well done, you've spotted my deliberate mistake. Good one, mate. Let's go and do what we both really love to do… fly."

We walked outside and headed over to EVC.

"How much fuel and oil do we have on-board, Kevin?" Bill said.

"We have full tanks, three hours safe and one hour reserve, which is probably a lot more than we need, right? Oh and the oil level is reading five and a half quarts," I replied confidently.

I took Bill through all of the safety procedures that I had been taught, which was totally by the book, of course. I talked my way through my pre-start and radio checks, then went onto the pre-flight and engine run up checks, followed by taxiing out to threshold two one.

"Kevin, show me a max performance take off, please," Bill said and gave me a rigorous test on the ground and in the air for an hour and a half.

This took me back to my driving test many years ago, when I was driving around Blyth Valley in the UK. I was very rigid and stiff during the test, but I made certain that I was doing the job right and passed first time. I knew everything backwards about driving and was doing exactly the same with flying today.

"Excellent work so far," Bill said. "Now show me what procedure you would do if you were caught in bad weather."

"Well, I could do a lot of things. The first thing that comes to mind is a reverse coastal turn. This basically entails me going back the way I came by picking a reference heading and turning exactly 180 degrees. I could also use a low-level flying configuration to fly below cloud. There is also a precautionary landing where I could pick a good spot to land and set down as a precaution or I could fly using my instruments. But that's not really feasible at my level of experience. I have however, been trained on instrument flying, which I could show you if you like," I smiled. I knew I was doing well, but didn't say anything.

"Nah, no need for that, mate, just show me the low-level configuration," said Bill.

I pulled back on the power and waited until the airspeed was in the green range of my airspeed indicator so I didn't rip my wings off as soon as I applied the flaps. I went on to explain that lowering the flaps would give me some lift at such a low altitude and continued flying as low as 500ft in this configuration until Bill told me to climb back up to the circuit rejoin height and then take us home.

"I have a few questions for you back at base and then we are just about done," Bill said.

I kept trying to look at Bill's clipboard to see how he had marked me. I couldn't really see anything, so I would just have to wait until the end of the test. The overhead rejoin into circuit was textbook. Followed by forced landing without power onto a crosswind runway, which was quite hard to do because of the number of things that I had to do all at once.

"Kevin, if you taxi us back and then tie her down by the clubhouse, I'll start on the paperwork for your licence," Bill said.

"So you mean I've passed? You're kidding me?" I yelled in excitement.

"Yes, you've passed, mate," Bill said with a smile on his face. "You're officially Captain Thomas."

"A pilot's licence! My God, I can't believe it."

Although I'd passed, it didn't really sink in and probably wouldn't for another few hours. The funny thing was that I had passed his flight test when I was completely stoned and I'd got away with it.

Now… who could I tell?

Dave and Karen were away on business and my sister was working, James would be unconscious from smoking pot, so it'd have to be my old mate, Kelly.

An hour or so later, I arrived home to a very excited Sly.

"Hey boy, get down, mate and calm down. I'm home now. Hello, what's this?"

I found a piece of paper that had been shoved under my door. The note was telling me that Dave's daughter and son-in-law were coming back from America and they needed a place to stay. This meant I had to move out. I'd been contemplating moving out for quite some time now, so this was just the excuse I was looking for.

CHAPTER TWELVE
FEEL THE FEAR AND DO IT ANYWAY

"Oy, you two," yelled Bert, "come here now. Where the fucking hell have you been? It's half past, your lunchtime is from 12.30 to 1pm, not 1.30pm."

"Do you know what, Kevin?" Kelly growled, "It's like being back at school with this prick. What's that, Bert? Didn't hear you, mate?"

"I said, 'where the fuck have you been?'" Bert yelled again, getting more and more frustrated by the minute.

We'd been to the local bookstore and become so engrossed in our reading that we'd lost track of time.

"Chill out, Kelly," I said. "He's not worth it, mate. Let it go."

She turned and looked at me. "Why the fuck should I let that prick talk to us like that?"

Kelly moved away from me and then looked directly at Bert. "I know we're late, Bert, sorry about that, it won't happen again," she said sarcastically.

"You're fucking dead right, it won't happen again. I'm docking you both half a day's pay," Bert roared in Kelly's face.

This was the last thing I wanted to hear right now. Not only did I have to change where I lived with deposit and rent expenses, but it was now looking like I had to find another job too. I snapped. I'd had it with this guy and this was the final straw.

"You fucking what? You one-balled, scruffy prick. What does it feel like to be hated by everyone on the fucking planet?" I yelled. "Yeah, that's right, mate! Everyone knows you've only got one ball."

This time it was Kelly who grabbed my arm. "Don't, man. Remember what you've just told me. Don't let him win, you're better than he is."

I walked away from Bert, despite the fact he was screaming at me to come back. Kelly intervened and let Bert have it big time.

"You fucking prick!" she screamed. "You just love to hurt people, don't you, aye?"

The entire workshop was staring at Kelly and Bert.

Ken, the service manager, had appeared on the scene and was trying to calm Kelly down. It was no good, when she lost it she would keep going and going until she ran out of energy.

"Calm down, Kelly, please," Ken shouted, which was very uncharacteristic of him as he was usually Mr Cool.

"You fucking arseholes," Kelly screamed. "You're siding with each other now, because we were a poxy half an hour late. Big fucking deal."

If you were to measure Kelly's voice level, it would have been off the decibel scale. She was absolutely screaming. To everyone's surprise, Ken was able to take the full brunt of her anger without even reacting. He just stood there and took it until she'd finished.

Kelly stopped screaming then got her second wind as another storm began brewing inside her.

"Fuck you and fuck Bert smelly man there. When are you going to clean your teeth and get a shower? You're a disgusting human being," Kelly screamed. "What does your girlfriend say about the way you look and smell, Bert?"

Bert looked at Kelly. "She says it's a turn on because I smell like a man, so I don't bother doing anything with myself."

Kelly went straight up to Bert and screamed in his face. "You're a fucking arsehole, mate, and I fucking hate you. I hate this job, so go and screw yourself! Both of you."

In the meantime, James was in the wash bay at the bottom end of the workshop, staring at the three of them screaming at one another over something so trivial. You could tell, even from a distance, that he was wasted. He could hardly stand upright. He was a complete space cadet and quite possibly on Mars right about then, but he occasionally came back down to earth to listen to the screaming match between the workers and managers.

"Well fuck off then if you don't like it," Ken yelled back at her.

"There's the fucking door, you bitch. Fuck off!"

Kelly burst into tears and stormed off to the toilet.

A few minutes later, she came running out of the toilet, past Bert and Ken, and then went down to the car park.

"Woah, man. What the fuck was that all about?" James had wandered over to my work bay and was now trying to pry the information from me about what had just happened between Bert and Kelly. "Hey, man," he said in a very relaxed tone of voice. "Try this pipe. I got it from Vicky market. It kicks ass."

"Are you mental, dude? I'm working," I said.

"Ah yes, my point exactly. Remember the day of your flight test, aye. I was the one who made you pass with flying colours. I got you relaxed, aye, aye, aye? I think you owe me a free flight, dude. Go on, take it, it'll chill you out big time," said James, trying not to laugh.

I took the pipe from James and took a huge drag.

Soon, I was on Mars too.

"Uh, what have you done to me, James?" I said softly, trying to get the words out.

"I mixed it with tobacco, it gives you a real head rush, yeah?" James said as he laughed at my discomfort.

James disappeared into oblivion and no longer existed in my mind. I was completely gone.

Knock-off time arrived and I left work dead on time, I'd had enough arguments for one day. On the drive home, I thought of Kelly and her temper. I thought I should perhaps give her a call to see how she was doing.

"Hi Kelly, it's Kevin. How are you?"

"Oh hey, Kevin. I'm all right, thanks for calling, mate, I appreciate that," she replied. "I'm bloody thinking about Ken and how much I went off at him. I've no idea what he's going to do to me tomorrow, it's the only thing on my mind. Lizzie's away in Hamilton again on another course, so I'm here by myself. Do you want to come around for dinner. Bring the Tasmanian Devil if you want."

She meant Sly, my dog.

"Oh yeah. I might do. In fact, yeah, okay then. Sly and I'll be there in say… an hour's time."

We arrived at Kelly's place just after 6pm. I drove down her long, gravel driveway and then parked my car outside the converted farmhouse where she lived.

Sly was going berserk, he was totally uncontrollable when he was like that, so I opened the car door and just let him go. He went straight for Kelly's dog, Sheppy, and began humping her.

As soon as Sly had finished with her, he ran around their garden at a million miles an hour until he eventually became bored with that and started peeing everywhere.

Kelly yelled from her balcony. "Come upstairs and bring the monster with you."

I walked up the steps at the side of the house and into Kelly's living room, where she sat smoking a joint, of course. This was Kelly's house… what else would she be doing?

"Hey, Kevin. Come on in and join me," she said.

Sly went bounding up to Kelly and began to lick her feet. He had a real fetish for feet and wasn't shy about showing it.

"Ah, Sly," she said, "don't lick my feet, mate."

I sat down next to Kelly and started rolling a joint from the bud that was on the table in front of me.

"Do you know what really got me about today?" said Kelly.

"Nah, what?" I replied.

"The way that bastard, Bert, yet again gets away with causing trouble and then someone else finishes it for him. The prick always does that. He never gets seen for what he really is. I hate him, do you know that, Kevin? I fucking hate the prick. I have no idea how I can get through the rest of the week knowing that he's caused all of this shit and made a big deal over something so small."

"Yeah, I know what you mean, Kelly, he's a toss-pot, all right. I don't know what to say really, other than just stay out of his way till it all blows over." I lit the joint and then took a huge drag.

"Awesome weed, Kelly. Here, take a hit."

Kelly took the joint from me and took a huge drag.

"You were so funny today, Kelly."

"I was? Why?" she said, frowning.

"Because the entire workshop was staring at you while you were screaming at Ken. Man, that was funny. Ken must have thought that you were a complete nutter."

"Oh, you're joking. Was I that bad, really?"

"Oh, yeah," I laughed. "James came over after you'd gone and said he could hear every word you were saying from the bottom end of the workshop."

"Oh, you're joking? Oh man, you're fucking kidding me. How embarrassing. Bloody hell! Look at the time, man. I have no sense of time when I smoke, but God knows what I would do without it. Come on, give me a hand with the dinner, will you?"

I grabbed the cutlery and took it into the dining room. There was silence in the room while we chowed on down. Sly sat deadly still in front of me, drooling while I ate my dinner. He wasn't going to get anything because he'd had his. Twenty minutes later, we'd finished and were back in the living room.

"I'll go, if you like," I said.

"You're okay for another half an hour. We'll have another joint before you go, if you like."

"Hey, Kell, I forgot to ask if you want to go flying next week," I said.

"Oh yeah, nah. I'm scared of heights, you know. I was only joking when I said you owe me a free flight."

"Aha, so you're bottling out, then?"

"No! I just don't like flying. I'm a ground person," she growled.

"Well, my dear, I do believe flying is what you fear and you need to just do it anyway. Yes?"

I was referring to Kelly's favourite book – Feel The Fear And Do It Anyway – which she would always go on about. She looked at me as if she wished she'd never given me that damned book to read.

"Okay, then," Kelly said apprehensively. "Just for a short time."

"Come on, you baby," I joked. "It's only flying, for Christ's sake. I've been highly trained and have a certificate on my wall to prove it."

"That's not really reassuring me. Okay then, next Saturday."

It was time to shoot off. I got up and made my way to the stairs.

"Thanks for feeding me, Kelly," I said, as I walked down stairs, dragging Sly as I went. "See you, Kelly, chill about tomorrow, won't you?"

"Drive safely, Kevin. None of your usual boy racer tactics, please."

"I'm gonna smoke this joint right now and get rid of it."

I lit the pre-rolled joint and sucked the guts out of it. I was already pretty stoned, but this joint put me on another level of astral plain. What I didn't realise was that I was only driving at 25 kph. Luckily, it was in the middle of nowhere and was 11pm. It took me over an hour to get home from Kelly's. This was normally a half hour's drive but I was too stoned to care.

Five days later, I began gathering my things together for flying and then put Sly on his lead outside in the garden. Saturday had finally arrived and it was time to give Kelly the thrill of her life.

I took it steady to Kelly's place, because I knew that I was a little early and wanted to kill some time. When I did arrive at Kelly's house, Sheppy greeted me with her normal fit of defensive barking. You only had to look at her the wrong way and she would bark her head off, so I just ignored her and walked straight past her to the front door.

"My God, girl. You look absolutely shagged. What time this morning were you smoking weed?" I said.

"Aye, yeah, nah. Fuck knows. Early." We went upstairs to her living room and sat down on her leather couch. Kelly came back into the living room a few moments later, smoking yet another joint.

"All right, Kevin. Fancy one of these?" she said, holding up a joint.

"You're kidding me. I'm flying the aircraft, remember."

"Oh, yeah, good idea. I'd best smoke it myself, then," Kelly replied.

Kelly went back into the dining room where Lizzy was sitting and then sat on her knee. She gave her a smoke and then gave her a big kiss on the lips.

"Got to go, darling," Kelly said. "My chauffeur is here to fly me around Auckland."

"Be bloody careful, Kelly," Lizzy growled at her. "I know that you're always in trouble and I don't want anyone calling me to say that you've been in an accident."

"I won't be, darling. See you later," Kelly replied. They gave each other a big kiss and then Kelly came into the living room and grabbed me by the hand, pulling me out of the chair and down the stairs.

"We'll take my car, okay?" Kelly said.

"Yeah, whatever, mate," I replied.

The drive to North Head didn't take too long with Kelly driving. She was a bit of a tear-arse and didn't take any prisoners in traffic. She parked her car outside the school and we walked inside to the reception area.

"I'll take you upstairs to the canteen, so you can have a cup of tea while I plot our course, check the weather and make a flight plan, okay?"

Within half an hour, I had plotted a course, planned and submitted it to Christ Church Information. "We're all good to go with the paperwork. I just need to refuel and do a pre-flight check, which should only take ten minutes or so," I shouted from the forecourt.

"Oh, yeah, whatever," Kelly shouted down to me. She finished her tea and then walked downstairs to the forecourt to join me.

"We're in EVC today," I said. "This is our baby here." I opened the passenger door for Kelly and went around to the other side, so that I could explain the safety procedure of the flight. "Okay, in the back you will find something called a ELT, which is an emergency locating transmitter. In the event of a crash and I'm unconscious, this could save your life."

"Okay, okay, you don't need to go on and on about it. I'm not stupid, you know."

Kelly climbed in the passenger's seat, while I helped her put her harness on and then climbed in myself.

I started the engine and then taxied out to runway two one holding point. Once I reached the holding point, I carried out some engine run-ups and pre-flight checks.

"North Head traffic, Echo Victor Charlie, rolling two one, vacating to the north."

I pushed the throttle forward and the Cessna roared into life. I reached fifty-five knots and then pulled back on the stick.

"Woah," screamed Kelly as we became airborne.

"Chill out, Kelly. It's not that bad, mate."

"You're used to it, I'm not," she said.

"Take off is surreal. It's the landing that I always have problems with," I chuckled to myself.

Kelly turned and looked at me with a deep scowl on her face.

"Just kidding… relax, will you?"

I climbed to 1,500ft and then levelled out. I changed heading to the city and began to track along the east coast of Auckland, which possibly has some of the best scenery in the world from 1,500ft.

Kelly was absolutely mesmerised by the scenery. She stayed quiet for the next hour, until she saw something of interest that made her speak.

"Oh shit, watch out," she screamed. "There's a bloody helicopter heading straight for us."

"Unidentified helicopter, Echo Victor Charlie, 1,500ft, five miles south, tracking north along the coast," I said over the radio.

"EVC, wpnz, 1,800ft, climbing 2,500ft, tracking south along the coast," the chopper pilot replied.

"Happy with that, Kelly," I said with a cheesy grin on my face.

"So that means he's going over the top of us at 2,500ft and we're below at 1,500ft?" said Kelly.

"It sure does, but never mind that now, take a look at the Sky Tower over to your right." I pointed to a large tower that looked just like the Telecom tower in London.

Kelly turned to her right and laughed. "I can see why you do this. It's absolutely unbelievable to have this perspective of Auckland city."

I decided that I had gone far enough along the east coast and made a slow roll to the left. It was time to go home.

"Once I've been flying, I don't want to land, because reality bites. This is much more exciting than anything on the ground that I can think of."

"I reckon," Kelly said, smiling.

"Do you see Mount Rangitoto to your right?" I asked.

"Oh yeah, I thought it looked familiar. Is that One Tree Hill in the distance?"

"Yep. You can see everything from up here, can't you," I replied.

"I love this, Kevin. I was shit scared to start with, but man, is it awesome. Cheers for bringing me, I appreciate it." Kelly was giddy with excitement at this point.

"North Head traffic, Echo Victor Charlie, 1,800ft, eight miles south east, will be joining over-head," I said over the radio.

I began preparing for landing by carrying out a few final checks then started planning my re-join into the circuit. Within a few minutes, I was flying over-head of the runway and starting to descend.

"North Head Traffic, Echo Victor Charlie, over-head, descending none traffic side runway two-one."

I began my final approach and Kelly was beginning to get nervous and was squirming around in her seat.

"Fuck, man, I hope you know what you're doing," Kelly said anxiously. "I don't want to die just yet. I'm really scared."

She was now seriously distracting me. Despite me asking her to keep quiet, she still insisted on making a noise. Asking her to keep quiet was like asking a bird not to fly, it was an impossible thing for her to do.

"North Head traffic…" I said.

"Ah, Kevin," Kelly screamed.

It was no use, she was completely freaking out and there was no way I could control her, so I ditched the radio calls and reverted to actually landing the aircraft.

I was already way off course and coming in far too fast, but I was too low to abort, so I had to go through with the landing. As I flew over the fence, I tried to level out, but the sink was too great and the Cessna dropped down like a lead balloon. We bounced, bounced and then bounced again, until eventually all three landing gears were on the ground. I stomped on the brakes and managed to make the last exit for the taxiway. I taxied to the clubhouse and then shut down the engine.

We went inside the clubhouse to fill out EVC's logbook. Kelly followed behind at her usual slow pace.

I snatched a pre-rolled joint from Kelly and lit it. I took a huge drag and leaned back in my seat.

"God, that's good, Kelly, I need this after going flying with you, mate," I said.

"Aye. I was a model passenger," Kelly replied.

We sucked the guts out of the joint until it was completely dead. We talked for a while and then Kelly decided that it was time to go. As she was driving along, she dialled Lizzy's phone number and told her that she had made it down safely.

"How is she, Kelly?" I said.

"Good, love. In fact, she said that she was stressing to the max the whole time that we were airborne, but she's relieved now," Kelly said.

The drive home through the Waitakere's was a slow one, because I was so absorbed in my thoughts. I loved the feeling of being stoned. In fact, as Kelly had kindly donated a bag of weed for my troubles, I was going to get even more stoned when I got home.

"Kevin?" Karen bellowed. "Are you there? Kevin, phone for you."

I went into the hallway and found the phone on the floor where Karen had left it for me.

"Urh, yeah… hello," I said.

"Hey, man, how's it?" Kelly said.

"Hey, Kelly."

"I've just been talking to Claire, you know, the new girl on reception at work. Well, I told her about our flying trip today and she's really keen to go with you, she'll contribute some funds. Will you take her?" Kelly said.

"No worries, mate. How about next weekend?"

"I'll phone her back and let you know you need to book the plane. She's dead adventurous and loves anything like that. So, what we plan is to make the flight out to Bethels Beach. Then I'll be there waiting for you, so I can wave to you both," Kelly said.

I returned the phone to Karen's place and went back to my flat to continue with my PlayStation game.

It seemed to me that everyone that I knew was reading this damned book, Feel The Fear And Do It Anyway. Now I was receiving phone calls, left, right and centre for flights, everyone wanted to feel the fear. People were actually paying me to fly and to log hours towards a commercial pilot's licence.

The hectic schedule carried on for over a month before I had a chance to squeeze Claire in for her promised scenic flight. But first, I had to get out of that damned house of Karen's. She was driving me absolutely insane with criticism of every stupid little thing I did. I just couldn't do anything right in her book. I had had enough of her shit and, enough was enough, I was leaving, besides Dave's daughter would be bringing her new American husband back with her from her 'ticky tour', Maori for 'long way around or holiday' to us Brits, so I had to leave anyway because they wanted the granny flat.

One of the last properties on my list was deep inside the Waitakere ranges.

I drove up the road from Karen's place to the little house tucked away snugly in the bush. I stood out on the road for a few moments, admiring the house. There were fifty odd steps, which led up to what would be best described as a tree house. I fell in love with it instantly. I had to have this place at any cost.

At six the following morning, I was up, dressed and packed, all ready to go. I was not a morning person by nature but something had come over me that day, I just wanted to go and get it over and done with.

I grabbed the weather report and sat down to thrash out a flight plan. I thought that I'd go to Pukakhoe first, which was only a small town, then onto the west coast to places like Manukau Heads, White's Beach and, most importantly, Bethels Beach, where hopefully Kelly would be waiting to wave to us.

I sat on the balcony for a while, enjoying my tea and relaxing with a smoke. I watched one of the commercial flights, Great Barrier Airlines, land and then taxi in to base. I loved the environment of North Head; it was just right in every way. There were no distractions and the most beautiful scenery ever.

I stubbed out my ciggy and then went downstairs to the reception area. When I got there, there was a very shy and nervous Claire waiting for me.

"You're early, aren't you?" I said.

"Yeah," replied Claire. "I thought I'd be ahead of time in case you were all ready and waiting for me."

Claire walked upstairs to the kitchen while I went outside to check EVC over. A short time later, I shouted up to Claire, who was now sitting on the balcony, to come on down.

I went through the usual safety talk I'd done with around a hundred people before, to explain to Claire the do's and don'ts, and what to touch and what not to touch, until I was happy that she had taken everything in.

The engine fired up on the first crank and ticked over smoothly.

"North Head base, Echo Victor Charlie, radio check," I said over the radio.

"Echo Victor Charlie," base controller replied. "North Head base, reading you five."

"North Head Base, copy five," I said. "So they read me clearly then, I guess."

I taxied out to holding point runway two one as I had done a hundred times before. I carried out my engine run up and pre-take off checks and then taxied to the threshold of runway two one.

"North Head Traffic, Echo Victor Charlie, rolling two one, vacating to the north west."

I pushed the throttle forward and the Cessna roared into life as it hurled along the runway and then rotated as I reached fifty-five knots.

"Woah. That's weird," Claire cried. "That feels weird, the take-off, I mean. It makes my stomach churn."

"Just relax and it'll pass once we're at a certain altitude," I said, trying my best to sound convincing.

I released the flaps and then levelled out at 2,000ft. I glanced across at Claire, who looked as though she was beginning to get used to things now. I set a course for the far west coast, following my visual flight rules precisely. I didn't want to stray off course on such a long journey, so things had to be right.

I loved the west coast. It was so untouched by man and was pure nature at its best. It had to be respected or else you would be taught a lesson or two. The beaches and tracks were quiet and you could spend weeks by yourself if you wanted to. It was perfect for your average recluse of the kind that I had become.

We made it to the coast and I swung the Cessna around so that I was parallel to land. There was absolutely nobody out there. It was deserted.

"I love it out here, Claire, don't you? You being a South Islander and all, you'll love it too, yeah?" The South Island is renowned for its scenery and rolling hills.

"Oh yeah, it's cool to get back to nature all right. The west coast reminds me quite a lot of home. I'd love to have a place out here someday."

There was silence for the next forty minutes or so, while we flew along the west coast admiring the scenery. It appeared as though we were not even moving, even though we were travelling at 110knots which, in laymen terms, was pretty close to 110mph. Cessna 172's are so smooth.

"There's Bethels Beach ahead. Get your cell phone out and call Kelly, that's if you can hear her above the noise of the engine."

"Hello. Can't hear you, dear. Hello," Claire screamed above the engine noise.

"Hi, Claire. Where are you?" screamed Kelly.

"Approaching Bethels now," Claire yelled.

"Ah shit. I've been out there once this morning, but I came back home. Hold on, I'll get my binoculars out," Kelly yelled. "Nah, it's no good, I can't see you. You're too far away."

"Anyway, we're moving on to Whites Beach," I said.

Whites Beach was renowned for its reclusive people, who sometimes enjoyed going naked for a swim and I was quite keen to see this but, unfortunately, never got the chance. Then onto Piha Beach, which was dead easy to see from the air because there were two, huge rocks straight ahead that looked like a lion's head.

I steered the aircraft in the direction of a small cluster of beach houses. It was going to be quite tricky to perform a U-turn once I had got in there, but I wanted to see them because this was where James had said he was living. In a shed at the bottom of someone's garden. I wanted to see it for myself. I didn't want to kill Claire and myself, just so I could get a shot of a shed from the air but I was game for just about anything really, so what the hell?

"You're not going in there, are you?" said Claire with a worried expression on her face.

"We can do it, Claire, you just need faith," I said.

I flew straight for the hill and then, at the last moment, started my turn. Almost straight away I had to apply full power to compensate for the drag that I was experiencing from down-drafts. The aircraft sank fifty feet before the power had a chance to make any difference.

"You see that shed?" I said, trying not to laugh. "That's my mate James's house."

"You're kidding me. It's… well… a shed."

"I told you it was a shed. What did you think I meant?"

"I don't know. I didn't expect it to be a real shed at the bottom of some flower-power girl's garden."

"You'd better believe it, living proof. Take a picture before I really start to turn this baby around. It's going to be a very steep turn in a minute, because we're running out of airspace."

Claire pointed her camera out of the window and down onto James's shed then took a few shots. She swore that she saw a blond-haired guy standing naked outside the shed.

"Did you get a shot?" I said.

"I managed to fire off a few. Now, quick, turn around before we hit that bloody hill," Claire yelled.

"Woah! That was exciting, don't you think?"

Claire just turned and looked at me in disbelief.

There weren't that many people on the beach today, just a few people walking their dogs or jogging, as I headed back to base, along the west coast. I had burned enough fuel for one day.

The trip back was a pretty dull one, compared with flying around James's shed, so I just sat back and enjoyed the scenery. It didn't seem two minutes since we had been flying around Piha and here we were in the vicinity of North Head.

"North Head Traffic, Echo Victor Charlie, overhead 1,500ft, descending none traffic side for two one."

I was quite proud of my landing.

Once we were down, I taxied off the runway and onto the forecourt.

"Do me a favour, Claire, tie down the wing on your side, while I tie this side."

We tied down EVC and then walked over to the reception area.

"That was an awesome day, Kevin," Claire said. "Cheers, mate. And here's a hundred and fifty dollars, so we're square, yeah? I really enjoyed myself, especially flying over James's shed."

"Listen, if you want to go again some other time, just give me a call."

Now that my business was up and running, I was always busy at the weekend.

Five of Claire's friends had booked with me to go flying, all paying $150 a pop. The aircraft cost $100 per hour to hire and, after the $15 landing fee, I made a profit of $35, not much, but I couldn't charge much more an hour for my regular customers because the average Joe couldn't afford it. But, at least it was something.

I now owed $56,000 on credit cards, finance, car and bank loans. I had no idea how the hell I was going to pay it off and it would probably be the end of me but I didn't care, I'd achieved my dream of having my own business and the best thing was, I didn't need my sister's help after all that. Maybe I'd just sell some more WOFs to Larne's dodgy mates and claw some of the money back that way.

It was only a pity Derek couldn't be a part of my dream.

I missed my friend at times. The laughs and movie trips were some of the best times of my life.

Still, if Derek was getting married, so be it… that was obviously what he wanted out of life.

CHAPTER THIRTEEN
WILD TIMES

I had just arrived at Norris and Sons estate agents to pick up the keys to my tree house.

"Hi, Kevin. How are you?" said Miss Fairmount. "Glad to see you made it. Are you all set to be Mr 10 Ponga Loop Road?"

She pulled out a pile of paperwork, which made me think that I'd be there all morning.

How could renting a house be so damned complicated?

Luckily, it didn't take long.

"Okay," Miss Fairmont said, "that's the paperwork completed and the house is all yours, Mr Thomas. How does it feel?"

"Excellent," I replied. I took the keys and shook Miss Fairmont's hand, then left the estate agents.

'I can move in later,' I thought, 'first back to Karen and Dave's to chill for a bit before the big move. Well, I'm $750 lighter but at least I'll be away from the wicked witch of the west. I'll actually be able to go home and relax after work or at the weekends. Do what I want when I want.'

I walked back into the flat to find a note that Karen must have left for me under my door.

"Please call James when you get in," the note read.

Oh shit. That meant I had to ask Karen for the use of her phone and talk to her. I'd had become more and more paranoid and reclusive over the past few months, not quite able to put my finger on what was causing it.

I knocked sheepishly on Karen's door. She shouted for me to come in, so I carefully opened the door. Inside, I found Karen sitting on her leather couch, watching Coronation Street, her favourite English import.

I said my hellos and goodbyes very quickly and then returned to my flat with the phone.

"Hey James, it's Kevin."

"Urh, aye, yeah, man. What's up, dude? Oh, Captain Thomas, I presume?"

"What's up?" I said, trying not to laugh.

"Got any weed, dude?" replied James.

"Nah, nothing. How about you?"

"Well, in that case, do you fancy legging it over to Danny's tonight to get some?"

"Aye. Are you mental? It's 10.50 at night, man," I said.

"If I phone him and arrange it, will you come with me?" James said. "The dude gives me the creeps."

"You call him and then call me back with an answer, okay?"

I put the phone down and jumped on my couch, waiting for James to call me back. Fifteen minutes later the phone rang.

"It's all set," said James. "Told you Danny wouldn't let us down. So, I'll see you in half an hour then."

James arrived at my place, exactly half an hour later, tactfully beeping his horn while, at the same time, wheel-spinning his van on Karen's gravel driveway. I ran outside and shouted at James to slow down.

"Will you stop thinking about her and think of yourself for a change?" James yelled. "You're moving out soon, so who fucking cares?"

"That's easy for you to say, mate, you don't have to live here for another ten days."

James revved the bollocks off of his van and then raced off along the driveway and onto West Bay Road. "Hey, man, if you go in the glove box you'll find my bamboo pipe and a bud wrapped in a bag. Stoke her up and we'll get lashed on the way. It's the only way I can deal with this guy. He's spooky. How do you think that he got those scars on his face?"

"Probably by sticking his nose in other people's business in a bar or something like that. I bet someone smashed his face in with a bottle for his trouble."

"Yeah, probably. Anyways, how's the peace pipe coming along, geezer?"

"Loaded and ready to fire, mate." I lit the pipe and took a huge drag until I began coughing heavily.

"I say, old chap, sounds like a bladdy good year to me. Bladdy good vintage indeed. This stuff is from a guy called Brian. He grows it himself using an awesome hydroponics set up in his basement."

I coughed and then nodded my head in agreement. "Here, take it before it blows my head off."

James took the pipe and took the biggest drag that I had ever seen.

"You sound like a fucking vacuum cleaner, James. What size are your lungs, for God's sake?"

We both burst out laughing, which made James cough even more. He was coughing so much that I had to take the wheel until James composed himself.

"Steady on, old chap," I said. "Just cough one of your lungs up and save the other one for Danny's place. You know that he's a very considerate sort of chap who'll offer us a sample before buying."

Sometime later, James had just about stopped coughing and managed a small nod in agreement.

By the time we arrived at Danny's, we were beginning to feel very introverted, paranoid and delusional from the weed and didn't want to go inside.

"Go on, then," James said.

"Go on, what?" I replied. "You're buying it, so you go in and I'll just wait here."

"Bollocks, you will!" James yelled. "You're coming in with me, Captain Thomas. You're going to be smoking it, so you can come too."

"Oh, for Christ's sake, you're like a bloody big girl's blouse, man."

We climbed out of the van and then staggered across the road to Danny's front door.

"Go on then, what are you waiting for?" said James.

"You knock on the door," I replied.

"Bloody hell, I'll knock then, shall I?" James knocked on the door and, within thirty seconds, a tall, scruffy-looking character with dreadlocks, appeared at the door.

"Yeah, dudes. Oh right, the English dudes. You've come for some stash, right?"

"Not too late, are we?" I said.

"No worries, dude, come in," Danny replied.

I turned and looked at James. This guy was Frankenstein's monster, only Dr Frankenstein didn't create him, it must have been his apprentice. Frankenstein's monster was prettier. This was one character that we didn't want to mess with, that was for sure.

"Sit down, dudes, while I find my stash. I sometimes forget where I hide it," said Danny. "Aha, here we are. Good shit this stuff. I was about to have a nightcap on the old water bong. Would you care to join me?"

"Erm, yeah, well, if you're offering," I said.

Danny began setting up his crazy-looking water bong in the corner of the room. I looked around the dingy room. There was a scruffy-looking mutt in a wicker basket. The curtains looked as though they were about to drop off and the room had a haze in the air of weed smoke.

"Okay, dudes, try this," Danny said.

James dived in first and then me. Danny refilled the bong and sucked the guts out of it himself and then the three of us sat back on the couch to enjoy the effects of the weed. My mind was racing with all sorts of weird and wonderful thoughts. One of them was that Danny would be incredibly generous with a $50 baggy.

After twenty minutes of staring at the ceiling, I eventually snapped out of my trance and made a decisive move. "Okay, mate, it's late and I have work tomorrow, so if you don't mind packing a $50 bag for us, we'll be on our way."

"Yeah, mate, no worries," Danny replied in a super-relaxed voice.

Danny emptied a huge bag of weed onto the glass table in

front of me and then grabbed five large buds and squeezed them into a tiny plastic bag.

"Oh shit," James yelled in delight. "Cheers, man, that's very generous of you."

Then the deal was done.

"Do you think we should get going, dude?" I said.

"Erm, yeah. I was thinking about blowing the whole lot in a tulip on the way home," James laughed.

"A what? Oh yeah, the Jamaican mate of yours that empties an entire baggy into one joint."

"Yeah, you got it," said James.

"James, why not just fill your pipe up and have a good smoke before we set off and then you can save the rest for next week, yeah?"

"Hmm, okay then," said James, not really wanting to.

We both went quiet while we explored our minds in great detail. This made the drive home seem like the most interesting journey that we had ever had. Time seemed to just stand still for me, until I suddenly realised that James had stopped his van outside Karen's place on West Bay Road.

"Oh shit, I'm home," I said.

"It seems that way, old boy. Who's driving the van is what I want to know?" James said, as tears streamed down his face.

"I'm wrecked, James," I said. "I need a few hours sleep before I go to work."

"Quit, man! It's just a fucking job, dude," said James, laughing uncontrollably.

"Easy for you to say," I said. "I owe shit loads and need to pay it off. Pot is just an escape for me while I do that. You use it to explore your mind because you're bored and have no real life."

"Okay, dude, see you later." James really didn't want to deal with his problems and usually just changed the subject whenever I talked about them. I said my goodbyes and walked across the road to my place.

"Hey mate, chill out. I'm happy to see you too, Sly, just calm down. Maybe you need some wacky-baccy to relax you, aye?" I said to my crazy hound.

I didn't have the energy to do anything, so I just crashed out fully clothed on the bed and went straight to sleep.

The alarm clock was set for 6.30 the next morning. I managed to drag my weary body out of bed and then get ready for work. The week at work dragged, all that was on my mind was moving into my tree house.

Several days later, Sly ran around the house sniffing every corner of the new house until he was completely satisfied he had smelled every nook and cranny. He ran up to me and sat down in front of me wagging his tail. He had given the tree house the royal seal of approval.

I began unpacking the boxes and then moved on to assembling my furniture, which continued all of Saturday and most of Sunday.

Once I'd finished, I sat on my brand new futon and looked around to admire my new surroundings.

Finally, I had my own space. I was delirious with excitement. I'd waited five long years for this and I was going to enjoy every damned minute of it.

There was a hammering at the door and I turned around to see a familiar scruffy-looking barstood standing on my deck.

"James!" I yelled.

"Orwight, geezer. Can I come in?" James replied.

"Yeah, yeah, whatever, James," I said. "Just be careful not to let the Tasmanian Devil out."

"Sly!" James cautiously opened the door and slid through the gap. "Orwight, geez, how's me old mucker then?" James bellowed in his London accent.

"Good, mate. I've settled in nicely. What do you think of the place?"

"It's one of the best places I've seen in NZ, geezer. Peace and quiet, mate, it's perrr-fect. Anyways, I've brought some stash around to christen the place."

"How the hell did you find me?" I said curiously. "I don't remember giving you an address. Did I?"

James sat down next to me and began rolling one of his famous tulips on the coffee table.

"You said Ponga Loop Road, the Waitakere's, so I drove around until I spotted your car," James said smiling. "Genius, right?"

"Oh yeah, good on ya," I said.

James lit the Cuban cigar-looking joint and then sat back while he inhaled the smoke.

"Cheers, James. Damned considerate of you, old chap."

Sly sat patiently watching us, thinking there might be some food for him.

"Want some of this, mate?" I said.

Sly jumped backwards and sneezed several times and then looked at me with a puzzled expression on his face.

"Sorry, mate. You know I share my beer with you, so I thought that I'd share my weed." Sly just frowned and then went to lie down in his basket. Over an hour later, we were still smoking the tulip. James was lying on the floor with his head resting against the couch and I was close to being asleep.

"Hey, Doysey. Do you want to finish the tulip?"

"Urh, aye. What? Fuck off, Thomas! I've had enough. You're mental. Just leave it alone."

"Oh God. I'm absolutely wrecked, mate, so I'm off to bed now," I said. "You can kip on the couch if you like."

"Oh yeah, cheers."

Within minutes James was fast asleep on the floor.

I liked James because we were both in the same boat… broke. We even tried eating dog food because we didn't have enough cash for food. Weed and dog food was all we could afford, so we shared the dog food with the hounds rather than starve. It was funny at the time.

I didn't even bother undressing. I just fell on the bed and went straight to sleep.

"James!" I yelled. "It's time to get up, mate." I wandered through into the living room. "Is your neck sore?" I asked, trying my hardest not to laugh.

"You barstood, Thomas," James yelled. "You could have woken me up last night. I can't even move my fucking head now, cheers."

I burst out laughing. "Sorry mate, it's bloody funny though."

"It's only funny because it's not you, you bastard," James yelled again. "Do me a favour… put the knives on the stove while I have shower."

"Fucking hell," I yelled jokingly. "Do you want me to smoke it for you as well?"

James went into the bathroom to have a shower while I put the knives on the stove.

After James showered, we finished off several balls of weed then we both jumped into my car. James had got himself a new job coaching at the local swimming baths so we had to go to James's work first and, after that, onto mine.

"Monday morning," I said. "I love it… not!"

"Oh shit. That's harsh man," James said, in between coughing fits.

"Why don't you move into my tree house? I can give you a lift to your work and we could share petrol costs on a regular basis. What do you think?"

"Nah, man. I'm happy living in my hammock under the house. Anyway, ta very much. Why don't you put an ad in your local dairy for a flatmate?" James said.

"I'd prefer someone I know to be honest. I'll manage I suppose."

There was silence for a few moments between us and then James broke the silence. "We need some music, dude. Rasta music okay with you?"

He pushed the tape in the deck and cranked up the volume. For the rest of the journey to James's work, there were nothing but mellow tunes and happy feelings in the air.

I sneaked in the back way when I eventually arrived at work, hoping that nobody would notice. I really couldn't be bothered to deal with Bert and his big mouth.

Kelly was opposite me with her finger in her mouth. When she did this, she was puzzled and was about to ask for help. Sure enough, she wandered over to me and asked if I'd had any trouble with misfiring Bluebird engines before.

"Hey," she yelled at me. "Are you stoned, Kevin?"

"Aye, what's that?" I replied.

"You are. You bloody stoner." Kelly nudged me with her bum and then smiled at me. "That's hanging out with James. Just be careful of that guy, he'll drag you down with him. He doesn't care about you. He's fucked in the head, so just you be very careful. You have a house and a dog to think of, okay?"

"Yes, mum."

Kelly walked away from me and went to ask Ross about her misfire job. She knew that she'd get no sense from me in my present state of mind.

Over the next two weeks, James went missing in action. He would simply disappear. The service manager, Ken, was asking me where James was. I just lied and told him that James was feeling sick and didn't think he'd make it in. I could tell by Ken's facial expression that he didn't really believe me but, to be honest, I didn't really care.

'Great,' I thought, 'James hasn't even told Ken he's changed jobs.'

It was a couple of weeks after that that James finally got in touch with me and came round to crash out at my place.

"I plan to do some work with my mum's friend's boyfriend," he said. "He's a bit of a nutter, but it's good money. Enough to buy a plane ticket and to leave this God-forsaken place behind. I'm gonna quit weed as well, it's doing me no good, I tell you. Mind-altering drugs, I can do without."

"You'll never quit," I said. " You love it too much. Doysey without pot? I don't believe it. You said another job… what job? And you said you're leaving NZ. Why? Don't you like NZ, James?"

"Oh I love it, it's the best place on earth but I don't see how the hell you're supposed to have a decent standard of living on the Joe jobs that are going here. You've got to be a friggin' brain surgeon to earn anything half decent, there's just no money here. Back home I'd have a minimum wage and, at least, I'd be earning something I could live on. Here it's just low wage city."

"Yeah, that's true, mate," I said. "It's hard to accept but I love money and NZ is not the best place to earn it really, is it?"

James didn't answer because he was fast asleep, so I decided to take Sly for a walk. I had neglected him over the last few weeks. The dog needed a good run.

The next day, at work, Kelly reminded me that her parents were due to arrive tomorrow night and that I had promised to take her dad out flying. As soon as she reminded me, I went into a panic.

"Oh shit! I forgot about that, Kelly. I haven't finished paying off my account yet, so I'm not too sure if they'll let me fly. What I'll do is give them a ring now and see if they have a plane available for this weekend."

"Okay, dude, whatever," she said.

I disappeared for a short while to make a phone call to North Head. Then I went back to the workshop and told Kelly the good news. She was over the moon with excitement and couldn't wait to tell her dad.

The following weekend, I took Kelly's dad on a round trip to the west coast. He never stopped talking about it for the rest of his holiday in NZ. I even made some money from the flight as Kelly's dad was a very proud man and wanted to pay his way, so I let him pay.

The extra cash really helped me out with my mountain of debt and, on top of that, James managed to get some money out of his dad in England, which helped pay his huge phone bill off.

Kelly's parents didn't stay long in Auckland, they wanted to explore the South Island and, hopefully, catch sight of some penguins and whales. They also wanted to see Stuart Island, which was basically just a large bird sanctuary.

"Hey, geezer," said James, leaning back on the couch, "I've now got enough money for my plane ticket to leave NZ. I plan on visiting my girlfriend in France. She told me to look her up and we'd go sailing on her boat."

"Oh yeah, sounds awesome, mate," I said. "So, then what?"

"I plan to do a yoga class and begin travelling again. This time by myself with no distractions… like women! Never get too attached, mate, because it's much too painful when you realise that the person you've been with for years isn't the one for you, like I did with my ex-wife in Canada. That feels like another lifetime ago."

"Oh yeah, I usually follow that motto anyways, mate, so no need to remind me of what I already know. I really don't want a girlfriend long term, or even at all. I can do without it, people think I'm weird, but I prefer life on my own. Anyways, Kelly's made tea, it's a free feed and no doubt a free smoke, let's go."

"Oh, for Christ's sake, man," said James, "whatever. I need a smoke first, so that I can deal with the emotion."

I put the knives on the stove to heat up, while James rolled some balls of weed. We had both become experts at doing this during the time that we had spent flat-sharing together, so it was a very quick process.

We were sitting on the couch, staring into space, living in our heads and exploring our minds, when the phone rang. I snapped out of it and went to answer it.

It was Kelly. "Are you two fucking stoners ever coming over tonight or what?" she yelled.

"Oh yeah," I replied. "No worries, mate, we're on our way."

"Bollocks! You're both wasted and are probably sitting, staring into space and not even caring that I've slaved my frigging guts out cooking for you. Get your fucking arses around here now."

I laughed out loud and told James what Kelly had just said to me on the phone. We both thought it was funny, typical Kelly.

"Come on, dude, we have to make the effort," I said. "Let's go before she sends a hit squad over to kill us."

"I fly out in twelve hours," said James. "I just want to relax."

"You're coming. Let's go," I yelled.

I grabbed James's arm and pulled him out of the chair. We then stumbled down to my car and fell in.

Forty minutes later, we arrived at Kelly's place. She appeared at the door and let us in.

"Come on, dudes, where've you been?" asked Kelly. "Dinner's on the stove and there's a joint on the table. Help yourselves."

We went into the living room and picked up the joint.

"More weed. Don't do it, Captain," cried James.

"Well, you don't have to smoke it, mate. Just watch me."

"Oh, all right, then. Light the bloody thing and I'll have some."

Kelly called us in for dinner, so we went through to the dining room and found a large plate of curry.

"Oh, excellent show, Kelly," said James. "Well done, old girl."

We all gobbled our meals down and then went into the living room to smoke yet another joint. Kelly rolled, while I drooled over it. James was trying his hardest not to look, he had had enough pot to last him a lifetime. He was sure it was driving him crazy, not to mention paranoid.

"Here, get this down your neck, James." Kelly passed the joint to James. He winced as if he was in pain, but took it anyway.

"God!" said James. "I'll be so pleased to get rid of this shit."

"You don't have to smoke it, dude," snapped Kelly. "I can always smoke it with Kevin."

"That's not what I meant," said James. "What I really meant is that I've been on this shit for eight long years and it's time to stop. I have all the information that I need to sort myself out and get on with my life, so I don't need it anymore."

"You talk as if it were a bad thing, James," said Kelly.

"It is. Don't you see that? It wrecks lives. It got me married when I didn't want to, it made me skint and I want to be rich, it made me a people person and I just want to be left alone. It's ruined my life and I really don't want to do it anymore."

"I think you're wrong," said Kelly. "It's the person who smokes it and, if you smoke it too much, then you ruin your life, not the weed."

"Oh, come on! Who's been brainwashing you with that shit? It's a mind-altering drug that changes a man into a woman and makes him all lovey-dovey. You know I'm right. You're just in denial in your own little world there."

"Shut up," said Kelly.

Kelly went quiet, while I tried tactfully to change the subject by asking what was on telly.

"Erm, don't know, Kevin. Put it on and have a look."

Over the next two hours, everyone was very quiet. We all knew that James was right but Kelly was pig-headed and stubborn. She just wouldn't admit she was wrong. The three of us just sat and watched the movie in silence.

"Okay, Kelly," said James, as we were leaving after the movie. "Thanks for the feed and the smoke. Wish you and Lizzie all the best, take care and I'm sure that our paths will cross again someday."

"See you, man. You take it easy and stay out of trouble." Kelly hugged James and kissed him goodbye.

The drive home didn't take too long and, before we knew it, we were home. I sat on the couch and was asleep within minutes, while James went around the house to check if he had left anything behind. He hadn't, so he joined me to have a few hours kip.

We were woken the next morning by a horn beeping, which made us both jump.

"That's my taxi," said James. "It's 6am already. I gotta go, dude."

"You grab your stuff," I said, "and I'll tell the taxi to wait, okay?"

"Okay, man. Whatever."

I raced down the stairs and then James followed a few moments later.

"Okay dude, take care and hang onto this place. It's a good spot. See you around someday."

"Okay, James, have a good flight and take care of yourself." We shook hands and James climbed into the waiting taxi. And that was the end of James Doyse.

CHAPTER FOURTEEN
THE VISIT

Not long after that, my family came to stay. I parked my car outside of my old granny flat and walked up to the back door. My worst fear came true, Karen answered the door.

"Hi, Kevin. How are ya?" she bellowed in her usual, loud voice.

"Hi, Karen," I replied.

"Come in and see your old place?"

I was quite surprised that she was so civil. I wasn't complaining, far from it. I went inside the house and knocked on my brother Mark's bedroom door.

Stephanie, Mark's wife, answered. "Hi Kevin, come in, dear. So, you guys are off flying today, then?"

"Yeah, that's right. Do you want to come?" I said with a big grin on my face.

"Nah, you're all right, thanks. I'm off to Takapuna Beach with Laura. I like to stay firmly on the ground, thank you very much!"

"Suit yourself. Where's Mark?"

"He's out the back looking at the scenery or something."

I opened the patio doors of the flat and went outside to the garden to find Mark, who was standing around the side of the flat.

"Hey Mark. How's it going," I said.

"I've got to be honest, Kevin, I'm shitting myself about today," Mark replied.

"Yeah? Don't worry about it, man. It'll be no sweat, bro."

We shouted goodbye to Steph and walked around the side of the house to my car. Laura's place was only a few minutes up the road, so it didn't take that long to get there.

"Morning. Are we all ready to go flying then?" I asked his parents.

"Mark's going flying, not me, mate. So don't bother asking me to go," said my dad.

"Whatever. You're the one who's missing out," I said. "Let's go, Mark."

Some forty minutes of driving and we arrived at North Head aero club. I parked my car and went inside the clubhouse with the family following.

"Okay, chaps, let's go flying," I said to everyone, feeling very confident with myself. Mark was looking as though he was having second thoughts, but there was no way I was going to let him bail out now. I pointed my parents in the direction of the stairs, which led up to the balcony and told Mark to follow me outside.

"Kevin, I'm really shitting myself man," said Mark. "I don't think I can do this,"

"Sure you can. It's a piece of piss, dude. It's like a 747 but smaller. I've checked the wind today and it's only two knots, which is nothing. Look at the windsock over there, it's hardly moving. If that baby was flapping around, then that's when you need to worry, Mark."

Mark didn't really look too convinced, but he had no choice, he was there.

I walked over to EVK and began checking the aircraft over. "Okay, mate, if you go around to the other side, I'll give you the safety brief."

"The what?" yelled Mark.

"Safety brief, standard procedure, dude. Just like on a 747, but there's usually a pretty girl giving a safety brief in the aisle. Okay, this is the life jacket."

"A what?" Mark snapped.

"Think about it, if a 747 loses its engine over an ocean, do you really think that a life jacket is going to save you in a free fall from 35,000ft at 800mph in a huge chunk of metal like a 747? Come on, get real! Who are they trying to kid anyway? It's a cunning plan that someone devised to make you feel safe. It's all bollocks, mate. Trust me, you wouldn't even survive the crash."

"Oh shit! I never thought of that before. Thanks, Kevin, you've inspired me with confidence now. Cheers, you bastard."

"I'm not talking about a Cessna, I'm talking about a 747. A

Cessna is really safe. If the engine fails on this baby over water, firstly it won't go higher than six or seven thousand feet, because the engines are not powerful enough and, secondly, it turns into a glider. Rough figures are: at 6,000ft, I can control my descent to a 1,000ft per minute descent pattern without stalling her. That would give me six minutes to find land or think of how to ditch her safely. 747s don't have that luxury, yeah?"

"Now that sounds better," Mark said. "Okay, let's go."

I ducked out of view around the side of the clubhouse and lit a joint.

"What the fuck are you doing?" Mark yelled.

"I always get stoned before I go flying. It makes me super-focused."

"You're fucking mad!"

I finished my joint and walked back to EVK. I went through my start-up procedure and then cranked the engine. It fired straight away. Then I taxied to runway holding point two one to carry out some engine run-ups and pre-take off checks.

"Okay, dude, wave to mum and dad. It's the last time you'll see them alive." I laughed.

Mark looked as though he was about to throw up. He just hung onto the door handle as if his life depended on it.

"North Head Traffic, Echo Victor Kilo, rolling two one, vacating to the training area."

I let it rip and then the Cessna roared into life along the runway until we reached fifty-five knots then I rotated.

"Oh shit!" Mark yelled.

"There you see, easy. We're now at 500ft, release the flaps and turning onto left base. As soon as I reach 1,000ft I'll keep climbing and make a radio call that I am vacating to the training area." I continued talking to try and reassure Mark. "See this lever, Mark. It controls the flaps. We are at 1,000ft now and need the flaps in the upright position, so pull the lever."

Mark pulled the lever into the upright position and the flaps raised.

I continued climbing until we reached 2,000ft. While I was

climbing I had scribbled something down on a piece of paper and handed it to Mark.

"Okay, mate, press the button on the stick and read back what I've just written."

"Erm, North Head Traffic, Echo…" Mark stuttered the words out.

"Victor," I whispered.

"Err, Victor, Kilo, airborne two one, vacating to the training area," Mark continued.

"Awesome, mate. Well done. Okay, we are straight and level now, so I set the trim wheel here to keep my hands free. Then we set the throttle to 2,200 rpm. All I have to do now is to steer the aircraft using my rudders, which is controlled by my feet. Want to steer her, Mark?"

"Oh yeah, give us a go."

"You have control," I said, sounding like a professional flight instructor.

Mark jumped on the pedals and pressed them left and right, which made the aircraft move violently to the left and then the right.

"Oh shit," yelled Mark. "I'm doing this! I'm really doing this!"

I let Mark fly around the training area for twenty minutes or so and then took control. Mark loved the east coast of Auckland. He couldn't get over the fabulous views and bright blue ocean.

I even managed to squeeze a few wing drop stalls in, followed by some steep turns, which was enough to give anyone a thrill. My brother had a permanent smile on his face. It was quite funny to see.

"It feels good to stare death in the face, doesn't it? It makes you feel alive."

"Fuck, yeah," Mark yelled back.

"North Head Traffic, Echo Victor Kilo, twelve miles north east, will be joining overhead," I said over the radio.

I aligned the aircraft in the direction of the airfield and began heading back to base. I began easing back on the power and descended to 1,400ft to join the circuit in the downwind leg. The circuit was dead. There wasn't even one aircraft out there.

A few moments later, I made a final approach radio call and then began our descent for runway two one. As I made my approach I spotted some traffic on the road, which ran parallel to the runway. I tried to ignore it by focusing on the threshold on runway two one.

"Hey look at that. We're gonna hit the bus," Mark yelled.

I was distracted only for a second but it was long enough to increase my air speed. This had a knock on effect to my descent. I was too high and too fast, so I quickly eased back the throttle and tried to raise the nose slightly in a desperate attempt to lose some air speed but it was no good. There just wasn't enough time to slow down.

The plane hit the runway full on at a hundred knots, which caused the aircraft to hit nose first and then bounce out of control. The aircraft twisted sideways and zig-zagged several times and then ended up on the grass, still travelling at a great rate of knots. As fate would have it, the grass was soaking wet, which made the Cessna skid from side to side a couple of times until, eventually, I managed to regain control and take off again amazingly.

"You okay, mate?" I asked.

"Wow, that was amazing. Shall we do it again?"

"Well, that wasn't exactly my plan, but at least you can say that I crash really well." I continued with a standard circuit and then landed safely the second time round. I taxied off the runway and up to the clubhouse.

I shut down the engine and opened the door. I tied down the aircraft and then shouted to Mark, who was still in shock. "Come on, let's go."

We went up to the clubhouse balcony to see our parents and found them sitting outside, enjoying the sun and the scenery.

"So… are you guys ready to call it a day?" I said. "After all of that excitement? I don't know about you but I'm going to call it a day. All I know is that I need a drink." The Thomas family left the balcony and walked down the stairs to my car.

The next day I took them up to Mount Eden. I turned into the entrance and drove up the steep hill, which led to a lookout point. Once I reached the top, I parked my car and got out to admire the views with the family.

"I can't believe that I've been in New Zealand several years now and I haven't been here before. It's an awesome view from up. You can see everywhere," I said to my dad. "There's Eden Park. Where they play international cricket."

"Oh yes, I'll have to go there," dad said with excitement. He loved sport, a real nut when it came to sport.

"I can see all of Remuera, the posh end of town, and there's the viaduct basin where the America's Cup was held. Not to mention the dirty great hole in the ground that I'm standing next too." The hole was, in fact, alive with lava at some stage in time but now it was just a grazing place for cows, a dead volcano called Mt Eden. I thought that Mt Eden was a good starting point for my family. "So here it is. What do you think?"

"Well, I suppose it's all right," dad said with zero enthusiasm.

"It's all right? It's a bleeding dead volcano! You don't get that in England, do you?" I replied.

'Auckland city was built on fifty volcanoes, some of which are still active,' the sign read.

"Well, that's a worry," I said to Mark. "What do you reckon?"

"No way, fifty volcanoes?"

"I guess once you've seen one dead volcano, you've seen them all. Time for the next place of interest now, ah… yes, Eden Gardens. Now let me see where Eden Gardens are on my map, err, yep, they're here somewhere."

I fumbled my way around Newmarket, trying my hardest to find Eden Gardens. It was amazing that I even passed my aircraft navigation exam.

"Aha, here we are, Eden Gardens. You'll like this, mum, nothing but pretty flowers and stuff."

After a morning of seeing every touristy place in Auckland, I had had enough. I just wanted to go home and relax for the rest of the day.

Later in the day once I'd sobered up, I met up again with Mark. "Hiya," I said cheerfully. "How's it going? Enjoying your stay with the wicked witch of the west… Karen? In my old granny flat."

He laughed. "Yeah, it's been a good trip and to be honest, I've hardly seen Karen. She comes and goes, says her hi's and bye's, that's it really. It's been quite good staying here, we've had a swim in the pool and a soak in the spa before bed, it's been great."

"Greg at John's works is organising a lads night out, you interested?"

"Oh yeah, what sort of night out? A get pissed and can't stand up type of night out?"

"Nah, Mark. Greg's a bush tucker man. He'll be going bush, mate. We'll start at his house that he's building deep in the Waitakere's and then go bush. Probably get very drunk as we tramp along and then set up on the beach for some snags, or sausages the rest of the world would say. We'll take the hounds with us and give them a good run, tire them out. It'll be good for them. Greg's a bit of a gobshite but he's harmless enough, should be a laugh."

"Okay, sounds different but I'm in. I'll look forward to it. Oh, what time?"

"I'll pick you up around six, okay, bud?"

"You got it, see you then, mate."

On Saturday afternoon, he climbed into my car with a bag of beers from Liquor Land.

"Good stuff," I said. "We're all set. I've got some snags, beer, pot and fags in my back pack."

"Got your priorities right, then?" said Mark.

"I know, let's get wasted."

"Count me out, I'm having none of that shit."

I pulled out a joint and lit it. "Ah, that's the stuff. Bloody good year if I say so myself. I know… let's have some tunes to drive with. Oh yeah, some techno. Got a beat and you can dance to it, awesome."

Within minutes, I was stoned and totally relaxed. The outside world was just a blur and my thoughts took precedence over my driving.

There was silence in the car for the next twenty minutes, I was living in my head and completely out of it and no doubt Mark was wondering whether he'd made the right choice to tag along.

We pulled up at Greg's driveway and drove down till we reached the house.

The house was mounted on huge stilts, set deep in the bush. From Greg's deck, there were awesome views of the Waitakere ranges and, in the distance, the city.

"G'day, mates," Greg bellowed from his deck. "Come on up, the door's open."

We walked through the garage where we saw Greg's handiwork… his lights. There must have been at least two hundred lights fitted in the ceiling of his huge garage. We went through the door, through his living room and up onto the deck.

Greg stood on his deck in his undies and Doc Marten's. "G'day, cobbers. How ya going?" Greg had spent ten years in Cairns Australia and had picked up the accent and sayings from over there. What a character.

"This is Mark, my brother. He's over on holiday from the UK."

"G'day, Mark. How'd ya like Kiwi land?"

"Oh, I'm enjoying myself just fine. There's so much bush everywhere, it's awesome."

"Yeah, nah, it's cool, aye? Hey bro, grab yourself a tinny and kick back. We're just waiting for John and a couple of boys from work."

We grabbed a Lion Red each and sat down in a couple of rickety old chairs to drink our beers. Greg's two dogs came straight up to us.

"Hello, Barney. How are you, mate?" I said to the little Staffy puppy, and gave the older dog a pat on the head. "How you doing, Amos?"

"Where's your Sly, Kevin?" Greg said in between supping another beer. He'd just thrown the old can on a pile of rubble in the garden from the build.

"He's in the car. He gets too excited when he meets new people and he'll rip your dogs to bits if they try and defend their territory."

"Righto cobber, we'll get the dogs together in the bush and then they'll have lots of space to run around in. Here we go, here's John pulling up the drive. Hey John, we're up here, mate. G'day, John. Come on up and grab a tinny, cobber. Fuck yeah, glugs the thing to get ya goin'."

John made his way upstairs to the deck, stepping over Greg's tools and piles of rubble as he went. He took one look at Greg's Lion Red and pulled out a bottle of Villa Maria Cellar Pinot Noir from his backpack. "I'll drink my own thanks, Greg, I like NZ wine best."

"Whatever you say, bro, grab a pew and look at the view. Fucking awesome from up here, don't you reckon?"

John took a sip of his wine and agreed with Greg and then pointed to the driveway. "Look guys, here's Corey and Glen."

"Yeah, nah, it certainly looks like them in their shitter. You can't beat a shitter. My old mitsishitters seen me right over the years, drop the oil every year and it always goes straight through a WOF. Fuck yeah, it's the only way to fly, I reckon."

"G'day, Greg, guys, how's it?" Glen yelled up to us.

"G'day, guys. Good. In fact, it's fucking awesome. A beer, a view and shit talk with the boys."

The two men made their way up to the deck and grabbed a Lion Red each.

"Fuck yeah, cobbers, get stuck into the tinnies and join in with the shit talk with the boys. You know Kevin, this is his bro over from England on his hols, aye."

"G'day, Mark," the men said in chorus.

"Hi there, how are you doing?" replied Mark.

This was the gang. Wherever Greg and John were, the other men followed, best of buddies, drinking buddies, bush-walking buddies, work buddies, they always ended up together.

Greg threw his empty beer can on the pile of rubble below and reached for his third beer since we'd had arrived.

"I'll finish this wine," said John as he desperately tried to down his drink, "and we'd best get going. Looks like rain, guys."

Greg jumped to his feet, gulped his beer down, burped and then threw his empty can on the pile. "Right! I'll throw some threads on and we'll get going shall we, boys?"

We supped up while Greg went into the house to put some clothes on, appearing a short time later fully clothed and wearing a backpack. "Got me snags and a few essential supplies, boys. Let's go."

We made our way down to our cars and everyone followed Greg out of the driveway.

Some twenty minutes later of driving around windy, country roads, Greg led us down a single-lane track to an open field, where we parked up. I opened my car door and let Sly out into the field. He went wild at the open space, running around and around like a dog possessed.

By then, day had turned to night. The winter nights had drawn in and it was dark by 7pm. Although New Zealand winters were like English summers, at night you could feel the temperature drop from 26°c to 10°c.

"Right, boys, stay close and keep an eye on the dogs as we go. Everyone got a torch? We have… good, let's go." Greg grabbed a beer from his backpack and cracked the beer open and then slurped half a can in one go. "Fuck yeah, this is the life, glugging and bush walking with the boys. Fuck yeah."

The dogs were being led by Sly who'd very quickly warned off Amos the old boy and whipped young Barney into shape. They were following him. Every sound or smell was of great fascination to the dogs, they loved every minute of the outdoors.

"Fuck, look at the boys go! They're lapping it up out here, wagging their tails and fully enjoying the exercise and fresh air." Greg burped then reached for his fifth beer, stamped on the previous can and then chucked it in his backpack. "Hey guys, check this out," he yelled to us. He pointed to some glow-worms on the hillside, glowing quite brightly.

"Wow, what's that?" Mark said in amazement.

"Glow-worms, bro. Cool, aye?" replied Greg.

Four hours later, I yelled ahead to Greg, "Any sign of this beach, Greg? We're all getting pretty tired here."

"What's that? Oh, yeah, nah, not long, bro. Just around the bend."

An hour later of tramping through the thick bush, Greg finally yelled out. "Here we go, bros. The beach. I knew it was around here somewhere, just couldn't remember where."

"More like the fifteen beers I've seen him drink clouding his judgement," Mark laughed.

We walked onto the deserted beach. Not a footprint. No man had set foot on Black's Beach in a hundred years.

'Pirates could have been the last people here,' I thought.

"Gather some driftwood, boys, and we'll have ourselves a fire to cook our snags. Shit yeah, cool aye?" Greg yelled to us.

The dogs plonked themselves down on the beach, puffing and panting. They were deadbeat.

Everyone was dragging their feet. We'd just done five hours of dense bush walking, along with ten beers each. Except John, of course, who was still on his wine, and we really couldn't be too bothered to look for driftwood.

After fifteen minutes of looking, we came back together and piled the wood on the floor then fell to our knees. "Fuck this shit, I'm beat," said Corey as he puffed and panted.

"Shit, yeah, that's it, boys! This is gonna be cool, aye?" Greg put the small pieces of wood at the bottom to use as kindling and then placed the larger pieces on top. He lit the fire and sat back on the sand. Once the fire had caught and the flames were roaring, he rummaged around in his backpack, pulled out some sausages and stuck them on a stick.

"Grab a snag and a stick, boys. Dive in."

We did the same and cooked snags on the open fire.

A bag of snags and more of Greg's shit talk with the boys later and all, including the dogs, were feeling very stuffed.

"Fuck me," said Greg. "I couldn't eat another thing. Them snags were cool, aye?"

"Does Greg ever get drunk?" Mark whispered to me.

"Well, he's on his eighteenth beer, so I reckon he never really gets pissed. The average Joe would be unconscious by now, but not Greg."

"Shit me, would you look at those waves, bro! I think the ocean is calling. I'm off for a swim, mate." Greg stripped off, down to his undies and ran into the sea.

Corey jumped to his feet and then pulled his top off. "Heck yeah, I'm off with Greg for a swim. Here I go." Corey stripped and then dived in after Greg.

"Those guys are mad. Fancy another beer, guys?" slurred John in a drunken stupor.

"Nah, not for me, mate." I turned and looked at my brother. "Mark? Fancy one?"

"Not for me, thanks. I've had enough."

"Fuck yeah, bro," Glen chirped up. "Throw one of those Lion Reds over here, mate."

John passed Glen a beer then passed out.

"Lightweight!" laughed Glen. "He's only had three bottles of wine, room for heaps more yet."

Greg appeared from nowhere, dripping wet. "Hey mates, what's happened to John?"

"He's a lightweight who can't handle his piss." Glen roared with laughter.

"Where's Corey?" Greg turned and looked around the beach.

"He ran in after you, Greg," I replied. "He said he wanted a swim."

Everyone looked at the water and began panicking.

"Where the fuck's Corey?" John suddenly chirped up.

We all ran to the edge of the water and began calling his name. "Where the fuck is he?" John yelled frantically.

"There he is!" Glen yelled as he ran in with Greg to pull the lifeless body of Corey out of the ocean.

"Quick, bring him by the fire to warm up." John pointed to the blazing fire.

We each grabbed a limb and carried Corey over to the fire and then laid him down.

"He's dead!" John yelled.

"He can't be dead," Glen said, as he checked Corey's pulse. "There's no pulse! He's fucking dead! What do we do? We're miles from anywhere."

"Don't panic," yelled Greg in a stressed voice. "He'll be all right, mate. I've got me cell phone with me. Fuck! No signal! Now what?"

"Kevin, you did that health and safety course at work in the UK. You told me about. Can't you do something?" John shouted in desperation.

By now, I had sobered up and was in serious mode. I leapt into action and recalled my CPR training from the UK. "Okay, check he hasn't swallowed his tongue, nope, check. Tilt his head back and make sure the airway is clear and then four breaths, then compressions on the centre of the chest to get his ticker working."

"No, nothing. For Christ's sake, keep trying, man," John was yelling in my ear.

"Okay, okay! I'm right here you know, just keep calm. Panicking won't really help anyone." I began compressions again, keeping calm as I worked.

Suddenly, Corey coughed and spluttered.

"Quick," I said, "put him on his side and let him spew out the water."

Corey continued coughing and spluttering out seawater and then opened his eyes. "What the fuck? Where am I?"

"You're on the beach and you drowned," I told him. "Your heart stopped for a bit, but we managed to get things moving again, no sweat."

"No sweat? You were fucking amazing! You saved his life. Sit him up and get his clothes on so he warms up." John rummaged around and found Corey's stuff near the fire. "Put them on, mate."

Corey spluttered again. "Nah, mate, I'll be all right." He sat up, grabbed his jumper and put it on.

"Right, let's just stay calm, crack open a tinny and think this through." Greg opened a beer and took a large swig. "Sit tight, cobber, and get warm, yeah, nah, that's the thing, get warm, bro."

My moment of fame had come and gone, Greg's mouth had taken charge. "Time for a smoke, I think. Staying relaxed is the best thing for it."

He lit a pre-rolled joint and wandered off to the edge of the water, looking out into the darkness and the moonlight reflecting in the water. "Mmm, that was quick acting, I feel wrecked now," he said. "What a drama this evening has turned out to be, ha, ha, ha. Gotta laugh, I suppose."

I turned and looked at the crowd of men. Everyone was hanging off every word Greg said. Dogs are pack animals and have a leader of the pack. Greg was the male leader and the men followed him like a pack of hounds. I knew I couldn't compete with someone like that, so I just let it go.

It only took Corey half an hour to recover and, within an hour, he was on his feet wanting a beer. "Right, let's get going. It's past midnight, so let's be on."

"Sure mate? We all had a bit of a scare back there and we've a five hour walk ahead."

"Yeah, nah, bro. I'll be sweet, aye."

Within half an hour we were tramping through the bush, dogs following, as if nothing had happened.

The next day, Laura called to say we were all invited to a lamb roasting at Eric's, Dave's business partner that evening. We went in two cars, Mark and his family with me in mine.

John tooted his horn as he drove past us, in the Kiwi tradition. They were all totally oblivious to other road users and every Kiwi loved tooting their horns with no regard for the road code: do not sound horn unless of an emergency situation.

My car roared into life as I followed John down West Bay Road and deep into the Waitakere ranges. It was getting dark when we arrived so the motion lights detected the approaching cars and it was like a sunrise of bright lights in the gravel driveway of Eric and his wife Janet's house.

"Orwight, geezers," Eric said, grinning and holding his hand in the air waving. "Come on in me, owld chinas. This way, through to the back yard."

The two carloads of us made our way round the side path to the back yard, which was already full up of people. There was a large trampoline to the right, belonging to Eric's kids and a net full of balls and toys. The rest of the garden was for grown-ups: a red brick barbie area, a couple of wooden tables and chairs and, of course, the spit in the centre of the garden.

"See me lambs?" Eric yelled to John. "Been on the spit all day slow cooking, cool aye?"

"Oh, really? All day you say? Surely they must be cooked by now, Eric?"

"Nah, I think another hour and they'll be done."

"Hi, Janet, how are you?" Laura yelled across the garden, waving frantically.

"Orwight, Laura. How's it going?" Janet replied.

Laura walked off to join Janet and the girls, while the rest of the family crowded around Eric, talking about his spit.

"That's not cooked, man," said John, sipping his Stein lager. "It's raw!"

"Well, it's been on all day as I said, so it shouldn't be far away," Eric said as he checked the motor and rotation of the spit.

I lit a cigarette and took a drag. "Ha, looks like it's raw lamb then, Eric. What do you reckon?"

"It'll be fine, leave it. Where's your beer, man, get stuck in, the beer is on the table over there." Eric pointed to a large wooden bench to the left of the garden, crates of Stein lager stacked on top of the bench.

"Orwight, geezers," yelled Dave in his cockney accent.

"Orwight, Dave. Orwight, darling." replied Eric.

"Hi, guys. Where'd you want this lot?" said Karen, puffing and panting.

"Stick them on the bench, darling."

Karen went to put the cases of beer on the bench while Dave swigged a Crown lager he'd liberated from her earlier.

"On the old Crown, Dave?" said John, smiling.

"Yeah, mate, it's man's beer, not like that Kiwi muck, that stuff is boy's beer. I got Karen to carry a couple of boxes for me, got to find some use for her, ha, ha, ha," Dave roared with laughter. "You not on wine?"

"Thought I'd try some Steiny instead. Just for a change, you know."

Everyone began laughing at Dave's 'I don't give a shit attitude' towards Karen. The great couple that loved to hate each other.

"That's not cooked, Eric," Dave said as he belly-roared with laughter.

"It fucking is cooked. Will you lot just fuck off, please. I'm calling it in an hour."

"You guys okay?" Karen had returned from her beer trip. "Where's Laura? Oh there she is, see you guys later."

I walked over to the bench and grabbed a Crown lager. I flipped the cap off with my lighter and then slugged the beer back. "Ah, Dave's right, it's Australian but it's good. Better than that crappy New Zealand Steiny stuff."

"All right, Kevin?" John appeared and began chit-chatting with me for an hour or so, knocking back the Crown lager this time, until we were both in a drunken stupor.

"Come and get it!" Eric yelled, with a large grin across his face. "Rabbit food and pastas over there and the lamb's all carved on the plates." Eric was proud of his achievement. He'd cooked several lambs on a spit like someone from medieval times.

Crowds of people were around the meat, and my family were starving so they pushed through the crowd and grabbed a plate of meat. "Don't forget your salad, John." John just smiled and left the crowd to find a quiet place to eat.

I found my parents sitting on the gentle slope at the top of the garden and sat down next to them. "This is good, isn't it? What would you have been doing in England right now? Watching telly, locked up, with the heating on, snuggled up because it's a freezing night.

"That's true," my dad said. "Is this meat cooked? It tastes funny."

I took a bite of the lamb and screwed my face up. "Great, it's raw. I can't eat this, can you?"

"Oh God, it is, it's raw," said my mum. "I can't eat raw meat. I know, I'll just eat my salad and say I've had enough."

"Good idea, I'm just gonna finish my beer and pretend I've eaten," I said, as I swigged my Crown lager.

"Well, I'm done, what now?" my dad said, as he gulped a Stein Lager. "I can't see us staying long now. I reckon a couple hours of this is enough."

"I'm gonna have a smoke. Do you wanna try some?" I said, smiling.

"Erm, okay then, if you think it's safe," said my mum, giggling like a schoolgirl.

"Sure it's safe. I've been on this stuff for ages and feel fine. It's a bit of a weird feeling to start with but then you get used to it and just feel great." I pulled out a joint from my shirt top pocket and lit it. After a long drag, I passed it to my dad.

"Oh, right, err, okay then." My dad took a drag and then coughed up a lung. "God, that's strong. A good vintage, is it?"

"Yeah, dad, it's weed le Kelly. Three months old, dried out and hand-picked. Great stuff. Take one more drag and let mum try, you only need a couple of drags if you're new to it."

Dad took his final drag and passed it to mum to try, who dived in and then passed it back to him. He took a long, hard drag and passed it to mum again. She put her head back and took a drag and then blew the smoke out after inhaling. She began enjoying it and began smiling, feeling great. She passed it to me. I sucked it back like a vacuum cleaner and then exhaled.

"Ah, this is awesome weed. Great feeling, don't you think?" Then I took another drag before the outer body feeling came over me and my eyelids became heavy.

"I meant to ask, how was your trip to Waitangi up north?" I said.

"It was great. All the chiefs' signatures on the treaty. All so New Zealand was part of the British Crown, the treaty house was a huge wooden hut full of Maoris with tattoos on their faces. Quite scary, really."

"Part of the Crown? What the hell would they sign that for? I heard the Maoris sold the South Island for a box of guns. Nah, I've been in New Zealand quite a few years and never been up north, to see the treaty house, so I don't know really."

"Right, let's go," dad said. "I've had enough, let's make our excuses and leave this joke shop and the raw lamb behind."

We rose to our feet and made an excuse that it was getting late and Mark's kids needed to be in bed and then left for my car.

I managed to get the team home some forty minutes later, super-slow driving. We had all had enough of Eric and his lamb.

'Time for a bedtime joint,' I thought.

The next day the family finally left New Zealand with fond memories and thoroughly convinced that I was set to stay in New Zealand.

CHAPTER FIFTEEN
CRAZY GIRL

The front passenger seat backrest thrust backwards and two intertwined bodies followed.

"Ooh, ah," cried Veronica, as I snogged her brains out. We were like vampires sucking the life out of one another.

I began unbuttoning her blouse, anxiously anticipating holding those firm breasts. "Oh my God, they're gorgeous."

"You're gorgeous," Veronica whispered in my ear as she nibbled my lobe.

I unhooked her bra clasp and flung the bra into the back seat. "Oh my God, they're so perky," I cried as I held on for dear life. I began caressing her.

She ripped my jumper off and then my shirt, her hands all over my chest. "You've got a great body, gorgeous. You make me hot!"

I unbuttoned her skirt and flung it away, not caring where it landed.

Veronica replied by undoing my trousers and put her hand down my boxers, having a good rummage around. "Oh God, you're the best thing that's happened to me in a long time, babe."

"Urh, aye?" My muffled voice came from her cleavage, my face fully immersed in fun-bag pleasure. I made my move on her and began making love. Wild passionate sex, screams of pleasure.

"Oh! Yes! Yes! Yes! Yeees!"

The windows in the car began steaming up with the passionate breathing from the couple. My car was rocking back and forth violently, putting strain on the suspension.

"God almighty! That was good! I haven't felt that good since I topped a thirty eight thousand quid pay packet in the early 90s back in the UK," I said as I laughed out loud, dripping in sweat. "Not a bad result, since it was our first date, don't you think?"

"Oh! Money! I don't even see why we even need money, do you?"

"Erm, I do know why we need money. Power, buying nice cars and houses for a start," I replied as I put my shirt back on.

"People and love are all I care about, don't you?"

"Err, I couldn't give a shit about people. Money, and loads of it, is what I care about," I replied, a big grin on my face.

"I think we just have to agree to disagree on this one," Veronica said, frowning as she put her skirt back on. "Anyway, tell me about your contestants to be Mrs Kevin Thomas. I'm curious why you chose me."

I pulled out a large joint, wound the window down and leaned back in the driver's seat and then lit it.

"Oh, you smoke weed?" said Veronica, coldly.

"Yeah. Why, like?"

"Oh nothing, go on with your story," she snapped. The change in her mood was not welcome but I continued with my tale nevertheless.

"Well, after Kelly helped me put an ad in the paper, I narrowed it down to three women that interested me. One, I finally decided, needed to be turned gay as she'd so many failed relationships. You're the second. And the third, I only met. We arranged to meet in McDonalds in Manukau city. We met, there were the usual greetings and small talk and then I tried to get out of it as I'd already made my mind up about you, so I went to the bathroom to think."

I took another drag in the joint then continued. "After I came out of the bathroom, I sat down with her and just told her straight that I don't think it would work. She asked me why, so I told her that I was not looking for a million kids hanging around me all of the time, that type of thing."

"That's not a nice thing to say, now, is it?" said Veronica with a deep frown on her face.

I took one last drag on my joint and nipped it out and then put it in my cigarette packet for a rainy day. I put my seatbelt on and started the car.

"Home James," Veronica said grinning.

I drove off, feeling very stoned.

The following morning, I tried my hardest to keep my mind off my big date. It was eating me up inside and I became very restless. I made it through to 4pm, when I began getting ready for it. I finished my shower and then put on my best threads.

On my way down to my car, I saw a girl sitting in a car. I hesitated for a moment, and just as I was about to get into my car, I heard someone call my name from behind me.

"Kevin," the voice yelled.

"Hi, Veronica." I pecked her on the lips and she replied with her tongue down my throat.

The movie theatre was only a stone's throw away, so the drive lasted all of five minutes. I parked my car in the large shopping mall opposite the movie theatre and walked across the road to Village Cinemas.

"What are we going to see?" Veronica said with a frown on her face.

"A.I… it's about a boy that is artificial and wants to be real, like Pinocchio, I suppose," I replied.

"Oh you're fucking joking, aren't you? It sounds shit."

I couldn't believe her. She wasn't like that yesterday. I shrugged it off as a one-off and continued walking.

"Hi there, mate. Two for A.I., please," I said to the nerd with large black-rimmed glasses in the kiosk. I grabbed a couple of buckets of popcorn and cokes and went in search of Veronica.

"Here you go, Veronica, some popcorn for you."

"Urh, how fucking disgusting. You can take it back," she said, aggressively.

I didn't know how to respond to this butch woman. She was swearing way too much for my liking, not feminine at all and I liked feminine. I was beginning to think that I had made a big mistake and it was only our second date.

We walked into the theatre to find a seat. I went straight to the back rows as I usually did. "Best seats in the house."

"Why are you going to the back?" snapped Veronica. "Let's sit at the front instead."

She didn't even wait for me to reply, she went straight to the front row and sat down. "Well! Are you coming?"

I sat beside her with two buckets of popcorn all to myself and tried my best to see the screen with a crooked neck.

"Oh shit, this is just impossible," I said. "How the hell are we meant to see the movie now?"

Veronica looked up at the screen with a crooked neck. "I can't see anything now. Come on, let's move to the back."

I couldn't believe this silly cow. She was like a jumping jack, all over the place, changing her mind repeatedly, not having a clue where she wanted to be. I was now one hundred percent sure that I'd made a mistake taking this girl out a second time. Veronica jumped up and ran to the back of the theatre, where I had originally suggested.

All the way through the movie Veronica was moaning about one thing or another. "Oh, this is crap. What's going on? I don't get this story."

I couldn't stand being around this woman any longer so I got up and went to the bathroom.

"Where are you going?" shrieked Veronica.

"I'm going to the bathroom. Is that okay?"

"Just asking. Off you go then."

I was beginning to feel déjà vu from the McDonalds date in Manakau city. I was going to the bathroom to clear my head, so that I could think of a way out of this nightmare. Once inside the bathroom, I found the nearest cubical and sat on the toilet seat.

Talk about déjà vu, this was ridiculous. This girl was worse than the other one. She was quite intelligent but she was all theory and she had no sense of reality. Also she ordered people around which I didn't really like. Not to mention her frigging attitude and how she thought she was right all of the time.

'God, I have to ditch the bitch. Okay, Kevin, what are you going to do to get rid of this stress," I thought to himself. 'I know.' I pulled out a butt end and lit it. 'Ah, just the ticket. A bit of wacky-baccy to chill me out.'

I sat on the seat for a few minutes thinking about what I

was going to do about this crazy girl. I had no choice but to go through with the rest of the evening and then just ignore her when she called again.

I left the cubicle and went back to the movie theatre, where a very impatient Veronica was waiting for me.

I saw the frown on her face from the entrance.

"Where the hell have you been?" she yelled. "I've been sat here for ages, all alone waiting for you. Call this a good time?"

"Oh, yeah, sorry Veronica. When you have to go, you have to go, pet."

Veronica was not impressed. She was so wound up, she was ready to explode at any minute. She was an iceberg waiting to find the Titanic and I just couldn't stand this girl for more than five minutes at any one time. I was dying to leave. I'd had enough of her bitching and moaning.

What an idiot I was for wasting her time with such a crappy movie, she told me.

"Okay, let's go," I snapped.

"No! I want to watch the end credits. They're the best part of the movie," she said, laughing out loud.

I almost wished that I'd stuck with the McDonald's girl. At least she had a great body and – the most important thing about a woman – she didn't talk a lot. This girl kept talking and talking and talking, until the cows came home. She was manic with conversation.

Finally, Veronica finished watching her stupid end credits and decided it was time to leave. I was beginning to think that it was role reversal here. She took the lead and I followed. We walked out of the picture house and into the lobby, where Veronica now decided that she did want some popcorn.

"Well?" snapped Veronica. "I'm waiting!"

"For what?" I replied.

"For you to buy me some popcorn. Come on."

I looked at her through my peripheral vision, I couldn't handle looking at her face-on. She would probably kill me with one of her evil looks. I was convinced that she was a she-devil. Instead,

I calmly put my hand in my pocket and pulled out a $10 bill and asked the nerdy guy in the kiosk for a small bag of popcorn, she didn't deserve a big bag.

"Okay, mate. Cheers." I took the popcorn and handed it to Veronica with a fake smile on my face. "There you go. Happy now?"

"What do you mean by that, Mr Thomas? Are you trying to say that I'm not a happy person?"

She was like a vacuum cleaner. She greedily sucked the bag dry within minutes and then complained that there wasn't enough. I ignored her and continued walking back to my car. I just wanted this nightmare to end.

I drove as fast as I could back to Veronica's car, back at Newmarket Nissan. I just wanted to get out of this situation.

"Is that all, Mr Thomas?"

"What do you want from me?" I yelled.

"I want … this." Veronica leaned over to me and gave me a sloppy kiss on the lips. As she kissed me, she grabbed my crotch and squeezed hard.

I was not ready for a girl like Veronica, this much was now clear. She was like a bloke. Sex was the only thing on her mind. All day, every day. She tried to hide it, but I could feel it about her, it was oozing from every pore.

"Okay, I'll ring you, my dear. Bye for now," Veronica said, chuckling away to herself, as she drove away.

It was all of two days later that she called.

"Hey, my sexy mechanic," said Veronica down the phone. "I've had a great idea! How about I take you out this evening? It'll be my surprise. Just bring your wallet with you."

'Why did I answer the bloody phone?' I thought.

"Bring my wallet? Is it gonna be expensive?" I replied, worrying about my finances as usual. "Okay, will do. What time? 6pm?"

"Yeah, six should be fine. I'll see you in Newmarket tonight then. Love you, my sexy English mechanic. Kisses, bye, bye."

"Okay, bye." I put the phone down and rolled my eyes around

in confusion. What was that woman up to now? Why oh why was I going out with this girl? I didn't even want a girlfriend, just sex every now and then would be ideal. Oh well, I'd find out tonight, probably an orgy, knowing Veronica, we'll see.

That evening, I walked down to the car park to meet Veronica, feeling very apprehensive.

"Hey, my sexy mechanic, don't you scrub up well? Come on, it's just around the corner, let's go." Veronica grabbed my hand and dragged me off down the street.

A few minutes later, Veronica stopped and began giggling uncontrollably. "Ha, ha, ha, there it is, my surprise to you, my sexy mechanic."

"A pub? We're going for a drink? I thought you had strict rules about drinking. You said anyone who has a couple of beers is an alcoholic."

"Nah, not the pub, the shop next door. Come on, let's go, my sweet."

"Love dolls, vibrators and beads? A sex shop? You've got to be kidding me, right!"

We walked through the door and down a narrow corridor to a black curtain. I pulled the curtain back and stepped inside. The lights were red, which made for a very strange atmosphere and I just knew I was about to have a weird experience.

"I've actually never been in a sex shop before, have you?"

"Nope, it's my first time. Oh, what's that? Lubricating jelly, strawberry flavour, Ha, what could you do with that? Aha, here we are… chocolate."

"What, chocolate! It says body paint. What the hell do we use that for?"

"Oh come on, Kevin, you're not that naïve, are you? Look, here's a paintbrush and we'll take four jars. We're gonna have some fun tonight, ooh baby."

"All right, mate, I'll… err… take four jars of the chocolate and two brushes please. What do I owe you?"

"G'day, mate," the rather seedy thirty something year old man said from behind the counter. "Oh yeah, nah, you and the missus will have some fun tonight with this stuff. Yeah, nah this will run you up $22 including GST, bro. I'll wrap it for ya, shall I?"

"Erm, yeah, mate, just put it in a bag. $22 right? Here you go, $25, cheers."

The man adjusted his black-rimmed NHS type of glasses as he stared at me, trying to suss me out. I ignored him feeling very embarrassed and secretly cursing Veronica for putting me in this situation. The man gave me my change and then I left the shop in a hurry, dragging Veronica with me.

"Thank fuck that's all over and done with. You really want me to paint this shit on you and then lick it off?"

"Ooh baby, you bet I do. I'm all wet thinking of my sexy mechanic licking some chocolate off my body and then making love to me. You're just a big tease, aren't you? You really know how to turn a girl on, babe, oh yeah."

We made our way through Newmarket and back to my car. I was very jumpy walking in the street holding a bag of body paint and having just visited a sex shop. 'Oh crap. If only people knew where I've just been,' I thought.

"Right, you take your little Mazda back to North Shore and I'll follow you in my motor, okay?"

"Okay, babe. And then we'll try out this awesome product."

All that I could think of during the drive over there was this damned body paint. How I'd have to perform with the nymphomaniac. She'd be the death of me. What a strange girl.

"Hi babe, did you miss me?"

"Erm, yeah, sure did. Come on, let's have a cuppa and watch a bit of telly."

"What? Don't you want to ravish my body and paint me?"

"Well, yes, but I'd like to just chill first."

"Oh! Anticipation, that's cool. Mmm, you make me horny just thinking about you doing me, on the rug or on the coffee table, yeah, baby." Veronica put the bag of paint on the table and went into the kitchen to put the kettle on.

Veronica was the most useless woman in the kitchen I'd ever

met, making coffee was a major exercise to her. I just knew it'd taste horrible, so I went into the kitchen to make it myself.

"Oh hello, my lovely man. Have you come to watch me make some coffee or have you come to have wild sex on the bench with me?"

"Ha, ha, ha, yeah, that's right. Let's do it right here."

Veronica pushed her hips and chest up against my body and gave me a long passionate kiss. "I love you, my sexy mechanic, you babe."

"Okay, calm down, dear. Let's have our coffee and chill on the couch."

We went through to the living room and sat down to drink our coffee.

"This is a good cuppa, my love. You're amazing at making coffee. I just know you'd be great at making love with chocolate body paint too."

"Aha, so I'm an amazing lover too now, am I?" I burst out laughing and then continued drinking my coffee.

Veronica just scowled at me. "I just think you're a great lover. Is that such a bad thing?"

"No, it's just you go on and on about it, that's all."

Veronica put her cuppa on the coffee table and then sat on my lap. "What do you want to do to me, lover? Do you want to have your wicked way?" She put her hand on my shoulders and then kissed me passionately. "Ooh, you're a good kisser."

I started to take control and unbuttoned her blouse and put my hand in her bra. "I love boobs. Boobs are it for me."

"Ha, ha, ha, you little monkey, you." Veronica pulled my t-shirt off and reached for the bag of body paint. She brushed it all over my nipples and then began licking it off. "Mmm, gorgeous, my love. I love your chest, so strong and manly."

I took control of Veronica on my lap and pulled her blouse completely off and then unclipped her bra. I reached for the chocolate and brushed it all over her boobs. I was in heaven licking it off, chocolate and boobs… my two favourite things in the world.

We began kissing passionately and undressing each other.

"Yes, yes, do me, my sexy mechanic. You're so big, aren't you? Oh yes, what a great lover you are."

I always thought that that sounded so corny and false but no, she really meant it and was genuine.

We made love on the rug in the living room, moaning and passionately embracing one another; becoming one.

"Oh that was fantastic, babe, and we've used only half of the chocolate. We'll save it for next time. Mmm, yeah, baby."

Veronica began getting dressed and adjusting her hair, while I sat at the patio doors in my boxer shorts, smoking, wondering if I could ever satisfy this woman. Probably not. I made a decision… run away.

'The first thing that I need to do when I get home is to change my phone number,' I thought. 'To hell with her.'

The answering machine light was flashing when I arrived home. Guess who had left me seven messages? Veronica, the psycho girl.

Suffice to say, I called the telecom company right then and there and changed my number.

The following day at work, I couldn't wait to tell Kelly about my experiences with psycho girl.

"You're fucking joking, aren't you?" Kelly said in disbelief. "She sounds crazy. What happens if she comes here to find you, Kevin?"

"I'll come get you. You can handle people quite well without losing it, so you're best qualified to deal with her."

"You can sod off, mate," snapped Kelly. "It's your problem, so you deal with it."

"Cheers, Kelly. You're a great help."

Kelly laughed and continued drinking her cup of coffee.

"Hey, Mr Thomas," a voice yelled across the workshop.

I cringed. "No, no, no!"

Veronica stood at the doorway with her hands on her hips, and a frown on her angry face.

"Hey, Veronica. How's it going?" I replied, screwing up my face.

"Have you changed your bloody phone number?" yelled Veronica. "I want your phone number… now!"

"Erm, yeah, nah. Have you met Kelly, Veronica?" I said calmly.

I shouted to Kelly, who was working on a car opposite me. Kelly had obviously figured out what was going on and who the girl was, so she came over.

"Who are you and what do you want?" growled Veronica.

"I'm Kelly, Kevin's friend. Kevin doesn't want to see you right now, so please respect his wishes and leave," Kelly said in a very assertive but calm voice while staring right in Veronica's eyes.

The two girls started arguing with each other as the entire workshop watched with great fascination.

"Please leave now!" I yelled. "I don't want to see you or go out with you, so please leave."

"What?" bellowed Veronica. "I need a reason why you don't want to see me. I can't just leave things this way. I need to know why."

"We haven't got any history together," I yelled. "We have only gone out twice and a few phone calls here and there, that's it, end of story."

Veronica stared long and hard at me and then left. She was out numbered two-to-one. Not to mention the entire workshop listening to her embarrassing behaviour.

I left work that night to find the words 'scumbag' written in lipstick across my windscreen. I walked round the car and groaned. "Bitch! She's keyed my paintwork as well, fucking cow."

I had become very close recently to Kelly, like an old, happy married couple, but without sex. Best mates, we knew everything about one another. Zero secrets.

She was having girlfriend trouble, another woman apparently. I often chuckled to myself that I'd gotten involved with Kelly. Guys cheated on their wives, women didn't cheat. Well, most women.

She didn't want to hurt her girlfriend but she'd met someone new and was cheating, a lesbian with a conscience. Hilarious when I thought of her predicament: a large farmhouse, two cars, two kids to pay for and she was living a double life with another woman.

'Women, they're all crazy! Let them get on with it I say,' I thought.

Later that night I was coming back from rock climbing, way out west, in some inhabitable part of the bush that weekend when I picked up my voicemail.

"Kevin, I'm home and I really need a friend right now. I'm about to leave home," the voicemail said.

'It's Kelly,' I frowned. 'She's leaving home and she needs a friend, strange girl. Why would she tell me that?'

I moved onto the next message. It was Kelly again.

"Kevin, I really need to talk to you."

The next message was the same and the next. Each time she had left a message, her voice had become more and more distraught. By the time I reached the last message, she was crying her eyes out and was obviously desperate to get in touch with me.

"Kevin, where the hell are you?" she yelled down the phone. "I came round to your tree house but you were out, so I had to have a crap in the bush. Please, call me."

I burst out laughing. I knew she was in trouble, but couldn't help laughing at her foul, butch mouth and lack of decorum. She was a real, stereotypical dyke at times but I loved her to bits anyway. I searched my phone for Kelly's number and hit the dial button. It rang a few times and then someone answered in a very quiet voice. It was Kelly.

"Hey, Kelly, it's Kevin. What's the story and where are you?"

"I'm okay, Kevin," she said in a softly spoken voice. "I'm at a friend's place in town.

"What's with all the messages on my phone?" I said, trying my hardest not to laugh.

"I've left Sarah," Kelly replied.

"You've done what?"

"I left her. I just couldn't stand it anymore. I care about her, but

I can't live there anymore. It's too much bullshit to put up with. It's one problem after another with her, nothing ever seems to come right and I just want someone to talk to. I feel like shit now."

Kelly began crying.

"Well I'm sure that if you have to go, you have to go. I mean why be miserable and stay? Don't feel bad because you're doing what you want, mate. Did you argue with her before leaving?"

"I did argue. I never got my stuff either."

"Well… you can stay at my place if you want. I have a sofabed and some spare pillows. No sweat."

"Can I? Oh that would be great. Can I come round straight away?"

"Sure, you can. Make sure you bring my tea with you. I like fish 'n' chips. And don't forget the onion rings."

What I really wanted was for Kelly to bring her weed with her. I knew Kelly would leave her things, her dog, her car, but she would certainly not go anywhere without her weed.

Sure enough, within half an hour, Kelly was around at my tree house carrying her worldly possessions under her arm. A bag of weed, a pillow, a blanket and a few clothes.

"You look knackered, mate," I said, trying not to laugh.

"You could have told me about the fucking steps, love. I'm absolutely fucked now. Let me dump my stuff and then we'll have a cuppa."

Kelly walked around the house. She dropped her keys on the video unit, her clothes on the back of the couch and her bag of weed on the coffee table.

I chuckled to myself. I thought it was quite funny how Kelly moved in within thirty seconds.

"Here you go. Tea fixes everything. We're English and you know when there's a major crisis, the English make tea."

Kelly laughed and nodded her head in agreement.

We sipped our tea and sat back and relaxed on the couch.

"Do you want some weed, love?" Kelly said.

"Well… hmm. Let me think… okay then, you've twisted my arm."

She lit a joint and passed it to me to try.

"So what's happened, Kelly?" I said anxiously awaiting her response.

"Kevin, I don't really want to talk about it right now, so just leave it, will you?"

"Whatever, mate. Just relax and think of good things. Besides, the weed will take kick in soon," I said, trying my best to help ease her emotional pain and failing miserably.

"I couldn't keep it in, Kevin."

"Keep what in?" I said, scowling.

"I've been having an affair with Claire behind Sarah's back. I had to tell her the truth. I don't want to hurt her, but had to be true to yourself, as they say. After she had calmed down, I tried to talk to her, but she wouldn't listen and told me to go. I didn't know what the hell to do, so I asked her if I could take some weed from the drawer at home, grabbed a handful of clothes and then left. I drove around for a while, thinking where the hell to go and ended up at a mate's place. Now I'm at your place."

"I was out most of the day driving," I said. "I love taking off and not having a care in the world. I just kept driving and driving until I spotted some rocks that looked like they needed climbing."

"Oh man, I'm sorry to hassle you like this but I had nowhere to go. I haven't really been getting on with my mate in town, so I'm very pleased that you rang."

"That's all right, Kelly, you fed me when I was starving to death and eating friggin' dog food with James in the past. As soon as I mentioned being broke, you had me round for tea and looked after me, so letting you stay is not really an issue."

Kelly leaned across and gave me a hug and then a kiss on the cheek. I felt quite embarrassed, but just shrugged it off as if it hadn't happened.

"You were what?" Kelly said. "You said that you were eating dog food with James."

"Oh yeah, pretty funny, isn't it?"

"Why the fuck didn't you tell me, aye?" Kelly yelled.

I laughed, but I wasn't sure whether I was laughing because

of the dog food story or because of the marijuana in my system.

"Anyway, I'm goosed, Kevin. Can I kip on the couch for a few days?"

"You know you can, mate. What time is it anyway? My God, we've been talking for hours and it's like 11.30pm. Let's get some sleep and worry about it in the morning, okay," I said, in my best 'concerned' voice.

I stood up unsteadily and walked over to my bedroom. I paused for a moment and then turned towards Kelly. "It'll be okay, mate. Just chill out."

"Okay, Kevin. Goodnight."

"Goodnight, Sly, goodnight Kelly, goodnight John Boy."

Kelly laughed and then lay down on the couch.

The next morning I was woken by a scream.

"Kevin! Come and get your bloody dog off of me, will you?"

I ran into the living room and saw Sly trying his hardest to hump Kelly's leg.

"Oi! Slyster, get over here now. What do you think you're playing at?" Sly put on his puppy dog eyes routine as he walked passed me to his basket as if to say, 'what?'.

Sly paused for a moment to have one last look at Kelly's leg and then did as he was told and climbed in his basket.

"Hey, erm. What do you want to do about sleeping… erm, I mean car arrangements, Kelly?"

"What do you mean!" replied Kelly.

"Well, it's pointless us both going in two separate cars to the same place, isn't it?"

"Erm, well to be honest, Kevin, I would like to take my own car. I like the freedom of having my own transport. You know how it is?"

Kelly stayed with me for a few days more. When she left, it felt like the feeling everyone gets after the Christmas decorations have been taken down. The room has life and is full of energy one minute, the next it's plain and bare.

A few days later, just as I sat down to relax, Sly began barking.

'Now what?' I thought. I stood up and looked out of the window. There was a car parked outside on my road that I didn't recognise. 'Hmm, maybe the people over the road have visitors?'

Just as Sly stopped barking, there was a knock at the door.

"Hello, lover. How are you?" said Veronica with a large grin on her face.

"Oh God. Will you ever get the message? I don't want to go out with you. Now leave or I'll call the police," I yelled.

Veronica burst out laughing and then forced her way inside.

"What the fuck are you doing? Get out," I yelled.

Sly ran up to her and began licking her legs. She pushed by me and into the living room and then sat on the couch. "Now, Mr Thomas, we're going to talk about this until we come up with a solution to our little problem."

"What problem would that be, Veronica?"

"Our relationship problem," she snapped.

"You're fucking nuts, man. Absolutely bonkers. Now please leave before I get mad." I sat down, hoping the psycho girl would go.

She did not.

"What we need to do is to figure out what is wrong and then fix it," said Veronica. "We are going to make this work, one way or another. Got it?"

I laughed, I couldn't believe this girl. She was completely crazy.

"How did you get my address?"

"From that man who smells. The one at your garage," she replied.

"Let me guess… Bert?"

"As I was saying… your main problem is what, exactly?" she insisted.

"You're always thinking of sex. Which is not a bad thing, it's just that you're too forceful with it. No man is ever going to go with a raving nympho like you. Your whole personality is like that. You just keep going and going until you run out. I don't want to be with someone who is like that. I only wanted sex here and there… have a laugh, you know, that type of thing. You're too direct and to the point, I like going slowly."

"Oh, fucking men are a bore. Just do it," snapped Veronica.

"Stop it," I yelled. "That's exactly what I mean, Veronica. You're a nightmare from Elm Street. You're as butch as a dyke. Ever thought of turning gay?"

"I'll show you gay!" she yelled in my ear.

Veronica squeezed my crotch again, even harder this time and then gave me a big sloppy kiss on the lips. She grabbed my left hand and placed it on her breast.

"Squeeze it, go on, squeeze it as hard as you like," she cried passionately.

I hated the situation that Kelly had put me in. I wished that I'd never put an ad in the paper now. It had been nothing but hassle from the start to what became the bitter end.

I sat back violently and yelled at Veronica. "Stop! Get the fuck out of my house, will you? I've had it with you, you stupid bitch."

Veronica stopped squeezing my crotch and sat back, shocked and flabbergasted.

"I don't understand. You're a guy, aren't you?"

"Were you listening to a damn thing I've just said?" I yelled. "I just told you what I wanted from you… sex sometimes! Not stalking or obsessions and I love you's or commitment or weird chocolate paint things. Why can't you just accept that and just let it be?"

"Because I always get something from a man and I want my fair share from you, that's why, boyfriend. Now take your pants off and we'll make love."

I was beginning to feel uncomfortable. Then as abruptly as she arrived, she left.

I sat down again and thought how lucky I was to have survived the nympho from hell. Just as I had become comfortable again, the door burst open and Veronica ran inside. She jumped on top of me and thrust her chest in my face. At the same time, she ripped her pants off and started thrusting her womanhood in my crotch area. "Oh baby. I ain't leaving until you give me some, so get started," she yelled.

It felt like role reversal. I didn't know what the hell to do, so I grabbed her butt and tried to move her womanhood off my crotch. It was no good, she was holding onto the back of the couch and wouldn't budge. If this were someone else, it would be hilarious, but of course it wasn't.

Panic had set in and I was beginning to suffocate. Some drastic action was called for, but what? She had me completely embraced, using her body as an anchor.

The only thing I could think of was to bite her in the hope that she'd release me.

"Oh yeah, that's it," Veronica yelled in pleasure. "Oh Kevin, you're a fantastic lover."

I couldn't believe it, she was actually enjoying it. Just as I had given up all hope of ever making it off my couch alive, my faithful companion Sly came to my rescue. He jumped on the couch and put his paws on her back and began having his wicked way with her.

"Get your fucking dog off of me!" screamed Veronica.

"Good boy, Sly. Well done, mate," I said, as I burst out laughing.

"You fucking what! You'd rather stick up for your dog than your girlfriend," Veronica yelled back at me.

"As I keep telling you, psycho bitch, I ain't your fucking boyfriend. Now fuck off." I stood up and opened the door. "Now get out and stay out, you silly bitch."

She pulled up her pants and left the tree house in a huff.

I laughed to himself and stood watching Veronica as she walked down to her sister's car, which was parked on the road.

"Thank God, she's gone, Sly. She's a crazy chick all right. Where does she get off doing what she does?"

I went to my bedroom, where my secret stash of weed was hidden and began rolling up.

"Boy, what a day."

CHAPTER 16
THE BEACH

'Yeah, this place is perfect,' I thought. I stood on top of a bush-covered hill, which overlooked Whites Beach in West Auckland, admiring the view. A few minutes of absorbing the scenery later and I decided to walk down the hill and onto the beach.

Sly ran down too and went wild with excitement. He loved the open space and freedom of it all. He was at home outdoors.

I, meanwhile, found a quiet spot in the far corner of the beach, next to a little cave.

"Home sweet home."

I shook out a blanket down, lay on it and sat there watching Sly run around.

A few moments later, I was smoking a pre-rolled joint.

'Ah, this is the life. Sun on my face, off my head on drugs and not a care in the world. Total freedom.'

Sly came running over to me, soaking wet from swimming in the sea and then rolled in the sand, ending up covered in sand from head to paw. He snuggled up to me and within minutes was sleeping like a baby.

"All of my life, Sly," I muttered, "I've paid my way and worked hard and where has it got me? On a frigging beach, that's where. God, I'm talking to a dog now, I must be cracking up." I closed my eyes and thought of how I had got here and how it had come down to this… homeless and sleeping on a beach.

It all started a week or so before, when debt collectors began pestering me.

"Hello, Mr Thomas, I'm Clare from National Bank credit cards. According to our records, you owe us $5,000. Can you tell me when you will be able to make a payment?"

"Yeah, well, I think I'll be able to make a payment next month of $200, is that okay?" I replied sheepishly.

"Not really, Mr Thomas, you haven't made a payment in over

two months now, so we really need to see something happening in the next few days."

"I haven't got it, so obviously you can't have it, can you? But what I will do, is to pay you $200 next month as I've just said," I snapped. I really couldn't be bothered with some silly little girl who was trying to pressure me into making large payments I didn't have.

"That's not really good enough, Mr Thomas, so what I'm going to do is pass this onto our debt collection department and they can take it from there, good day, Mr Thomas."

I had spent the past several weeks trying to stay out of trouble and keeping a very low profile. I just wanted to get on with my life and try and figure out what I was going to do about my national debt.

"Hey, Kelly, how's it going?" I had said to a very busy Kelly on the ramp opposite me.

"All right. What's wrong with you?" replied Kelly.

"I've just had a phone call from one of my many credit card companies, asking when they can have their money back. I can barely pay the rent and feed myself, let alone pay the thousands that I owe these people. I'm thinking of sleeping on a beach to save money," I said, giggling as I spoke.

"You won't! Not if I have anything to do with it, mate," yelled Kelly. "Stop being silly and go and sleep at Veronica's place. I mean, she wants it big time, so just give it to her. Use the bitch."

"You think? I know I could do that to a bank or a company, they rip people off every day, so I don't feel guilty, but the psycho nympho girl… I'd be worn out."

"Well, whatever you do, you're not sleeping on a beach. Do you hear me?"

"Maybe, if I gave up my tree house and then cut a key, I could go back and squat rent free. What do you reckon?"

"Kevin, stop being so bloody stupid and sort your shit out, will you?"

I laughed and then went back to work. Little did Kelly know, I was very serious about giving up my tree house and then squatting until someone else moved in. I was at the point where I really couldn't care less what happened to me.

Just as I was thinking of my fantastic plan of free rent, Burt appeared, carrying the workshop phone. "Hey, Kevin, one of your girlfriends, mate," he said grinning as he said it.

"Aye, who is it?" I snapped.

"No idea. Some woman."

"Hi, this is Sam from ANZ, I'm inquiring about your credit card re-payments. When can we expect to see a payment from you, sir?"

"Erm, yeah, that would be in about a month's time. Is that okay?"

"Yes, but we need at least $550 from you," replied Sam.

"Erm, yes that's fine, thank you, bye." I put the phone down abruptly, hoping that would buy me some time until I thought of something.

'This woman is dreaming, of course, I haven't got shit to my name.'

I started laughing. I'd had enough of this shit and was ready to quit everything that I had hung onto for years… my life in New Zealand. I just couldn't afford to live here anymore.

I had to leave.

The rest of the day was just a bore. There was nothing that really interested me. I was about to have one of my brainstorms, that usually ended in some major catastrophe but I just didn't care. I had nothing to lose and everything to gain.

'Kevin! Where the hell can you stay to save money,' I thought to myself. Then it hit me. Why didn't I move back in with my sister, underneath the house in the garage and extension area? After all, she was the bitch that brought me to this penniless land without telling me that I couldn't earn a decent wage. I'd never forgive her for her lies. Ever!

I'd made up my mind… somehow I was going to persuade Laura to let me stay in her house but, not yet. I had some mileage left on the beach.

Over a period of a week, I had handed the keys for my tree

house in to the estate agents. I just couldn't afford to pay the rent anymore. I told my landlady that I was moving overseas, so I had to let the place go. She agreed and gave me my bond back, which was enough for a plane ticket back to England.

The following morning, I was awoken by Sly licking my face.

I sat up and began rummaging around in my backpack for some dog biscuits.

"There you go, mate, chow on down," I said to my faithful companion. After breakfast, I packed up my things and called to Sly, who was going bonkers with excitement on the beach. I had to go to work to earn some cash unfortunately.

"Come on, Sly. Let's go, matey," I yelled across the beach.

I began the long walk up the side of the hill and back to my car, hoping no one had pinched it. Because of the remoteness of the beach, anything was possible.

It took me half an hour to make my way back to my car. When I finally did make it, I was completely knackered and ready for a rest.

"In you go, Sly. I haven't got all day."

Sly jumped in the car and curled up into a ball, then went straight to sleep. Because I was now homeless, Sly had to go to work with me and stay in the car. It was wintertime and the weather was quite cool, so Sly would be okay in the car, however, if I was still there in the summer, I'd have to do something else as it'd be too warm for Sly then. God only knows what he'd do?

I had been living on the beach for over a week before Laura called me at work one Thursday afternoon.

"Hello," I said.

"It's Laura, I'm just ringing to see if you're okay. The last time we spoke, you said you were going to cash your bond in to the tree house and live with Kelly," bellowed Laura.

Just then, Kelly walked into the office where I was talking to Laura. She put her head against the receiver and listened in on the conversation.

"Yeah, I'm staying with Kelly. Why do you care?" I replied.

Kelly looked at me and grabbed the phone.

"Hello, Laura. This is Kelly from work. Kevin is sleeping on a beach out west somewhere. He's not at mine. He's lying."

I grabbed the phone back and frowned at Kelly.

"Kevin, what the hell is going on?" Laura yelled down the phone. "Just listen to me for once in your life. Come around to my place and I'll feed you, okay?"

"I don't need you, Laura, so please leave me alone, will you!" I yelled back.

Kelly grabbed the phone again from me. "He'll be there straight after work, Laura." Then she put the phone down. "You're a fucking idiot, Kevin. Do you know that? Your sister is trying to help you. Can't you see that?"

"She's a bitch that left me to suffer with no money and starve to death, so it's her problem, not mine! Just butt-out, will you?" I yelled.

"Are you trying to make her feel guilty?" Kelly said.

"You got it," I yelled. "She ruined my fucking life by bringing me out here, promising me great things. I have zero money or life because of her lies. I don't want anything from her at all."

Kelly shrugged her shoulders and walked away in disgust. Then she paused and turned around. "You're bloody going tonight, even if I have to drag you there myself!"

"You pay for the petrol, then, because I have enough to get to my beach and that's it."

I drove straight to the beach and headed for the cave near where I'd slept the previous night. It was raining cats and dogs that night, so I'd had to sleep in the cave.

"This is all right, isn't it, Sly? Cosy and warm in a nice cave. It's our little den. Cool or what?"

I had propped himself up against the cave wall and sat down, thinking of the women in my life.

I had a nympho psycho girlfriend, a lying bitch of a sister, a complete tart of a secretary shag and now a lesbian friend. I began laughing uncontrollably, Sly stared at me with a puzzled look on his face.

"Eeek!" came a sound from the bottom of the cave. I could see something shinning in the dark, staring at me. Sly began to growl and then began barking into the darkness.

The two shiny things grew closer and closer, until I decided to grab Sly and retreat to the entrance of the cave, where we'd be safe.

"Eek, eek," came the sound again from the darkness.

"What the fuck are you?" I yelled with fear in my voice.

The shiny things suddenly appeared at my feet. It became obvious that they were the eyes of some angry animal warning me off.

'It's his home, not mine is what the critter is clearly saying. Fuck me, it's a possum. The bloody thing scared the living daylights out of me.'

I didn't like the look of the violent little critter so I decided to spend the night in the car.

"Urh. Oh, fuck. My bloody neck is killing me," I moaned, as I awoke in my car the next morning. "Right! That's it, I've had enough. I am not staying in this damned car another night! It's straight to my sister's and take the piss by staying as long as I can from now on."

A day later, I pulled up on Laura's drive and went inside to face the music.

"Hey Laura, how are you?"

"You fuckwit, Kevin. What the hell are you doing sleeping on a beach?" Laura yelled in disgust. She was sitting, surrounded by case files of her pregnant patients.

"Trying to survive, what's it to you?" I replied.

"Oh, you know what? I just want to get on with you and move on, so just chill."

"Fine. What's for tea? Anyways, you seem to forget the first thing, sister dear. You know the bit where you promised me the world in New Zealand and I got jack shit in return. You left me for dead, never coming to check on me to see if things were going according to plan, always working. You never even came to my house or phoned me in over a year. Not once! That's what I'm talking about!"

Laura started crying. She had twisted things around so that it was all my fault. I knew that it was her. No matter what she told my family and friends. She was an evil person who ruined people's lives at the drop of a hat.

"Laura, stop crying will you," I yelled.

"Kevin, are you still mad with me?" Laura said, as she wiped away the tears.

"A hundred years from now I'll still be mad with you for wrecking my financial life. You never even warned me about the low pay here. I might forgive you if you let Sly stay in your house until I have enough money to bail out of this crap-hole place," I replied aggressively.

"Sly is not staying! No way, Kevin," Laura yelled.

"Why? He's as quiet as a mouse and no trouble whatsoever."

"Kevin, no!" Laura yelled. "You know that I hate dogs, so he goes in the kennels and that's that!"

I stared at her for what seemed like an eternity, which was really only twenty seconds. "Okay, I'll sort something and then I'll be back in a few days to stay here."

Laura nodded her head and went back to the phone calls she'd been making before I had arrived.

There was no way I was going to put Sly in the kennels. I called Greg, explained what was going on and asked if he could take in another dog. Sly had got on brilliantly with Barney and Amos, and Greg agreed straight off. I wasn't happy as I dropped Sly off but it had to be done. I gave Greg what cash I could, to contribute to food, gave Sly a big hug and left with a very heavy heart.

I couldn't get Sly off of my mind on the drive home but I had to do it, there was no other choice. I made it to my sister's place deadbeat and really didn't want to deal with her shit. I just wanted to have another joint and go to sleep.

"Hi, Kevin. Sid you drop Sly off in Hamilton," yelled Laura down the stairs.

"Yes," I snapped. I couldn't be bothered explaining.

"Okay, I was just asking. You can have dinner with us tonight if you want to."

"No, thanks," I replied. "I just want to sleep and be by myself tonight."

"Oh, well," yelled Laura. "Okay, then. Whatever you want. See you later."

I jumped on my bed and lay there for a while, thinking about my dog and how everything had turned to shit over the last few years. I loved the country but hated the crappy pay packet that I received as a mechanic. My only choice was to go back to the scene of the crime, so to speak, and start all over again from my parents' house in England.

'Yes, that'll work.'

It wasn't long before I fell asleep.

I was at my sister's place for a week, before her nagging began. Any excuse and she would nag away for hours… on and on until she was blue in the face. I was sick of her. I kept telling myself that I only had a few more weeks of her shit left and then I was on my way to England to start again.

"Kevin," yelled Laura.

"Yeah," replied Kevin, with attitude.

"Phone!"

It was a Friday night, which meant that I had been smoking pot heavily with the guys from work. I grabbed the phone from Laura and went back downstairs to the garage. I was hoping my sister hadn't noticed how wasted I was but she did notice and she looked at me as if it was the end of the world. Steam was coming out of her ears she was so annoyed.

"Hello, Kevin speaking." I held the phone against my ear and shoulder as I lit a joint.

"Hello, son. How are you," my dad said.

"Hey, dad. Good, mate. What's up?" I said, hauling on a big joint.

"I've been offered a job in Saudi Arabia and there's an opening for a warranty claims supervisor. Do you want to come?"

"Do I? You bet I do," I yelled. "I've got enough for my ticket to England now. I'm just working out my notice period at work and then I'm gone."

"So where are you staying?" asked dad.

"In Laura's garage. She won't let me stay upstairs and she's got me down here. Don't really know why."

"You what?" yelled dad. "Put Laura on the phone now!"

"It's okay, dad, don't worry. I don't care anymore. I just have to wait a few more weeks and then I'll be back in England with you guys."

"Take care, Kevin, and I'll see you soon. Bye for now."

I returned the phone to Laura upstairs. I couldn't even be bothered to talk to her anymore. She had changed over the years and into something I hated with a passion.

Over the next few weeks, I cruised at work. I was missing Sly like crazy and it had only been a few weeks since the dog had gone to Greg's.

My last day at work was actually quite disappointing. When I had left England six years ago, I was complimented and awarded gifts by the general manager. In New Zealand, I was a nobody with no money, hardly any friends and jack shit to show for my six years there.

Ken, the service manager, hadn't bothered to tell anyone that there was a training course after work until the last minute, so I spent good money on some goodbye beers for nothing.

Bollocks to it! I was taking the beers home with me.

I didn't even say goodbye to anyone. I just left.

I had to get a taxi home, because the finance company was chasing me for a payment on my car, so I left it on the roof of Newmarket Nissan.

When I arrived home, I went straight down to the garage and lay on my bed.

I grabbed one of the beers and flicked the top off with the base of my lighter. I swigged a large mouthful and then burped.

It was awesome, just what I needed after six years at that shitty job. In fact, I thought I had some weed left. I might just smoke a large joint.

I climbed off my bed and moved to the little room at the back of the garage. The room was originally meant to be a bathroom but the previous owner hadn't finished it before he sold it to Laura and John.

'I lurvvv weed,' I thought, taking a huge drag on my joint.

I collapsed on my bed, my eyelids heavy. I went straight to sleep and was soon in a total dream state.

The following morning, I didn't wake until 10am. I was leaving the country at 3pm, so I needed to get up and pack my bags. I found a note from my sister on the outer door of the garage, telling me to be ready by 1.30pm, because John was taking me to the airport.

It didn't take me long to pack up my stuff and put my bag by the front door. I left most of my stuff behind because I was toying with the idea of coming back to New Zealand someday. I loved the country but hated the lack of money and needed to make a fortune before I came back. Whenever that may be.

Sure enough, dead on 1.30pm, Laura and John arrived, almost simultaneously, in separate cars.

"Kevin, come on," yelled Laura through the doorway. "I have six pregnant women to see after I've seen you off, so let's get a move on."

I grabbed my bags and loaded them into my sister's Jeep, then climbed in the back seat. John backed out of the driveway and headed off for the airport.

Laura practically threw me in the queue for Hong Kong airlines. "Okay, take care," she said. "As I said, I have to go now because I have mums and their babies to see. You're more trouble than you're worth, so off you go!"

And that was it.

I couldn't believe how cold-hearted she was towards me. I had lost everything because I'd been fooled into moving to New Zealand and now she couldn't care less if I was gone or not.

'Bitch!' I thought.

She'd changed over the years, we used to be best mates growing up, but now we had nothing in common.

I was so pleased to get away from her. How the hell did John put up with her? No wonder they led separate lives.

'A strange relationship… John must just be drunk all the time.'

"Hello, Mr Thomas," said the lady behind the check-in desk. "How are you today?"

"Now that you mention it, I'm feeling pretty good, thank you," I replied with a large smile across my face.

I handed her my passport.

Finally, I could get out of here and go to a place where I could earn some decent money.

"Okay, Mr Thomas, there you go and enjoy your flight." The lady handed me my passport and I walked through to the departure lounge, where I found Kelly and Claire waiting for me.

"Oh, what are you guys doing here," I said.

"We thought we'd come and see you off. What do you want? A beer?" asked Kelly.

"I wouldn't mind," I replied. "If you're buying, of course."

Kelly went over to the bar and ordered me a beer. "Here you go, mate. Get your laughing gear around that."

I grabbed the beer and took a swig. "Ah, that's good, man."

"So what are you going to do in England?" said Kelly.

"My dad's got a job lined up for me in Saudi Arabia as a warranty claims supervisor in charge of four branches. Good money, so I can pay off my national debt and maybe come back here some day. To be honest, I don't really care. I just want to leave this mess behind and fix it from a distance. But first I'm stopping off in Hong Kong for a few days, so I'll make the most of that, I assure you."

"I see. Here… a little gift for you," Kelly said as she passed me a box, covered in bright blue wrapping paper.

I took the gift from Kelly and opened it. Inside I found a large note pad with a picture of New Zealand on the front of it.

"Every time I see you, Kevin, you're writing something down, so I figured that you could use this."

"Oh cheers, Kelly. Very thoughtful of you."

"Final call for flight CA187 to Kowloon," the voice over the intercom said.

"You'd better get going, Kevin, or else you'll miss your flight, mate," Kelly said, a tear in her eye.

I rose to my feet and hugged Kelly, then Claire.

"Take care of yourself, Kevin, and behave yourself in Saudi. Do you hear me?" Kelly said as she put her hand on my shoulder.

"Yes, mum," I replied.

"Hey, I'm just concerned, that's all," said Kelly. "Now off you go and have fun in Hong Kong."

I left the two girls and walked down the tunnel to the aircraft.

'Well, that's New Zealand done with,' I thought.

I paused and turned around, towards Kelly and Claire, smiled and then I carried on walking down the tunnel to my future.